Caylen's Journey

A Caylen Helms Adventure

by

Robert B. Marchand

Argus Enterprises International, Inc.
New Jersey***New York

Caylen's Journey © 2010
All Rights Reserved by Robert B. Marchand

A-Argus Better Book Publishers, LLC

For information:
A-Argus Better Book Publishers, LLC
Post Office Box 914
Kernersville, North Carolina 27285
www.a-argusbooks.com

ISBN: 0-9846195-3-4
ISBN: 978-0-9846195-3-5

Book Cover designed by Dubya

Printed in the United States of America

Caylen's Journey

Main Characters and Places,

- Caylen Helms, Adahy, or "Lives in the Woods"as a boy, Mato Honl, or "Brave Wolf"as adult

- Lora Helms, Caylen's mother gave birth to Georgina, Caylens half sister.

- Sania, Caylens dead native guide and mentor, The Whakan Powwaw or Sacred Priest that befriended Caylen. (124 years old at death)
  (*Caylen can talk with the deceased Sania in cases of extreme danger but cannot see him.*)

- Sanias, younger brother, Komali or "Spirit Guide"

- Village of Oraibi on Third Mesa, Arizona, Sania's Pueblo home in Arizona

- Sania's granddaughter-Aponi's mother, Sihu or "Flower".

- Sania's great-granddaughter, Aponi or "Butterfly ".

- Shilah, Caylen's hired Hopi handiman.

- Loknl, Brother of Wildflower.

- Kosuml, Brother of Wildflower.

- Northwest Mounted Policeman, Sgt. Bill Tomkins who has married Lora, Caylens mother. Named their daughter Georgina

- Viktor Lubak, Younger brother of Fariss.

- Warrior, Caylens wolf dog or "Cheveyo"meaning "Spirit Warrior".

- Chilam, Snow Bird, or "Snow"female white wolf. Mate of Warrior.

- Qaletaka, The Great Spirit--"The Sacred Guardian of the People".

- Wendigo, The evil spirit of the forest that devours evil men.

- Serenity Island, Caylens island.

- Serenity Mining Co. Miners, Honaw or Bear-The boss and Lopi or Cedar Bark and Istaqu or Coyote Man and Honani or Badger and Lanse or Lance.

- Caylen's And Aponi's Twins, Boy, Kele or Hawk. Girl, Catori or Spirit.

- Serenity Mountain, The big mountain on Serenity island

- Tranquility Harbour, The little bay on which they built their home.

- Tranquility Place, The name that Caylen and Aponi give their home.

- Mystic Cove, Caylen and Aponi's favourite site on their island.

- Matah Kagml, The wild forest people. (Known today as Sasquatch)

- Talisa, Beautiful Water. Girl baby gift from the Matah Kagmi

Powers Bestowed on Caylen by the Great Spirit,

➢ The power to insert part of his mind into the mind of any other creature including the Matah Kagml, except another humans.
➢ The power to be able to see through those creatures eyes.
➢ The power to be able to guide and control the movements of those creatures who's minds he has entered.
➢ The power to be able to move his soul from his body to the distance permitted by his "thread of life".
➢ The power to be able to see the aura of humans and to be able to tell by the colour of their aura if they are good or evil persons. (The darker the colour, the more evil the person is) The meaning of each colour is thus , red is anger, blues and purples are sadness, yellows and oranges are happiness, green is restfulness, with brown and black the colour of evil.

Powers Bestowed on Caylen by the Aliens ,

- ➢ The power to speak to others through his mind. The power to see ghosts of those who have not passed over.
- ➢ The power to move objects with his mind. This power will evolve into bigger things.

Prologue

Caylen's Journey is the saga of young Caylen Helms life and his many intriguing adventures as he strives to uphold what is right in the world and to defeat evil wherever he finds it. In the first Caylen Helms novel, Caylen's Quest, young Caylen and Lora, his beautiful youthful mother, finally managed to escape from her evil, abusive husband Faris Lubak and their remote Northern home. Having gone off on his own to avoid Faris's abuse, Caylen soon discovers a extremely rich gold mine. Young Caylen's many dreams about an old Indian man and a huge black wolf eventually leads to Caylen and his pet wolf dog Warrior being summoned to the wilderness lodge of an old Hopi sage, Sania, who teaches Caylen the use of the supernatural powers bestowed upon him by the Great Spirit Qaletaka during a Vision quest. Caylen, using some of his newly found Powers, then assists the Police in tracking down the evil Faris after he murders a fellow Policeman who has come to investigate the disappearance of a former live in Indian girlfriend. After the death of Sania, Caylen visits the old man's home reservation in Arizona where he meets and falls in love with Sania's great-grand-daughter.

In Caylens Journey, Caylen and his new wife Aponi build their beautiful new home in Caylen's beloved Northlands. From this isolated home he travels with his

pet wolf dog far and wide, utilizing the powers granted him by the Great Qaletaka to bring to justice criminals of every kind. He also soon discovers that life in his new wilderness home on a remote Northern island is filled with mysterious and bizarre events.

Chapter 1

Wedding Bells

Caylen's return to the Hopi village of Oraibi on the Third Mesa in central Arizona created great excitement amongst the entire Reservation population. It was well known by the entire tribe that Sania's great granddaughter had been corresponding with the young white man who possessed great powers and who was known to them as Mato Honi for nearly two years now.

All of the tribes eligible young bachelors had been especially aware of the beautiful young Aponi's single-minded devotion and loyalty to the man that she loved who had, two years past, assured her that he would one day, return to her.

The numerous eligible young men's advances towards Aponi were always politely received but then quickly rejected by her with a simple statement, My life-mate, my Mato Honi will soon be with me. I have promised that I will await his return and his love. My life and my love will to be his and his alone."

Aponi's faith in Caylens return never ever wavered. When her mother, several months after Caylen had left to return to his beloved North, advised her that she should perhaps, consider another young man as a suitor, Aponi replied without any hesitation whatsoever, "I have already given my heart, my love and my life to my man, my Mato Honi. I have no want or need of another man in my life.

While Aponi's open and obvious displays of loyalty and love for Caylen finally caused her family and her potential suitors to cease in their attempts at seeking her favours, her inner resolve was even stronger. She had, the day following his departure, taken a paper tablet and marked off one-hundred and four weeks. As each week passed, she drew a heavy line through that week and wrote beside the following week, the number of days remaining until his expected return. She sent one letter per month to him, writing something in it, each and every day, telling him what she had done, what she was about to do and also telling him shyly, of her great love for him. Each night, before sleep claimed her, she would take out the big gold nugget he had given her and clasp it tightly to her breast, whispering softly."Where are you, my love; what do you do at this very moment? Please hurry back to me, my love, before my heart bursts apart in my loneliness,

As the months passed and the date of Caylen's promised return grew nearer, Aponi began, each and every afternoon, to walk down the steep trail that led to the rock ledge in the hidden nook where she and Caylen had attested to their love for each other. She would stay here for hours, looking out in frustration, over the desolate but beautiful semi-desert lands for any sign of her Caylen returning to her.

It was one week short of two years when she saw, as she sat waiting on the rocky ledge one bright day in mid March, the reservation bus stop at the end of the roadway that led from Flagstaff. As she watched, she saw a tall light haired young man with a heavy back pack exit the old bus and begin walking across the arid countryside towards her. Unable at the great distance to positively make out his facial features, she still knew, without even a moment's hesitation, that the figure approaching her was her beloved Caylen, her Brave Wolf. She could also see what appeared to be an enormous, jet black wolf dog walking along beside him.

As she sat quietly waiting for him, Aponi could feel her heart beginning to beat faster and faster in her chest until she thought it would surely burst in anticipation of seeing her beloved after her long two year wait. As Caylen neared she saw him look up towards her. She saw the sudden flash of recognition on his face and watched as he stopped, threw aside his big pack, and begin to run just as fast as he could up the steep rocky trail towards her.

***

It was quite late that evening before Aponi and Caylen arrived at Aponi's mother's pueblo. The couple's initial meeting had taken up the better part of the warm afternoon after which they then had to go back down the trail to recover his pack from where he had thrown it.

Aponi had not told him about it in her letters, so Caylen was deeply saddened to find out that Aponi's father had passed away suddenly, not long after Caylen had left the village to return to his far away northern home.

Aponi's mother Sihu welcomed Caylen with a big hug and a, 'Welcome back to my home, young Mato Honl, your arrival here has brought great joy and much happiness to my little Aponi. As you promised two long snows past, you have returned to us with your big wolf dog. Have you yet explained to my daughter Aponi the reason for your return?"

Caylen's face immediately turned a bright beet red. He suddenly decided that he would express his intentions openly and honestly to Sihu and Aponi before another moment passed.

"I have returned to your village and to your pueblo because I wish to become the husband and lifemate of your Aponi. I care deeply for her as she does for me. I seek her and your permission to undergo the marriage ceremonies of your people that will place us together and make us one for all time."

"We are pleased that you would like to take part in our traditional marriage rites as you become one with our Aponi." said Sihu."Our traditions, however, require that she, as well as you, comply with all of the rituals of our people. As Aponi's birth father has gone to be with the Great Spirit Qaletaka and cannot advise you, I will send you to live with her uncle, my brother Nikan, who shall speak to you of all those things that you must know of if you are to be accepted as Aponi's lifemate."

"I am here to do whatever must be done so that Aponi and I may be as one for all time, " said Caylen.

That same evening Sihu and Aponi led Caylen to a large nearby pueblo where he was introduced to Sihu's older brother Nikan. Sihu spoke at length with Nikan in the Hopi language so that Caylen could not understand what she was saying.

Aponi and Caylen sat, holding hands until Sihu finally beckoned to her."Come, daughter, we must return to our own robes. The sky is now black and the time for our sleep is here."With that Sihu and Aponi left to return to their own pueblo.

"So, young Mato Honl, you seem to imagine that my sister's daughter is interested in becoming your lifemate? I think perhaps you have eaten of the Sacred priest's magic powder and that your mind is not at all well." said the smiling Nikan to Caylen as he spread out his sleeping robes.

"I do not imagine anything," said Caylen."I know as surely as I know that the sun shall rise in the morning sky that Aponi loves me as I love her. I know also that she, as do I, wishes nothing more than to become my lifemate."

"If you are as certain of this as you now sound then you must follow the ancient tribal traditions and let the people of this tribe know of your and her wishes in this important matter."

"And how do I go about doing that?"asked Caylen.

"I will," said Nikan, "when the sun rises after our sleep, bring you to my cousin Talisa who is the best sewer of buckskin that I know of. You will tell her of your heart's wishes in this matter. She will then ask you for a gift. You will give her one American gold piece, whereupon she shall then make for you a pair of white buckskin moccasins and other items of clothing that you must leave on Aponi's doorstep. Only if she accepts and takes this bundle of clothes that you leave for her, will you and all of the people of the Third Mesa know that Aponi is considering becoming your lifemate. If Aponi then agrees to become your lifemate, and her mother approves of such a match, Aponi will make and bring to you a loaf of her bread."

"Whew", said Caylen."Is that all there is to it?"

"No, there is much more to do but we shall wait until all of these rituals that I have spoken off, are completed before I thicken your young mind with more," said Nikan."Now sleep and think your sleep thoughts of your beautiful Aponi."

Caylen was up and waiting after a fine meal of corn bread and goat butter when the sun finally rose over the painted desert. The reds, yellows, greens and blue colours caused by the rising sun over the rolling sand hills mesmerized him until Nikan's deep voice brought him back to the day's reality.

"Wake up, Mato Honi. You must have all of your senses about you if you wish to be the lifemate of a woman such as the beautiful young Aponi. If your mind thickens like this when you are about her, she shall surely lead you about the lands like a small puppy on a leash! "

By that evenings main meal, Caylen had made arrangements with Talisa for the bundle of clothing and the moccasins intended for Aponi. When he asked her how she would know what sizes to make the clothing and moccasins, she just smiled and said: "I know."

It took Talisa four days to sew the various items of clothing for Caylen. Caylen and Nikan had just finished their evening meal and Caylen was about to go to visit with Aponi when Talisa came to Nikan's pueblo to present Caylen with the gift of new clothes for Aponi.

"You must now take these to the pueblo of Aponi's mother and place them in her doorway. If the beautiful Aponi takes them up into her arms you shall know that she will accept you as her future husband."

It took Caylen only a few moments to get to Sihu's and Aponi's pueblo. Laying the bundle of clothing in the doorway, he scratched the leather door loudly.

"Who visits the home of Sihu?" said Sihu from inside.

"It is I, Brave Wolf, here to speak with your daughter, Aponi," said Caylen.

Without further ado, the pueblo's door flap was thrown back to reveal Sihu, Aponi's mother, standing in the doorway. Looking down, she quickly spied the bundle of clothes and the moccasins that Caylen had just placed there. Bending over, she reached for the bundle, saying quite loudly as she did so, "Well! Aponi, come quickly! There is a handsome young man with a very large dog at our door and he has left me a bundle of white buckskin clothing and a pair of beautiful white moccasins!"

With those words, Sihu was suddenly and hastily shoved aside by Aponi who grabbed the bundle and clasped it to her breast saying, "Mother, do not tease my Mato Honl, can you not see how red his cheeks have become? Can you not see that his tongue is now thick and he is unable to speak?"

"Please enter our pueblo, Brave Wolf, and be welcome to our fire. Have you eaten your evening meal? Aponi, fetch this hungry young man some of that sweet cornmeal bread that you made this very day."Aponi's mother said.

As Caylen sat down by the little fire in the centre of the pueblo, Aponi handed him the entire loaf of sweet cornbread. As Caylen accepted it he noticed that it was still quite warm and had obviously just came out of the stone baking oven.

"Well! " said Sihu."We now have, in our humble little pueblo, a handsome young Mato Honi and a beautiful young maiden called Aponi, who it seems have just proposed marriage to each other! It also seems that both Aponi and Mato Honi have each accepted the proposals of the other!, The Sacred Guardian of the people, Qualetaka, will be pleased to bless this marriage and the many children that will come of this union."

Caylen sat quite still. Unable to speak, it took him a more than a few moments to realize what had just occurred. As Aponi sat down beside him, she took his big hand in hers and whispered in his ear.

"I would be very pleased to become your wife and your lifemate and to bear your children, my big Brave Wolf. Are you also pleased with your choice of the daughter of Sihu as your wife?"

"I am very pleased and very happy, my love, are we now as one, are we now married?"

"Ha," said Sihu."You are very fortunate, Mato Honl, that you are not of our people. If you were of our people's blood you would be made to do many more things before you would be permitted to bed your Aponi in this pueblo. The Elders, however, have decided to permit the remaining marriage ceremonies without you having to perform the many rituals normally performed by a Hopi man before his marriage."

"I am willing to do as I am instructed, I would do anything that is required of me." said Caylen.

"Then you must leave the home of your Aponi before the next setting of the sun and not return until fourteen suns have passed. At that time the women of Aponi's family shall wash your and her hair in one basin of water and then they will braid your hair together. After this is done you shall both go to the rim of the Mesa to observe and pray to the rising sun. Once these prayers are completed you shall be as man and wife forever and may then move into my home."

***

The following morning Aponi met Caylen after their morning toiletries and breakfast were completed. The couple roamed about the Mesa and talked of their future together. Caylen expressed his desire to return to the North of Canada and make their home together in the land he so loved.

Aponi readily agreed to this move even though she had never been anywhere except to Flagstaff and the Third Mesa. Her only hesitation about such a big move was that her mother would be such a long distance away and hard to contact.

"No problem!"exclaimed Caylen."She shall come with us. I am sure that she shall soon learn to love the North as shall you. You both shall be amazed at how green everything is during the summer months and how white and clean it is in the winter months."

"But where shall we find the monies of your people to do all these many things that you speak of?"asked Aponi.

Caylen, at that point, thought to himself, I *guess now would be a good time to tell Aponi just how rich we are. I don't know if I can explain to her just how rich we are but I must give it a try.*

"I do not think, Aponi," Caylen began, "that we, or our children or their children's children, will ever have to worry about having money. Do you know how much money four million dollars is?"

"It must be all the money in the world," Aponi said."It would take a lifetime to just count that much money."

"Well, that's about how much money we have and it increases by about one million dollars each and every year ". said Caylen.

"You must not make fun of me, Mato Honi. A man would have to own a very large and very rich gold mine to have that much money." said Aponi.

"I am not making fun of you, my little Butterfly, I am such a man that you speak of. I do own a very, very rich gold mine far away in the Northlands of my country. From where did you think I got that big gold nugget that I gave to you two years past?"

"I thought that yellow stone was just that -- a big yellow stone." said Aponi."I never, for a moment thought that it might be real gold."

Caylen spent the remainder of that day telling Aponi the details of his life in the distant North. He told her of his experiences with Fariss, the attempts on his life, the sad story of Wildflower, of his leaving home and his discovery of the gold mine.

He also went into all the small details of his life with Sania, her great-grandfather and his vision quest on the sacred rock. He told her everything about the granting of his powers by Qaletaka, the details of his instructions from Sania on the use of those powers, the sad passing of the old man, and finally the murder of the policeman. He went on to tell her of the chasing down of the evil Fariss and his terrible death at the hands of the Wendigo. He also described to her, his find of the gold-laden stream and the subsequent development of the rich mine by his mother Lora, her new husband Bill Tompkins and the native brothers Kosumi and Lokni.

He also talked at length of his love for the North. He described to her in detail the beautiful Northern Light displays that would light up the northern skies for hours on end during many of the long cold winter nights. He told her of his dreams of becoming a policeman so he could put his many powers to good use. He also told her of his dreams for the two of them and how he wanted to show her the place that he wanted to build their dream home.

Aponi listened intently to everything that Caylen said. When he, after three hours of speaking, finally said, "And that's about all I can think of right now. Now it's your turn to ask me whatever you wish and to tell me of your deepest desires."

Aponi took both of Caylen's hands in hers, looked deeply into his eyes and replied in a very low, soft tremulous voice."Mato Honl, you are to be my lifemate as well as my husband. I have heard you speak many times of your past life in the Northlands. You did not really need to tell me of your love for that far away place as I could hear your love in each and every word you uttered. Your voice alone announces your love for all that is in and about that place. I have no wish or desire to be anywhere on this land or to do anything with my life unless I am with you and doing it with you, my Brave Wolf, my Mato Honl, my Caylen Helms. I will go with you as your wife, your lifemate, your partner and your friend to do as you do, forever and ever, my love."

Caylen found himself quite speechless. He stared lovingly at Aponi and felt as though his heart would surely burst out of his chest.

"My heart is also yours forever, my little Butterfly. My heart sings with my happiness at what you have just said. I wish that I could take you away with me to some far away Garden of Eden even as we speak. My birth mother and her own new lifemate cannot help but love you as I do. We shall chose the placing of our home together and we shall welcome the presence of your mother in our home for as long as she wishes."

"I must soon go to my mother's house, my Brave Wolf. As you know we must not see or speak to each other for fourteen suns after which we shall be as one forever. I now wish to take you to meet our Sacred Priest, Komali who has said to me that he wishes to speak to you of Sania, his older brother."

"His brother "exclaimed Caylen."Sania never said anything about having a younger brother. How old is this Sacred priest, this Komali?"

"I am uncertain of his real age but our people say that he has seen at least one hundred snows." said Aponi.

"Take me to him." said Caylen."I have much to tell him about his brother Sania. Why did he not speak of his brother when I last was last here?"

"I know not the reason he did not speak. Others of the Third Mesa have also asked that very question, but none have received Komali's reply. What all the people do know is that Komali was, for many years, ashamed to speak of his older brother, as he, those many years past, was banished forever from the Third Mesa and the lands of the people."

"Well, the Sania that I knew was a good and righteous man who would harm no-one." said Caylen.

"Perhaps the many snows that he lived away from this place changed him from the Hopi Medicine man that he once was into the Hopi man that you knew in the northlands of your Country " said Aponi.

"You know, Aponi, you are a very, very smart lady and also a very, very beautiful woman. I am a very lucky Mato Honi."

"Yes, you are!, now come quickly, I must take you to Komali's pueblo and return to my mother's pueblo before she sends a war party after you!"

Aponi led Caylen across the Hopi village and out to where the northern edge of the mesa dropped off steeply to the desert floor that lay about twelve hundred feet below. Perched on the rim stood a small rounded pueblo with one leather flap door facing out over the desert below. As Aponi and Caylen approached, they could see a wizened old man with a multi-coloured blanket draped over his shoulders, sitting on the ground just outside the pueblo's door watching them as they approached.

"I welcome you, daughter of Sihu and great-granddaughter of my brother Sania. I welcome you and your future lifemate to my pueblo. My home is your home." he said."I have seen your coming and have expected your arrival now for four hands of the sun's passing." he said."Now tell me this young man's birth name so that I may speak to him of many man things and counsel him to beware of the ways of pretty, bold young Hopi maidens searching for a lifemate."

"Do not tease me so, Great Uncle, you cause my face to become hot and red! " exclaimed Kosumi."He is called Mato Honi and he is to become my lifemate."

"And that reddening of your cheeks was my very intent, my beautiful young Butterfly, daughter of my brother's wife's daughter. Now leave us and go to your mother's pueblo, so that I may begin this poor young man's training and make him wise in the ways of young Hopi maidens."

With that, Aponi gave Caylen a hug and whispered to him."When next we speak to each other, my Brave Wolf, it will be to pray to the rising sun as man and wife. Until then I shall dream the dreams of a lonely, unfulfilled Hopi maiden waiting alone for her man.

"I also, shall dream many dreams as I await our final day of marriage," said Caylen as Aponi hurried off.

***

"What did your words mean, Komali, when you said that you must begin my training?"asked Caylen.

"You are, Mato Honl, to hereafter only speak when I, your Great Hopi Spirit Guide, Komali, gives his permission for you to speak. You are here with me so that you may discover the length and breadth of the powers that you have been granted. I, the Great Komali shall examine your knowledge of those powers and I shall further instruct you in their proper use. My Brother, the Great Whakan Powwaw Sania, taught you many things, but he did not teach you all that you should know of your powers. That is what I shall now attempt to do."

"May I now speak?"asked Caylen.

"Speak." said Komali.

"Just what is it that you think you can teach me?"asked Caylen in a slightly bold and sarcastic manner.

"I shall teach you much, Mato Honl. One of the first lessons shall be to teach you how to curb the challenge that your voice reveals when you speak. A challenging voice used incorrectly or at the incorrect time can cause much pain, not only to your essence but also to your body. It can also cause much anger in the one to who you are speaking who just might in turn, inflict upon you much pain. Now, Mato Honl, go to your evening toilet and then to your night robe. The father sun appears very early on this, the Third Mesa, and you must have my hot morning tea prepared by sun-up or I shall be a very angry old Spirit Guide."

Chapter 2

Expanding Powers

Komali made Caylen fast for three days and nights, allowing him to drink only water that had been steeped with sage during that time. On the fourth day he sat across the pueblo's fire from Caylen and asked Caylen to, in detail, describe each of his powers, his limitations surrounding with each power and how he, Caylen, felt about using his powers. The pair spent two entire days discussing the powers, how they were initiated by Caylen, their intended uses, their limitations and their effects on Caylen as he used each of the powers.

Komali explained to Caylen that while he, Komali had some limited use of some of the same powers as Caylen had been bestowed with, that he much feared to use them as he was afraid that his essence would be unable to return to his physical self and that he would then simply cease to exist.

"I do not have that problem," said Caylen."My problem is that I do not know of my limitations so I really don't know the extent of my powers. I believe that Sania knew of his coming death and that he had not the time to teach me fully about my powers and their many uses."

"These things that you say are the truth, Mato Honi. The Essence of my brother, Sania, has come before me during the last snows to tell me of your coming to the Third Mesa. He asked that I assist you and broaden your knowledge of the powers that you now possess. He asked of me that I show you the many things that he, Sania, had wished to himself show you, had he been permitted to stay longer on Mother Earth. Unfortunately for Mato Honi, the great Qaletaka called Sania to his side before his teaching was completed."

"You spoke to Sania last winter! How could that be, has he not been with Qaletaka now for nearly three snows?" said Caylen.

"There are many things you know nothing of, Mato Honi. The great Sania has powers greater than any man. The end of his physical life on Mother Earth was not the end of his essence. Did he not explain that to you? Did he not tell you that he would always be near you?"

"No, he came to me and spoke to me only once after he had gone to be with Qaletaka. He said at that time that he would never be permitted to speak to me again."

"The Great Qaletaka now permits our Sania to, on certain occasions, speak to an earthbound one such as you and I." said Komali.

"Is it possible for me to speak with him?" asked Caylen.

"Earthbound souls cannot initiate speech with such as Sania. Only the spirits can begin such talk. However, if the spirit opens a talk with a earthbound one, that earthbound one may also enter into that talk."

"Does one such as Sania have any knowledge of my wishes to speak with him?" asked Caylen.

"And how do you think that one such as Sania would have knowledge of your wishes? Sania would know only of your wishes if you went to a sacred prayer site and fasted, drinking only water, for two passing's of the sun. Only then, if you asked for, and obtained Qaletaka's permission, might you be allowed to speak with Sania's essence. He will also have knowledge should your life be in extreme danger. He may on those occasions, also initiate speech with you. Do you now have wishes to speak with the great Sania?"

"Not at this time, I only wished to know if it was possible to do." replied Caylen.

"Enough of this talk! We must examine all your powers and learn of your knowledge regarding those powers that you now have. Tell me now of your powers."

"Okay," said Caylen."The power that I seem to use most of all is the one whereby I can see colours around other person's heads. I see them at all times as though it were a normal thing. All I know about these colours is that the darker they are, the badder that person usually is."

"Then that is where we shall begin." said Komali."The main, or prevalent colours you see about a person's head is a revealing of that persons inner being only at that very time. The meaning of these colours is not so simple as you describe. Each of us, good or evil, may reveal dark, light or any colour at different times depending upon our thoughts at that time. A black colour seen about my head does not necessarily mean that I am evil. It simply means that I am, at that particular time, experiencing dark thoughts. As well, a white colour does not mean that I am good or pure. It may mean that I, at that particular time, am having good and pure thoughts. We, all of us, are all things. We all have, at different times, bad thoughts as well as good and pure thoughts. Therefore, the prevalent colour you see at any particular time does not really tell you of a person's true inner self."

"Then how do I know how to judge a person's character from just the colours about his head?"asked Caylen.

"You must look for the colours that exist very close to the persons skull," said Komali."This is the area of coloration that truly reveals the inner self of a person. If the person is truly evil, his or her colours at or close to his or her skull shall always be dark no matter the outer more visible colour. If the person is truly good this colour shall always remain light no matter the outer colours. The extent of a person's evil or goodness is shown by the intensity of that colour that is closest to the skull. You must observe closely these colour differences. Only through close observations, time and much practice shall you be able to be certain that your conclusions about any persons character are correct."

"Okay, I understand all of that but what of the other outer colours that I see; the reds, the yellows and the blues?" asked Caylen.

"Each of those colours will tell you something of the persons true thoughts and inner self at only that time. The meaning of each colour is thus , red is anger, blues and purples are sadness, yellows and oranges are happiness, green is restfulness. Browns and blacks are the colours of evil. You will remember these colour meanings and you will forever be able to easily determine, with only a glance, any persons state of self and inner being at that very moment. This great power, as with all of your powers will only become greater with time, practice and careful observations.

"Enough of the colour power! " said Komall, "Let us move on to the next of your most used powers."

"The next most used one is similar to the colour power in that it is something that I cannot control. It is something that just happens and it sometimes frightens me." said Caylen."I see things that others cannot see and that I wish not to see. I see transparent people who walk through things and that can be walked through by others. I have seen terrible ugly creatures such as a Wendigo that others cannot see."

Komali replied at length."Those transparent people that you see are the spirit essences of people that have passed from the world of the living and are no longer among the living but for some reason are unable to move on and be with Qaletaka, The Great Spirit. They are searching for the way to him or else they may have unfinished work to do at this level. These spirit essences are not necessarily evil and cannot harm you or any other beings such as you or I. The other, terrible looking creatures and monsters that you see are evil spirit essences from the dark world of fire that lies far below us in the fires of the earth. Even these terrible creatures cannot harm you, I or any other good person. The only beings that need fear these creatures are those who are evil themselves. Some of these creatures are called a Wendigo by many of the world's peoples. They survive on this world of the living by consuming other evil beings and can exist forever as long as there is evil available for them to consume. Other evil creatures are also to be found. Most of these creatures are simply known by humans as devils or spawn of the devil."

"Do I have to see all of these dead people and evil spirits at all times? asked Caylen."It can be very distracting at times."

"You shall, with time and practice, teach your mind to ignore these spirit essences as they appear. They are not aware that you are able to see them and are to be pitied as they search for whatever it is they are searching. It is, however, important that you be aware of any evil spirits that are in your area. One way of knowing of their presence is by their odor. Their odor is that of a sun-rotted fish. You shall be able to detect this odor even before the evil becomes visible to your eyes. You must be aware of one more thing about these evil essences." said Komali.

"And what is that?"asked Caylen.

"The evil essences are not always ugly creatures. An evil essence could easily take the form of a beautiful maiden or any other being."

"Then how will I know them?"asked Caylen.

"No matter what form they take or what they appear to be, they will always smell-like a sun rotted fish." Komali replied."Now let us discuss your other powers."

"The power that I like to use is that of placing my essence into the mind of a wild creature and controlling that creatures actions." said Caylen."I especially like to travel in the minds of eagles and hawks as they soar high above the lands looking down at the world below."

"Ahh, yes, this power is one that I, Komall, also possess. I have not, however, ever been able to take over the complete control of the creature who's mind I have occupied."

"It's simple, ' said Caylen, "you just tell him to do as you wish and he does."

"Ha! if it were really only that simple." said Komali."Are you able, when you have occupied another creature's mind, to control that creature in every way? Are you able to enter the minds of any creature or only those that are within your sight? Are you able to, even when you are in a creature's mind, still fully control your own mind and body?"

"I can do all of those things." Caylen replied."The only thing I am unsure of is how to return to my own body, the part of my essence that is within a creature's mind when my body is not within sight of the creature when I decide it is time to leave it. I am ever afraid that my essence will not be able to locate my body if I am not within sight and that it will be forever lost to me."

"You must not fear this thing." said Komali."Your essence will always return to your body no matter where it is when it leaves a creature. Your body is like those metals that are called magnets that are drawn to each other and are then difficult to separate. We shall practice this part of your power so you will have more confidence in this ability. Now tell me about your other powers."

"I am able to move my complete essence only to the distance permitted by my 'thread of life'. Sania warned me not to exceed that distance for if I did, my life's thread would break and I would be unable to return my essence to my body." replied Caylen.

"Tell me, Mato Honl, when your essence is out of your body do you still retain control of your body?"

"It is as though I am asleep and dreaming of what I am doing." said Caylen.

"Aha! " said Komali."You have much to learn about this power. It is possible, with medicines made from the Peyote plant, for one with such powers to be able to travel much greater distances from your body. It is also possible, by using this same medicine, to remain awake and in control of your body when your soul is travelling out of your body. Again, we shall practice the use of this power as well as your other powers as you await your wedding ceremony."

For the next two weeks, Caylen, under the guidance of Komali, practiced over and over the extended uses of his powers. After the first few days, he found that using and interpreting the powers as Komali had described to him, became easier and easier. He found that the use of the Peyote drug enabled him to take his essence much further than he had been able to previously. He also found that by taking a small amount of the drug, that he was able to now remain awake and in control of his physical body when his essence was travelling. An added benefit was that his entire body, as well as his mind, seemed much more aware and sensitive to his surroundings for hours after using the dried Peyote powder.

Chapter 3

The Homecoming

Caylen's Wedding Song to Aponi,

> *My Little Butterfly, My Aponi*
> *Come fly with me*
> *My little desert Butterfly*
> *Fly with me across this land*
> *Fly with me across wide waters*
> *My little desert Butterfly*
> *Come fly with me*
> *Spread your wings and soar with me*
> *Soar with me to other lands*
> *My little desert Butterfly*
> *Give to me both of your hands*
> *As we soar to these other lands*
> *The World is ours to take*
> *My little desert Butterfly*
> *Fly with me, Soar with me*
> *Take my hand, take my love*
> *Dance with me, Fly with me*
> *My little desert Butterfly*
> *Dream with me*
> *My love is yours and yours alone*
> *Forever and ever, my love*
> *My little desert Butterfly*

Aponi's Wedding Song to Caylen ,

My Love, My Lifemate, My Caylen
I Fly as you fly
My man, My Husband
Where thou go'est, Shall I Go
I Fly Wherever you fly
I Soar as You Soar
My Man, My Love
I Follow Wherever You Lead
My love, My Man, My Husband
Your Lands are My Lands
I Follow as You Lead
My Man, My Husband
I Walk Forever by Your Side
I am Your Desert Butterfly
I am Your Love
I am Your Wife
I am Your Lifemate
Forever, My Caylen

Caylen and Aponi's wedding ceremonies were attended by the entire population of the Third Mesa. Elders from other nearby villages were also in attendance to witness the marriage of the long famous Sania's descendent to the white man who possessed powers that were usually only possessed by a few Sacred Hopi Priests.

Following the marriage, Caylen, after he and Aponi had sung their wedding songs to each other, spoke at length with the Elders of the third Mesa about what he wished to do for the village to thank them for their generosity to him. After much discussion, he managed to convince the Elders that they should permit him to, at his expense, have a brand new four room schoolhouse for the education of the Tribe's children constructed on the Mesa.

Caylen then travelled to Flagstaff and through a local bank, hired a well known, reputable contractor to construct and furnish the schoolhouse for the tribe. Once he was sure that his instructions regarding the schools construction would be followed, he sat with Aponi and her mother to discuss their upcoming move to the North.

After much discussion the trio decided that Caylen, Aponi and Sihu, Aponi's mother, would travel North together to select a homesite and oversee their home's construction. After the other tribal members found out that the trio were to soon be leaving the Third Mesa for their new home so far away, a three-day feast was given in their honor.

At this feast, four men from the tribe approached Caylen about going North with the trio. Caylen, at first, dismissed this possibility, but after discussing the men's idea with Aponi, he discovered that one of them, a single man named Shilah, was about Sihu's age and had previously and openly displayed a romantic interest in her following her husband's death.

Caylen and Aponi decided to ask Sihu herself what she thought of the idea of Shilah going to the North with them as a employee of Caylen and Aponi. As they asked, they could see from the sudden reddening of Sihu's cheeks and the sudden soft tone of her reply that she would only be too happy to have the handsome Shilah accompany them on their long journey.

***

It was nearly a month later when the foursome left the little village of Carcross in the thirty-six foot, gas-powered launch that Caylen had purchased in Carcross and loaded with provisions that he had shipped down from Whitehorse. They enjoyed a leisurely cruise across Nares Lake onto Tagish Lake and then east on Graham Inlet to the river that led them to the huge Atlin Lake. Once on Atlin

Lake, Caylen turned the boat South towards the Northern tip of a huge isolated Island. As they neared the Northernmost rocky point of the island, the foursome stood on the deck in utter awe as they took in the spectacle of the enormous snow covered mountain and its thickly forested slopes that leveled off about a mile inland before sloping gently down to the lakeshore.

"Ohh, Caylen, this has to be the most beautiful place in all of Qaletaka's land!" exclaimed Aponi."Mother, Shilah, do you not think this is the most beautiful place? Caylen, can we not build our home on this place?"

"I have never seen so much water and so much green. It is surely Qaletaka's own home." replied Sihu.

"I wonder what kind of food animals live in such a place." offered the ever practical Shilah.

"There are many good-eating wild things that live and grow in this country." said Caylen."There are moose, caribou, beaver, black bear, brown bear, five different kinds of salmon, lake trout, grayling, whitefish, geese, ducks, grouse, rabbits and many other meat animals as well as wild berries and wild mushrooms that are also very good to eat."

"You will have to show these food things to us so that we may gather our winter's foods before the cold arrives and the snows that you speak of cover the lands." said Shilah.

"You all will all soon be most familiar with this land and all its bounty." said Caylen."We will go into this little bay and anchor for the night. Tomorrow we shall search for a good place to build our new home."

"Do you not suddenly have a strange feeling Caylen? Aponi asked."I began to have a strange calming come over me as we grew near this place."

"Yes, this island seems to have that effect on anyone who comes near it or steps on its shores. There are many local native legends about it and some natives even say that it is a holy place where good spirits live and all things bad or evil are forever banned and forbidden."

"I, too, am suddenly feeling quite relaxed and calm." said Sihu."Up until a few moments ago I was quite apprehensive and concerned about living in such a place. Then this strange calming seemed to come over me as though I was being told that all would be okay and that I had nothing to be concerned about. I don't really understand it."

"I also have suddenly become more acceptable and calm." said Shilah.

"I cannot explain it." said Caylen."Perhaps the legends are true. We should now name this island as it all belongs to us and us alone."

"What do you mean, it belongs to us?" asked Aponi.

"It belongs to us because I purchased it from the Government when we were in Carcross." replied Caylen."I bought the entire island for twenty thousand dollars in gold. We, Aponi, you and I, now own approximately fifty square miles of the land that forms this island and its big mountain. It is all ours, and ours alone!"

"I have the perfect name for it." said Aponi."We shall call it Serenity Island and we shall call the mountain Serenity Mountain."

"Perfect!" said Caylen."And we shall call this little bay that we are entering, Tranquility Harbour and our home shall be named Tranquility Place."

"I like it." said Aponi."It is such a beautiful place. it deserves a beautiful name."

The following morning Caylen, Aponi and Sihu waded ashore to the sand beach at the back of the bay. They soon discovered a ice-cold stream about five feet across and two feet deep, tumbling over a gravelly bottom before emptying into the bay. Caylen pointed out to Aponi and Sihu the shapes of the many-coloured grayling that darted back and forth in the cold stream and lake waters as they searched industriously for food.

"Those fish are called grayling and they are delicious cooked in any way. Look! did you see that huge fish that just swam by? That was a lake trout and they can get large enough to feed a hungry man for ten or more days. That one was probably about thirty pounds and was trying to catch one of those grayling for its supper."

They then followed the stream up a few hundred feet to where it ran through a clearing of about three hundred feet in diameter. The big lake was clearly visible to the north while the entire southeastern horizon was filled with the most beautiful snow-capped mountains that they had ever seen. They all stood silent for a few moments, just taking in the sights, until Sihu finally broke the stillness.

"I think, daughter, that if you do not chose this very place as your home, I shall think that you have lost your mind and I shall return at once to the Third Mesa!"

"I also think that this very place will be where our home should be placed. It feels like home to me even as I speak." said Aponi.

"I agree," said Caylen."We shall proceed at dawn to Atlin to hire a carpenter and crew to construct our home on this very spot. We must make haste as the winter snows come early in this country. You must now begin to plan the rooms of your home so that the carpenters will know what materials to bring."

By noon of the following day they were in the little village of Atlin attempting to hire a crew of skilled carpenters. Caylen's usual good luck prevailed, and the next morning they had in their employ, three carpenters, two stone masons and four workmen with building experience. In addition, Caylen discovered that another carpenter with considerable design and supervisory knowledge was also available for hire. Making this man his foreman, he gave to each man a one-hundred dollar advance payment and the promise of another two thousand each on completion of the house. He then took the foreman to the Atlin Bank and authorized the bank manager to provide whatever funds were needed to the foreman so that he could purchase the needed building materials and to also rent a tugboat and barge so as to transport the men, materials and supplies to the island.

The barge, the work crew, the building supplies, tents, cookstoves and two work horses arrived on the island ten days later. By nightfall of the following day, the camp had been set up and the crew was ready to begin work on the main house.

***

"Just what is going on here?" asked the foreman on the third day after his and the work crew's arrival on the island.

"What do you mean?" replied Caylen.

"Well, when we got here, everyone felt as though they had been given a drug to calm us. All of us felt as though we were on a vacation and not here to work."

"I don't know what it is but this place seems to have that same effect on everyone who steps foot on this place, including us." replied Caylen.

`"Another thing," said the foreman."Four different workers have told me that they think someone is watching them from the forests. They say that they haven't really seen anyone but they can sense the presence of something. This also happened to me just a little while ago when I went down to the barge for something."

"Yes, all of us have also had the same feeling from time to time since we arrived here but we have never seen anyone else here." said Caylen.

"I'm sure you have heard some of the stories the local natives tell about this island," the man said.

"Yes, I have heard most if not all of the stories," replied Caylen, smiling as he spoke."I especially like the ones that say that there are nothing but good spirits living here and that all things bad or evil are banned from here."

"Well, I'm certainly glad that they are only stories," the foreman said with a smile."Cause if they were true, I would be in a lot of trouble!"

"Wouldn't we all." replied Caylen.

***

Caylen and Aponi had spent their time poring over sketches and drawings of their new house. After much bantering back and forth as well as asking advise from both Sihu and Shilah, they finally reached some agreement of what they wanted their home to be.

The house was to be sited in the clearing about seventy five feet to the east of the stream on a low knoll. It was to have a partial basement that would contain a heating room and also a large cold-storage room. The home would be heated via a hot-water circulating system that was to be comprised of steel piping and a large two-hundred gallon hot water tank located above the firebox in the heating room.

A second, one hundred gallon water tank was also positioned above the heating rooms firebox. This tank was to provide hot water for domestic use in the household. A steel pipe was to be dug into a deep, ice-free well that would be located upstream of the house site, close to the flowing stream. This system would ensure that the home had a steady, year-round source of good potable water in their home. The well was located so as to permit gravity feeding of cold water to the entire home. Small hand pumps were to be installed in the bathrooms and kitchen that would bring the hot water up from the heating room. Two flush toilets were also installed in the two bathrooms. These toilets would flush into a large underground septic tank and then into a disposal field installed below frost level in the clearing to the north.

The house itself would be constructed of rock and logs with the entire rear and end walls of large local rocks cemented together. The main chimney would be located at the approximate midpoint of the rear wall with two smaller stacks at each end of the house. The main stack would extend through to, and serve the heating room as well as a large fireplace in the great room. One end of the home was to contain three bedrooms and a sitting room. This area was to be Caylens and Aponi's living area and was to have a smaller fireplace. The opposite end also contained three bedrooms, another small fireplace as well as the kitchen and eating area. This part of the house would be Sihu's and Shilah's and any visitors living area while the great room with its vaulted ceiling and huge rock fireplace would be used by all.

The front of the big house faced the northwest with the large triple-glazed windows providing a spectacular view of the big lake and the snow capped mountain peaks that lay just to the west. The views from the rear-facing, stone-surrounded windows, offered awe-inspiring scenes of the southern nearby mountains and the thick green forests that lay in that direction.

Caylen also had his stone masons and carpenters construct three other much smaller structures near the main house. These were to be used as a stone smoke house or drying house, a bear-proof stone food storage shed and a wood frame firewood shed.

As Caylen had instructed his carpenter foreman to construct the smokehouse and other out-buildings before beginning construction on the main house, he, Aponi, Sihu and Shilah were able to spend their time gathering, smoking and drying meats, fish, geese, ducks, berries and firewood for their use during the coming winter months. Aponi, Sihu and Shilah were astonished at the quantities of food that was readily available on their huge island and lake.

Shilah quickly became a proficient hunter and fisherman and quite enjoyed these tasks. He also became adept at handling one of the large freighter canoes that Caylen had brought to the island.

Sihu and Aponi, meanwhile, seemed to revel in gathering the wild mushrooms and berries that seemed to grow everywhere.

Caylen spent most of his days rushing about, ensuring all went well with the building process. He was forced to make two more supply trips by water and rail to Carcross and Whitehorse before summer's end. In mid-September, he and Aponi made a third furnishings-buying trip to complement the hand-crafted furniture that the talented carpenters had constructed for their home.

***

It was early October and the nights were beginning to get quite chilly when the carpenter foreman informed Caylen that their home and accessory buildings were now complete. Caylen took the little group of men back across the lake to Atlin and paid them each their full wages. As they thanked him and turned to leave, he called them back and gave each man a cash bonus of five hundred dollars.

"You all have done a great job for me and I think you deserve this," he said as he handed the extra monies over. By that evening he was back home on Serenity Island with his new family in their new home.

***

"This sleeping room that we have in this house is, by itself, larger than the entire pueblo that we all lived in

Oraibi." said Aponi as she walked about her newly-completed and fully-furnished house for the first time.

"It is our home now," said Caylen."This place is no longer a house as it has now become our home, yours and mine and all of our children's."

"My Brave Wolf, my Mato Honl, you make my heart swell with my love to where I am, on many the occasion, unable to speak." replied Aponi.

"What does your mother now think of all this?" asked Caylen.

"She has told me that she has much love for our home, especially the kitchen. She is astonished that we have such easy access to both hot and cold waters. She does, however, still have some fear of the white stone objects that are called 'flush toilets'. The rushing waters still frighten her so she continues to use the outdoor toilets."

Laughing, Caylen said, "She will soon get used to using them, especially when it gets down to forty below zero outside and the frost is one inch thick upon the outdoor toilet seats and the snow lies three feet deep on the ground."

***

With all of the winter preparations and the construction now complete, Caylen and Aponi spent the beautiful sunny fall days exploring their new island home.

"How big is this island that we have built our home upon? It appears to be as large as our Third Mesa lands." Aponi asked Caylen.

"It is probably larger." replied Caylen."But why don't we go and see."

"Whatever do you mean?"Aponi asked.

"If you wish to see just how big our island is, we should travel around it by canoe." Caylen said."We will camp out under the Northern Lights and enjoy the scenery."

"That sounds wonderful; I shall begin to pack immediately!"Aponi exclaimed.

***

The following morning, Caylen and Aponi paddled off down the southeastern shore of the big island. Their canoe held sleeping robes and enough supplies for a two week trip. It also held fishing supplies, gold pans and a canvas tarpaulin to be used as a tent if the weather turned nasty.

In less than seven hours the pair found themselves in the shadow of the huge snow-capped mountain that dominated the centre of the northern half of their island. The view from the canoe was so awesome that the couple could barely speak. They paddled slowly, stopping every few moments just to stare at the rocky, snow-covered peaks that seemed to dominate the entire western sky.

"This land of yours is so beautiful," whispered Aponi."This must be where the Great Qaletaka makes his home!"

"I do not know if the Great Spirit lives here but if I were he I know that I would, at the very least, visit here often." replied Caylen.

As they gazed in wonderment at the big mountain, the afternoon sun slowly turned the western sky a blood red as it began to slip behind the more distant mountain range that lay far off to the west. The scene changed from moment to moment as the sun slid even further behind the tall snow-capped spires of the granite peaks.

"I cannot believe that anything could be this beautiful." said Aponi as they came across a particularly beautiful cove."We must remember this particular place forever. We must give a name to this place and keep this day in our hearts for all time."

"What name would you like to give it?" asked Caylen.

"Why don't we call this cove, Mystic Cove?" said Aponi.

***

Caylen and Aponi took eight days to circumnavigate Serenity Island. They camped under the stars and explored every inlet and stream mouth that they saw. Caylen taught Aponi how to pan for gold, how to fish for the delectable multi-coloured grayling and how to navigate by the nighttime stars. Every point of land on the island that they rounded led to one spectacular view after another.

At one little weed-filled bay, they saw a mother moose and her two calves feeding on the lily pads that floated in profusion in the shallows.

"Watch the calf on the right Aponi." said Caylen as he projected his mind into the calf's. Aponi watched in fascination as the young moose turned and waded towards them, coming to a stop only a foot or so from where Aponi sat completely spellbound.

"Did you make him do that?" she asked.

"I must confess that I did. Would you like to scratch my nose? It's itchy from when I ate that last lily pad." said Caylen, with a grin.

***

It was when they rounded the southerly tip of Serenity Island that Caylen spotted another creek running into a little bay that contained a sandy beach. As it was getting late in the afternoon he suggested to Aponi that they camp there for the night. Later that evening, Caylen took his gold pan and walked upstream on the little stream to where a small pool had formed at the base of a short rapids.

As soon as he lifted the first pan of sand and pebbles out of the icy water, he yelled at Aponi to join him. When she approached, he tilted the pan of now partially-washed gravels so she could see the bright gold nuggets and golden sand that covered the bottom of the pan.

Aponi picked up the largest of the bright yellow stones and examined it closely."It is quite heavy, is it not?" she said."Is this the gold mine that you spoke of having?"

"No, I have never been here before. This is a new gold find that has not yet been developed. We shall camp here for a few days and investigate it further. If it is worthwhile, we shall stake out claims for you, myself, your mother and Shilah and I will register them at the gold office in Atlin when we return home."

***

It took only one more day for Caylen and Aponi to establish that the gold find was quite extensive and quite rich. By the end of the day on the creek, they had about three pounds of nuggets and dust and had panned upstream from the lake about one-half mile, with no lessoning of the quantity of gold. They spent the following morning preparing and setting out their claim stakes on both sides of the stream. Caylen, decided, as he placed the stakes, to include six more claims, explaining to Aponi that he would register two additional claims in his mother's and Bill's names.

"I will register the other four in the names of four of your people from the Third Mesa in Arizona," he said in reply to Aponi's questioning look."Your entire village shall share in the wealth of this mine They can build new schools and hire better teachers for the children of your tribe. They can also use some of it to build new or better homes for themselves.

"But how will we get the gold out?"asked Aponi.

Caylen replied."I shall ask Bill and Mom to come out and look over the site this fall. Then next year we shall ask some of your tribal people if they would like to come up and learn how to placer mine. That way they will be able to keep track of all the mines earnings."

***

It was late in the afternoon three days later when Caylen and Aponi turned into the little bay where their big boat was anchored. To their surprise, they could see a sleek two-masted white sailboat about thirty six feet long tied up beside their power boat. On board, watching as they paddled up, were Caylen's mother, Lora, and Bill, waving to them as they approached.

"When did you get that thing?"Caylen shouted."It sure is a beauty."

"I had it shipped up from Vancouver where it was built by a famous boat builder from Italy." said Bill."Come aboard and have a look at her; we will take you out for a sail tomorrow if you want. It handles like a dream and will outrun anything that sails." he added proudly.

***

It was late in the evening before everyone was up to date about everything that had occurred since they last saw one another. Caylen briefed Bill and Lora about the new gold find they made on their exploratory trip, telling them of their ideas as to the sharing of the profits with them and Aponi's tribe.

Both Bill and Lora thought that Caylen's suggestions about sharing of the future mine's profits was a great idea and would benefit Aponi's tribe greatly.

"Now, we have two things to tell you both." said Bill."One of them you will, I think, like; but the other is not quite as pleasant."

"What is it?" asked Caylen."Tell us the good first."

"I think I will let your mother tell you." said Bill, smiling at Lora.

"There is only one way to say this." said Lora."We will, in about six months or so, have a brand new member in our family and you will have either a baby brother or a baby sister. Now what do you think of that, young man?"

"Oh, my gosh!"exclaimed Aponi."Your expecting a baby! Wow, that's just fantastic. Isn't that great, Caylen?"

"That's really great news, Mom. Congratulations, Bill. Will you be okay, Mom? What does your doctor have to say?"

"He thinks it's grand. I am only thirty-nine years old and according to the doctor, I'm as healthy as can be."

"Well, that's really super; we will have to come out when he or she is born and welcome him into the family," said Caylen."Have you decided on a name yet? Now what was the other thing you had to tell us?"

"Our mine workings were recently attacked by a mob of claim jumpers. They killed three of our workers and wounded Kosumi. He is okay, and is recovering in the hospital in Whitehorse. But they got away with two weeks take of gold. Lokni estimated its value at about fifty thousand dollars." said Bill.

"Have the police investigated yet?"asked Aponi.

"They sent three men out. Apparently, they caught up with the robbers who managed to ambush and kill one young constable." replied Bill."The other two constables wisely decided that they were outgunned so they brought their dead partner out. Since then we have had reports that they have robbed three other placer miners, killing two more men in the process."The Superintendant also asked if I would consider signing up again and leading a chase group to apprehend this band of killers. He asked me as I know this country better than most. He also suggested that talk with you to see if you might be interested in joining us."

"I have to tell you that I am not too happy with Bill over this." said Lora.

"We certainly don't need the seventy-five dollars a month salary that I will make."Bill said.

"I know just how you feel." said Aponi."You are not going to go with Bill are you, Caylen?"

"I pretty much have to; this is what I trained for. It's our mine that they robbed and it was our men they killed." replied Caylen.

"I knew that this was exactly the way it would go, that's why I came out with Bill." said Lora."I will stay here with you, Aponi, while these two roam around looking for that gang."

"I can be ready to go by to-morrow morning." said Caylen."We will take our power boat as it is much faster than your sailboat. We'll also take the big canoe to use in the shallower waters. Do you have any idea where to begin this hunt, Bill?"

"That's why I came to you. They have been operating in both Atlin Lake and Tagish Lake over the past few weeks. All we know for sure is that the last reported robbery was on the east end of Graham Inlet and the one before that was just to the west. It appears that they may now be here on Atlin Lake somewhere." said Bill.

"What shall we do about our new gold find?"asked Aponi."Shall we wait until you get back before we do anything?"

"I'll make a quick trip over to Atlin and record our claims before we begin our manhunt." replied Caylen."You should write a letter tonight to your tribe's elders explaining the gold find and our idea regarding some of them coming up and working it. That way we will know if they are at all interested in becoming gold miners and if they are willing to come up and work the mine. If you write it now, I can mail it when I get to Atlin. I don't really know why they would not come up but it is a long way from their home.

Chapter 4

Manhunters

Caylen spent the remainder of the day preparing for the manhunt. He stowed sufficient food on board his boat to last Bill, himself and Warrior for three weeks or longer, if supplemented by fish and any small, edible game animals or waterfowl that they might shoot or catch.. He also topped up the boat's fuel tanks and lashed an extra two hundred-gallons of the boat's fuel on the deck. By eight o'clock that evening he was fully prepared and ready to leave.

* * *

Later that evening, Caylen asked Shilah to accompany him for a walk on the sandy beach of the little bay."We will be gone for some time, Shilah, and I want you to look after things here while we are away. You have the keys for our gun locker and I want you to carry a loaded revolver with you at all times. These are some really bad people that we are searching for and they just might be in this area. Our location and the fact that we are quite wealthy is common knowledge in the Atlin area so these men just might try to rob us." Caylen said, adding, "You should probably not sleep in the main house either. If they do try something, it would be best if you were away from the women."

"I shall protect our family with my life." said Shilah."You may have noticed, Caylen, that I said 'our family', as that is how I feel about all of you. I feel that I am now part of your family. Is this feeling of family 'belonging' on my part acceptable to yourself or is it wrong of me?"

"It is not only acceptable, Shilah, it is an honor. I gladly accept you as a member of our family. I would also be honored if you were to agree to become my brother and allow our blood to mingle as one."

"I, too, would be honored by such a ritual." said Shilah, drawing the small razor-sharp knife that he always carried on his person. It took only a few minutes more and a small cut on each of the their hands. Holding their hands together so as to make their blood mingle, the two men pledged their lives to each other to complete the ritual.

I also have one more thing that I would like to ask of my brother, Brave Wolf, on this day." said Shilah.

"And what is it that you wish to ask, Shilah? Do you know that that is the first time in ages that anyone has called me 'Brave Wolf'." said Caylen.

"I have watched you closely ever since my arrival in this wonderful land and know that the great Sania chose well when he decided that you should be called by the name Brave Wolf." replied Shilah.

"I thank you, brother Shilah, for your kind words. Now what was it you wished to ask of me?"

"I wish to ask of you, as the chief of our little band, that I be permitted to become the lifemate of Sihu." said Shilah.

"It's not me that you need to ask." replied Caylen."Have you spoken to Sihu of your wish to become her lifemate?"

"Many times, Brave Wolf. And each time her reply is the same. She insists that I must obtain the permission of yourself before she will consent."

"Well, even though I cannot understand why you would need it, you certainly may have my consent. I, and

I am sure Aponi will agree, am really happy for you and Sihu. We were wondering what was taking you so long to ask for the hand of Sihu, I only hope for your sake that she accepts your proposal." said Caylen.

"If she does not, I shall return at once to the Third Mesa, ancestral home of my people." said Shilah.

"I am quite sure she will accept." said Caylen."When are you going to ask her?"

"I shall not ask her until your safe return from your hunt and your capture of those bad men." said Shilah."Now, my brother, I must prepare myself for this keeping safe of my family."

* * *

When Caylen was alone with Aponi, he told her of his conversation with Shilah and how Shilah had asked about Sihu. He also told her about his becoming blood-brothers with him.

"I'm glad," she said."Mom was beginning to wonder if he would ever get up the courage to ask you if he could ask her."

"Well, he's not going to ask until I get back from this manhunt. I have asked him to stay away from the main house and to do patrols about the area. We do not know where these characters are right now. They just might decide to show up here."

"I wish you were not going. This could be a dangerous hunt and I will miss you." said Aponi.

"I will visit you every chance I get." said Caylen. Watch for a raven or an eagle that seems to be too friendly to be a wild bird. That will be me looking in on you. I will have a twig in my beak that I will give to you so that you will know it is I."

"I will watch for my love each and every day until you return to me." said Aponi, holding Caylen tightly in her arms.

"I don't expect this to take more than a week." said Caylen."We will find out where they are by using my powers and then all we have to do is catch up with them, take them into custody and deliver them all to the Whitehorse jail."

***

Caylen, Bill and Warrior were on board Caylens power-er boat at dawn. They had also decided at the last minute to take two eighteen foot freighter canoes with them in the event they had to travel in shallow river waters. By noon they were in Atlin where Caylen mailed Aponi's letter to the Third Mesa elders informing them of the gold find and inviting them to send a crew up to work the mine for a substantial share in the profits. He also stopped at the recording office where he recorded all the mining claims pertaining to their new find.

Following the claim recording, Caylen met Bill at the Atlin police station where he found him being briefed by the local Corporal of the North West Mounted Police.

"Corporal Ward, this is Caylen Helms, the young man I was telling you about. Caylen, meet Jamie Ward. Jamie worked for me in Whitehorse for a year before he was stationed at the White Pass summit to monitor the gold hunters coming into Canada. He's a good man and has much to tell us."

"Bill has told me all about you, Caylen, and your famous wolf dog. Where is he? Did you bring him with you?"

"I hope he didn't build me up too much." said Caylen, confident that Bill would tell no one of his powers without his permission."Warrior is just outside if you would like to say hello."

"I would very much like to meet him before you leave." said Corporal Ward.

"Jamie has much to tell us about our murdering mine robbers." said Bill."It seems they have recently been here and have been bragging about their amazing good luck at mining. He also has something really interesting to tell us about another matter that you will find very interesting, Caylen."

"How long ago were the mine thieves here and why did you not arrest them?" Caylen asked."And what is this other matter that I will find interesting?"

"There were five men here a few weeks ago that were bragging about all the gold that they had found. Unfortunately they left before I got word of the robberies and I had no idea where to look for them." said Corporal Ward.

"The other thing that you might find interesting is that there was a mean, ugly fellow around here for a few days asking a lot of questions about you. Questions like, if you were still around here, where you lived, if there was anyone living with you. All kinds of questions like that. He was also asking about a woman named Lora. Isn't that your wife's name, Bill?"

"Yes, it is." replied Bill."Did this guy have a name and is he still around?"

"His name was Viktor Lubak and he said he used to have a older brother who was prospecting up here somewhere. He got himself a outfit and took off last week somewhere to the north in a eighteen foot freighter. Said he had a score to settle and some gold to find."

"I'll be damned." said Caylen."Fariss never spoke of a brother but I can't believe that there could be more than one Lubak in this world. I wonder if he knows where my house is?"

"It's pretty common knowledge in Atlin that some really rich young man has built himself a mansion over on the north end of the big island and lives there with his beautiful Indian wife, her mother and another Indian man." said Corporal Ward.

"Well, if we come across him we will have a really serious heart to heart conversation with him. We will try to convince him that this country will not be conducive to his good health and that he should be moving on." said Bill.

"I'm not too sure that I could be that friendly towards him until I know just what it is that he wants." said Caylen.

"Well, we had best get our gear under cover and then do some snooping around to see what we can find out about our murdering robbers. Will we see you later today, Jamie?" asked Bill.

"Why don't you and Caylen come over to the house for supper?" said Jamie."I'm certain Gail will not object and will be glad to see you again."

"We will only be too happy to eat anything that great cook you married has prepared for us, How is that beautiful wife of yours doing?, I'll bet she has her hands full with those two boys. They must be about seven or eight years old now." Bill replied.
"They are eight years old and they are always asking why their Uncle Bill never comes to see them." Said Jamie.

* * *

Bill and Caylen spent the next few hours visiting Atlins' many bars, talking to the bartenders and any customers that they found. From what they could ascertain, no-one seemed to know just who the five murderers were, where they came from or where they had gone. At the end of the day all they knew for sure was that there were five men who were spending a lot of money and bragging about their rich gold finds a few weeks earlier and that they had left by canoe in a westerly direction across the big Atlin Lake. They also got a vague description of the five men as well as an even more vague description of the man who claimed to be Viktor Lubak. Before going to Corporal Wards home for supper, Bill stopped at the Atlin general store and purchase two kites, one for each of the two boys.

***

Following a delicious meal of roast caribou, mashed potatoes with gravy and a large piece of apple pie, Bill and Caylen informed Jamie of their immediate search plans while the twin boys wrestled and played with Warrior who seemed to revel in all the attention. It seemed that no matter what the boys did or how rough they were with him, Warrior just played on, seemingly shrugging off any minor hurts the pair bestowed on him. On one occasion, when one of the boys stepped on his tail, he did stand and utter a low growl as if to say, "Okay, guys, let's just slow down a little."

***

The sun was just starting to rise over the Eastern mountains when Bill cast off the boat lines and Caylen steered his boat out into the open waters of the big lake. Once they were well out onto the lake, he spun the wheel, turning the big boat onto a northern heading. They reckoned that since the robbers had come from Tagish Lake after robbing placer miners there, that they would now be heading for new grounds on the northern reaches of the big Atlin Lake.

They discussed at length how Caylen could use some of his powers and finally concluded that the best way was for him to use ravens or eagles to scout ahead and examine closely, the eastern shoreline of the lake, searching for any sign of the robbers.

"Can you read in the minds of the birds or animals that you occupy what they have seen in the near past? For example, if they had seen this group of bad men yesterday would you know that from the minds of those birds or animals if you were to occupy their minds to-day?" asked Bill.

"I have never attempted that." said Caylen."Normally I am just using whatever I am occupying as a vehicle for my essence and am seeing what they are seeing at that particular time. I shall try that on the next raven we see."

"What about occupying more than one creatures mind at a time?"asked Bill."Have you ever tried that?"

"No, I haven't ever tried that but I will also try that and see what happens. To do that I would have to be in control of myself and each of the creatures that I am oc-cupying. I think that might be a bit too much."

"There is a eagle way up there, just to the right of us near the shore line." said Bill, pointing at the high flying raptor.

"Okay, I will take over his mind and have a look see up the coast a ways." replied Caylen.

For the next few hours Caylen, inside the eagle's mind, directed him to fly a zigzag pattern for about forty miles up the lake. Seeing only one lone prospector pan-ning for gold at the mouth of a small stream he soared back to the boat where he left the eagle's mind and rejoined his own.

"Well, I saw only one old man that looked about se-venty years old panning at the mouth of a stream about ten miles up." he said to Bill."From the state of his camp he's been there for some time so we should probably go and speak to him and see if he has seen anything."

***

Bill and Caylen arrived at the camp of the old man about two in the afternoon. Questioning him, they dis-covered that he had been camped at that same location for at least three weeks and had, during that time, seen only two other canoeists paddling southward along the shore line. As they had not stopped, he did not know their destination or where they had come from.

"Well, where to now?"asked Bill once they had gotten underway again."Maybe we should cross the lake and head back southward along the western shore."

"Sounds like a good idea. Maybe we will see someone over there who knows or has seen these characters." said Caylen, turning the boat to the west as he spoke.

***

By nightfall Caylen and Bill were anchored just offshore another small creek that flowed into the lake from the western mountains. The pair were soon feasting on the four grayling that Caylen caught within a very few minutes in the creek mouth.

Both quite tired, the pair were soon snoring away in their respective bunks while Warrior dozed quietly on the open boat deck.

***

It was about three am when Caylen woke with a start. He lay quietly for a few moments, collecting his thoughts and listening to the soft snoring of Bill. His thoughts then went back to his long ago stay with Sania. He remembered the many teaching sessions that the old man had given him following his vision quest and the granting of his powers by Qaletaka, the Great Spirit and Guardian of the people. As he lay quietly, recalling the many pleasant and good times that he experienced during his stay with the old man, for some reason he suddenly remembered something that the old man's spirit had said to him when he visited his body following his death.

"I shall leave with you, for all time, a small piece of my essence so that you may never forget of me and so that, if need be, you may speak to me, but you shall only see me again when the Great Spirit finally brings you be-

fore him." Sania's spirit said. *"I must go now, for the Great Spirit again calls."* said the spirit of Sania as he slowly faded from sight.

"I wonder why I just thought of that."Caylen said aloud to himself.

"You thought of that moment, young Mato Honl, because I just reminded you." a loud familiar voice said in Caylens mind.

Startled for just a moment, Caylens mind raced as he suddenly realized what was now occurring."Is that you Sania, my brother?, is that really you?" he said aloud.

"Yes, it is I, your blood brother Sania." said the voice in Caylens head.

Fully awake now, Caylen looked over to where Bill still lay unmoving and seemingly, still sound asleep."Why have you come to me, my brother?, do you wish of me something?"

"I have come to speak to you of my granddaughter Sihu and my great-granddaughter Aponi for they are in mortal danger. Even as I now speak to you, evil men plan to harm them. You must make all haste to return to them and rid your world of these evil beings that wish to harm them. Qaletaka, the Great Spirit has granted me this boon to warn you of these evil men. Now rise and make haste to return to your home less these evil men harm our loved ones. I must go now, my brother, the Great Spirit again calls to me.

Caylen quickly jumped out of his bunk, yelling at Bill as he did so."Bill, Bill, get up, we have to leave for home right now! "

"What on earth is going on?"queried Bill as he sat up on his bunk.

"We have to get back home as fast as we can, the men we are after are going to attack my home and possibly harm Sihu, Aponi and Mom. Come on, let's get going!" Caylen replied.

"Now just hold on, young man, you are acting really funny. I listened to you a few minutes ago talking to yourself and now you say we have to turn around and head home. What's going on?"

Caylen hesitated for only a moment before explaining to Bill Sania's promise that he, Sania, would speak to Caylen from the after-world if he or his loved ones were ever in extreme danger.

"They must be in danger or he would not have come to speak to me. I was not talking to myself, I was asking him why he was here. I did not realize that I was talking out loud. When he speaks to me he speaks to me through my mind, not with a voice that anyone can hear, but with thoughts that are silent. I can speak to him in the same way, through my mind."

"Well, I know enough about you and your powers to know that it would be foolish of me to not believe you, so let's pull the anchor up and get this boat into high gear." Bill replied.

It took only a few moments for the pair to hoist anchor and get underway in the early light of dawn, heading south at the boat's best speed. It was nearly twelve hours later when they began to see the dark shape of the Island's shoreline ahead of them. As they grew closer, Caylen could feel the icy cold fingers of fear for his family begin to inch up his back.

"Maybe I should have rode a raven down here earlier so that we could know what was going on." he said to Bill.

"Now you listen up young man. You may have all those 'powers', but I have nearly sixteen years as a policeman and I learned, long ago, the most important thing that every policeman must learn if he is to be a good policeman."

"And just what is that?" asked Caylen.

"You must never, ever, try to second guess something that you have said or done on a case. Once you start to second guess yourself, you're finished as a policeman because you will soon begin to doubt everything you do and you will end up losing all confidence in yourself."

"That makes a lot of sense."Caylen said."But I still wish I had flown down earlier."

"All that is too late now because we are here. You could not have done anything anyway, even if you had flown down in a eagle or a raven. Isn't that Shilah standing there on the dock?" said Bill.

"Sure is, I guess he saw us coming and came down to greet us. I wonder if he has seen any signs of the bad bunch." Caylen said.

"Well, I see the women standing on the porch waving at us so I presume that the bad guys have not been here, or they have come and gone." Bill replied as they pulled up to the dock.

"You two will not believe what has happened here since you left." Shilah said as he tied the boat to the dock.

"Right now I'm ready to believe just about anything." said Bill."Tell us."

"Well, first of all, we now own two nice freighter canoes, five men's gear and about seven pounds of gold." Shilah said."Secondly, the reason we now own all those things is because the owners are all dead and lying in the bushes about three hundred yards southeast of here."

"Did you kill them all?" asked Caylen, in astonishment."What happened?"

"No, I did not kill them, I did not even get a chance to fire one shot. They were all dead when I found them."

"What do you mean, they were all dead when you found them? What killed them? Maybe you should tell us the whole story." said Caylen.

"Well, I was around the corner at that little rocky point watching out to the north when I saw the two canoes coming up along the shore."Shilah said."I hid in the bush waiting to see what they did. They landed just off the point and came ashore with their rifles. They stood around for about twenty minutes talking about how they would approach the house. They did not realize that you were not home and they finally decided that you would not give up without a fight. They decided that they were going to kill everyone here, steal whatever was worth stealing and then burn the place down."

"Oh my God." exclaimed Bill."What happened next?"

"I knew that I had to warn the women so I took off back to the house to make sure all the windows were shuttered, the doors locked and that they all had loaded guns to protect themselves." Shilah said."Then I went up on the roof deck to wait for them to show up. I meant to shoot them all as they came over the bridge. This all happened early yesterday afternoon. I waited for about two hours before I heard it."

"Heard what?" asked Caylen.

"The screaming!" answered Shilah."The most ungodly screaming I have ever heard in my life!"

"What was the cause of it? Was it the bad guys?" Caylen asked.

"That's what I thought at first, but after a minute or two the screaming had stopped. Then it began again. I soon realized that the second period of screaming was different than the first and I really began to get confused. I waited for about an hour after all the noise had stopped before I ventured out for a look-see." said Shilah."I found all five of the would-be crooks dead with their necks quite obviously broken. Their bodies were all together on the ground, laid side by side in that little clearing just in from the point where they originally landed. I looked all around the area but whoever or whatever killed them was long gone. I was still checking the area when I heard more of the particular weird screaming that I heard at the start. This time it came from much further away and from two different directions. I don't need to tell you that I was terrified, I have never heard such an awful sound."

"Can you describe the screaming to us?"asked Caylen, thinking back to the noise that the Wendigo had made as it attacked Fariss.

"I will try." Shilah said."Here it comes, "Aagooooooouummmmmm ". The long, drawn-out deep eerie scream that Shilah let out caused both Caylen and Bill's neck hairs to stand erect for a moment before the screams echo returned from the southern mountain, *Aagooooooouummmmmmm Aagooooooouummmmmm* The sound reverberated and echoed loudly through the forest and clearing, carrying out and over the lake.

"Did you hear that echo?"asked Bill.

"I sure did, but the second scream was not an echo." said Caylen."I think the second scream was a response to Shilah's scream. I don't think that we are alone on this island. Something out there killed those men and then left."

"Are we in danger?"Bill asked."What do you think we should do? Do you think it might be another Wendigo?"

"No, I am sure it is not a Wendigo." said Caylen."Remember that a Wendigo must consume evil in order to survive. This thing, whatever it is, did not eat any of those men."

"It was a Matah Kagmi Man." said Shilah with a sudden realization."They are here!"

"What do you mean, Matah Kagmi Man?" asked Caylen.

"The Matah Kagmi are the wild people of the forests. They are big people who stand eight feet tall and are covered from head to toe with thick hair. They are normally a very gentle, reclusive people who try to avoid the real people. They eat the roots, mushrooms, and forest vegetation but will occasionally eat meat. They do like fishes and will come down to the streams and lakes when the fish are running."

"If they are a gentle people why did they kill these men but leave you guys alone?" asked Bill.

"It is known by our people that the Matah Kagmi do not mind living near the real people as long as the real people are peaceful and permit them to live as they wish. It is also well known that they, like the Wendigo, can sense evil in a person, and once angered, that they will take whatever means necessary to rid the earth of whoever has angered them." said Shilah."It is thought that the Wendigo was once a Matah Kagmi who so displeased the Great Spirit through his actions that the Great Spirit turned him into a Wendigo who was then banished by the Matah Kagmi to remote areas of the forest to live by himself forever. These bad men were, from what I overheard, camped about three miles down on the eastern shore of our island for about two weeks. They must have done something to anger the Matah Kagmi so that when they came here the Matah Kagmi decided to end their existence."

"Where do you think they live and how many would you think there are?" Caylen asked."Can we expect them to give us problems now that they are aware of our presence?"

"They usually live in family groups of no more than seven or eight in big caves up in the mountains. They are probably what we could all sense when we first arrived here. I am sure that the Matah Kagmi were well aware of our presence very soon after we arrived. I do not believe that they will bother us at all. I think that we are fortunate that they are here and that they came to my assistance when they did. I am not positive that I could have stopped them by myself." Shilah said.

"Maybe we should go up the mountain to meet them and thank them." Caylen said.

"That would not be wise." Shilah said."They are a very shy people and might not like us moving through their territory. It would be much better if we just left them some gifts of their favourite foods. Dried and smoked fish as well as salt and tanned leather are some of the things that they like. If we leave some of those things out, they will find them. If they like what we leave they will let us know that by leaving us something in return."

"That is easy to do." Caylen said."We shall take some of those things out tomorrow and leave them on the rocky point where the crooks landed. Now I guess we had better go and take those men and bury them before the wolves get to them."

***

Bill, Shilah and Caylen decided to bury the five dead robbers in the small clearing where they had found them.

"This will forever be this island's cemetery." Caylen said."We shall bury these men properly and shall utter a prayer for them even though they were evil. Perhaps our prayers will convince the Great Spirit that their souls are not all bad."

***

Three days later, Bill and Lora left on their sailboat. Their plans were to cruise about on both Atlin and Tagish lakes enjoying the scenery and the fishing before returning to their Whitehorse home. Before leaving, Bill accompanied Caylen in his powerboat down to inspect the gold find that Caylen and Aponi had found on the southern tip of the island. It took only a few hours of panning before Bill said to Caylen, "I'm sure that you have found another *'Bonanza'* Caylen. This is a really rich find and I am sure it will make everyone richer than we already are. I also think it's a great idea to have Aponi's tribe mine it for a share. It will really help them out.

Chapter 5

Romance

It was only a few days later when Shilah reported to Caylen that the gifts of dried fish and tanned caribou hides were missing from the rock on which they had been left for the Matah Kagmi people.

"They left some dried berries and mushrooms in their place." said Shilah."That means that they are not our enemies and that we shall still be tolerated here." he added.

"Good," said Caylen."We shall continue to, on occasion, leave them something at that same place. By the way, Shilah, have you asked Sihu if she will become your lifemate yet?"

"No, I have not." replied Shilah."Our custom is for a man to approach the father of the woman he wishes to marry. The father, if he approves of the man, goes to the woman and asks if she is willing to become the lifemate of the man. If the woman's father approves and the woman agrees to the marriage the man must thank the father with gifts of some great value to the man. The gifts may not be of value to the woman's father but must be of great value to the man."

"Are you suggesting what I think you are suggesting?"asked Caylen.

"Your words confuse me, my brother." replied Shilah."What I wish to ask of my brother is if he will approach Sihu, mother of Aponi, on my behalf. I would ask that you tell her of my heart's thoughts and that I wish for her to become my lifemate. I would also ask that you tell her that I wish to hear of her heart's wishes on this matter of importance."

"I would only be too happy to approach Sihu on your behalf, Shilah. You are a good man and my brother. I shall consider it a great honor to take your offer to her. You will make her a good lifemate and husband. Do you also realize that once you are married to Sihu that you will not be just my blood-brother, but also my father-in-law?"

"Yes, that is a good thing. Our families shall then be as one and shall be blessed by the Great Spirit forever." said Shilah.

"When would you like me to speak to Sihu, Shilah, and would you like to be present when I do?" asked Caylen.

"You may speak to her when you please but as for my being present when you do, I do not think that would be wise. If Sihu is displeased and chooses to not become my lifemate, I shall be very sad and shall not wish that she see me in that state." Sihu replied.

"As you wish, my brother, I shall speak to her of your heart before this day is done. You shall know her heart's wishes before the moon rises." Caylen said.

"I thank you, my brother. I go now to prepare myself for the reply of my love and to think on a gift for my blood-brother for his respect and his caring ways."

"You don't have to thank me with anything, Shilah, you are my blood-brother and my friend. I do not do this thing for you for gifts. I do it because you are my friend." replied Caylen.

"I must give you a gift of much importance to only myself." Shilah said."It would dishonor Sihu and my own family were I to not present you with such a gift. While my gift may be of no monetary value to you or any other being, it must be of great personal value to myself."

"Alright, "Caylen said."You may, providing Sihu accepts your proposal, present me with such a gift. I would be honored to respect your wishes and your traditions."

Later that evening, Caylen informed Aponi of Shilah's wish to wed her mother. Aponi's response to this information was as expected.

"Oh, I'm so happy for Mom, I must tell her immediately. She was beginning to wonder about him." Aponi said as she rose to her feet.

"Hold on, Aponi, I am the one who is supposed to ask her for her hand in marriage on Shilah's behalf. He wants to go along with traditions as much as is possible and has asked me to approach Sihu for him." said Caylen, beginning to get into the spirit of the moment.

"Okay, " said Aponi."I will go out to the kitchen and let her know that you want to speak to her. I will not let on that I know what you are about to ask her. She will be so happy!. I am also going to eavesdrop on you from the hallway when you talk to her. Do you know where Shilah is? Is he in the house?"

It was only a moment after Aponi had left the room before Sihu appeared, holding a damp dish-drying towel in her hands.

"Did you wish to speak to me, Caylen?" she asked, sitting across from him in the large leather easy chair.

"Yes, Sihu, I have a couple of things we need to speak about. Have you written to the Elders at the Third Mesa about the gold mine to ask them if they are interested in our proposal?"

"Yes, I have, my letter to them was in that batch of mail you took over to Atlin when you and Bill went looking for those bad men." Sihu replied.

"How long do you think it will take for them to decide if they wish to send a mining crew up here?" asked Caylen.

"We should hear from the Elders within a few weeks. They will need to tell everyone and then find enough young men who are willing to go so far from their homes."

"Okay, thanks, Sihu. And oh, by the way, Shilah has asked me to ask you, on his behalf, if you will marry him?"

"You're welcome --- what did you just say?" Sihu exclaimed, not at first entirely grasping all of what Caylen had just said.

"I just asked you, on Shilah's behalf, and as his chosen spokesperson, if you would agree to become his wife and his lifemate and to love and care for him just as he loves and cares for you." Caylen replied with a smile just as Aponi burst into the room from where she had been eavesdropping on Caylen's conversation with Sihu.

"Oh, Mom, I'm so happy for you and Shilah!" said Aponi before Sihu had any chance to reply to Caylen.

"Well, young man, you go out and tell that cranky old Hopi Indian that I thank him for his offer but he will get no reply of any sort from me until he finds the courage to ask me himself! " said Sihu as she stormed out of the room, leaving Aponi and Caylen staring at each other in wonderment.

"I think I blew that!" said Caylen after a moment."What am I supposed to tell Shilah now?"

"No, I think you did fine," said Aponi."I think, though, that Mom was just surprised that Shilah proposed in the old tribal ways. I think that she was hoping that Shilah would ask her himself. She thinks doing it that way would be much more romantic. Mom may not appear so, but she is a real romantic at heart."

I suppose I had better go and tell Shilah." said Caylen with a grin."He is going to have to find the courage to do this himself!"

"Oh, Caylen, it's not funny! You're acting as though you're having fun with this." Aponi said.

"Well, I am." Caylen replied."This whole proposal thing is turning into a real comedy of errors!"

With that comment, and after he and Aponi had stifled their laughter over what had just occurred, Caylen left to find and inform Shilah that he would have to personally present his proposal to the miffed Sihu.

***

Shilah and Sihu were married two weeks later by a Justice of the Peace in Atlin. Shilah, following his proposal to Sihu on bended knee and her acceptance, had asked Caylen to represent him as his best man with Sihu asking Bill to give her away. Having studied the marriage rites of Christian whites, she had become enamored with the idea of being married in the ways of a Christian-Canadian with Shilah eventually but reluctantly agreeing.

During their Atlin visit the mail service delivered a response to them from the Elders of the Third Mesa reserve concerning the operation of the newly found gold mine. They indicated that they would be only too happy to accept Caylen's generous offer and would be sending, in early spring, four hardworking young men to work the mine.

***

Following the marriage of Shilah and Sihu, Bill and Lora returned to their Whitehorse home with a promise from Caylen and Aponi that they would make every effort to travel to Whitehorse to attend the birth of Lora and Bill's child, due in early March.

Shilah, on the day after they had all returned to Serenity Island and Tranquility Place, approached Caylen as he stood on the pier casting a dry fly out to the voracious grayling that were always cruising around the bay searching for food.

"I have come to thank you for all your help in arranging for my marriage to Sihu." he began.

"Your very welcome, my brother, is your marriage all that you hoped for?" Caylen asked.

"It is that and much more." replied Shilah. I also am here to give you the gift that I promised."

"You do not need to give me anything." said Caylen."I am your brother and as brothers we do things for each other without seeking anything in return."

"As I said before, you would dishonor me if you refused my gift." Shilah said.

"Then, Shilah, I gratefully accept your gift, whatever it may be." Caylen replied.

"My gift to you, my brother, is the gift of my loyalty and my friendship forever. No matter what troubles might come between us, I pledge my lifelong service to you and Aponi, the daughter of Sihu and the daughter of my wife. That is the gift of thanks that I give to you, my brother." Shilah said.

"Wow!" said Caylen."That is a huge gift that you have given me. I know that your traditions bind you to these rituals but that is really a huge boon that you have given. I thank you my brother. I thank you with all my heart and I wish you to know again that my heart swells with my pride and the honor in having such a brother as you."
**

Chapter 6

More Romance

It was mid-September when Caylen and Aponi first noticed that Warrior was missing overnight. He often went roaming about the island forests but was always home for the evening meal. He seldom, killed anything for food now but he still enjoyed the thrill of the chase. As there was always plenty for him to eat and drink at Tranquility Place he saw no need to kill for food. Still, he would go out and just run for hours on end, going wherever he pleased around the big island. He would not now, however, venture more than about five hundred feet up the slopes of the big Serenity Mountain. He had, on one occasion, followed a caribou cow up about a thousand feet or so but when he suddenly encountered a strange powerful odor that actually caused him to choke, he broke off the chase and returned to a lower elevation where the strange unpleasant smell was not present. He returned to the same area a few weeks later to find that the strange pungent smell was still present and was just as bad as it had been on his first venture into the area.

"Have any of you seen Warrior this morning?" Caylen asked of everyone present at the breakfast table.

Warrior did not normally sleep indoors unless the weather was so cold that Caylen, afraid he would freeze if left outdoors, called him into the big house before he retired for the night.

"I haven't seen him since yesterday morning," Aponi replied.

"I have not seen him since the day before yesterday." said Shilah."I was out in the forest collecting mushrooms with Sihu yesterday. Warrior usually comes with
us but we did not see him at all yesterday."

***

Warrior, early the previous day, decided to take a
run down the western side of Serenity Island. He was
about an hour run from Tranquility Place when his sensitive nostrils detected a unfamiliar yet somewhat pleasant
smell. He stopped immediately and ranged about in the
thick coniferous forest until he determined the source of
the smell. Once he had found the scent trail he took off
again, at a slower lope, following the unfamiliar, yet
strangely appealing scent that grew ever stronger as he
closed in on its source.

***

The big young white female arctic timber wolf had
made up her mind earlier that year to leave the protection of her home pack and strike out on her own. The big
grey dominant female of her pack, was always trying to
pick a fight with her in order to display her dominance
over the much larger white female who did not wish to
fight her for the coveted position of dominant female and
the right to mate with the dominant male and the overall
leader of the pack. Finally realizing that she must either
fight the dominant female to the death or leave the pack,
the big white female wolf finally decided to strike out on
her own. She trotted in a northeasterly direction for
three days before arriving on the shores of a huge ex-
panse of open water. Deciding then to turn north, she
followed the shoreline of the big lake until the dark line
of trees that marked the distant western shore of Serenity Island appeared to her to be within swimming distance. Without a moment's hesitation, she leapt into the
icy waters of the big lake and began swimming towards

the bright sun that had just peered over the far-away line of trees. She had been swimming for about three hours before the realization came over her that she was now in deep trouble. Her legs were beginning to grow numb in the frigid water and she could barely feel her feet. With the far shoreline only marginally closer at this point, she was contemplating turning about and returning to her starting point when she spied, just ahead of her, a large spruce tree that was floating in the cold lake waters. Turning towards it, she soon managed to grasp the limbs of the big tree with her numbed front legs and to pull herself out of the icy waters and onto the big trunk of the tree. Now high and dry, she stretched herself out on the trees warm trunk and was soon fast asleep in the fall sun as the big tree, pulled ever northwards by the lakes current moved closer to her destination of Serenity Island.

**

Several hours later, the big she wolf came awake with a start. She had now recovered completely from her near-hypothermia and found herself quite hungry. She looked off to the east and to her amazement saw her destination shoreline only a few hundred feet away. Again, without hesitation, she leapt off the tree trunk and into the cold waters of the big lake. Within a few moments, she was shaking the water from her thick fur and was sniffing about, exploring her island home and looking for food. Within a few more minutes she was happily dining on the snowshoe hare that she captured with only three quick leaps.

The large wolf, after a busy two weeks of exploring her new territory, decided that she was completely alone and that there were no other wolves claiming the area she now occupied. She did, on one of her exploratory trips, detect a very faint scent of another wolf but with absolutely no indications of any territorial spotting she soon claimed a large tract of the forest as her own, travelling around her chosen area every few days, renewing her scent marks on rocks, logs or any other prominent feature she could find. As wolves are normally quite social, she did find that she was now beginning to miss the company of others of her kind and wondered if she had done the right thing by leaving her far away home pack.

The young wolf had no way of realizing that her body was now, as a mature, fully-grown Northern female timber wolf, coming into estrus and that she would, as such, be quite receptive to a mature male timber wolf. All she really knew was that she now really craved the company of another wolf.

***

A few weeks after the white female wolf's arrival on Serenity Island, Warrior, travelling southward on one of his frequent island romps, suddenly came to a stop so fast he nearly fell forward and over onto his face. The slight, very pleasant, unfamiliar scent he had been following was suddenly and without warning, now overwhelming in its intensity. His sensitive nose curling up slightly, he sniffed about until he located the log that the female wolf had, that very morning, urinated on to mark her new territory.

It took Warrior only a moment and two or three deep sniffs to decide that the strangely appealing scent marking had been left by a mature lone female timber wolf who would soon be receptive to a male wolf's sexual advances. Now five years old, Warrior, a pure black Northern timber wolf, was in his prime. At approximately two-hundred and fifteen pounds, he was exceptionally large for his species and would make a great catch for any willing female wolf. With his emerald green eyes that appeared at times to be luminescent, he seemed able, as had been his father, to mesmerize thoroughly and completely any animal that looked directly into them.

***

The big white female wolf was fast asleep, lying on a warm grassy knoll just a few hundred feet from the lakeshore when the loud croaking of a pair of big ravens roused her from her dreams of a handsome young male timber wolf. Lying quite still with only her eyes moving back and forth, she thought for a moment that she was still asleep and dreaming. Just in front of her, about fifteen feet down the slope from where she lay, sitting on his haunches staring at her with beautiful large luminescent green eyes was the, biggest and the most handsomest, jet-black wolf that she had ever seen. She blinked two or three times to ensure that what she was seeing was in fact real before she jumped to her feet and stood, staring down at Warrior.

Warrior could also not quite believe what he was seeing. Lying on the warm grass, obviously sound asleep was the whitest, most beautiful, she-wolf that he had ever beheld. At the sudden clamoring of the ravens, he saw her big blue eyes pop wide open and fix on him.

Snow stared back at him in a unbelieving fashion for a few moments as she came fully awake. She thought for a moment that she must be dreaming. She had never seen another wolf as black, as big, or as handsome as the one that now sat gaping at her. The big white female wolf rose to her feet to stand directly in front of Warrior, not quite knowing what to expect from this strange beautiful male wolf who was obviously in prime condition and totally lacking in fear at finding another wolf on his island.

Warrior slowly approached her in a stiff legged fashion with his long, black, bushy tail held high behind, prepared, if necessary, to enter into battle with her.

She stood quietly, awaiting his detailed inspection of her entire body as he circled her, sniffing and staring into her sky-blue eyes with his own green, luminescent eyes until she could stand it no longer. With a sharp yelp, she leapt into the air and began to prance about Warrior in pleasure, showing her desired friendship towards this big handsome wolf that had found her.

Warrior, sensing almost immediately that this pretty, snow-white she-wolf was alone and pleased to see him, could also contain himself no longer. In less than a moment, both he and she were prancing around each other making, pleasurable yelps and yips at each as they became further acquainted.

Warrior soon decided that they had played about long enough. He decided that it was now time to find out if this pretty she wolf would follow him and accept him as her leader or if she would remain independent and alone to make her own way about in the island forest.

Although both Warrior and female wolf did not, and could not possibly realize what was occurring between them, the rituals that they were performing were as old as time itself. Since the beginning of time, unattached wolves of the opposite sex had roamed about on their own with no affiliation to any pack. These lone wolves were normally animals who for any number of reasons, had left the security and the familiarity of the home pack to make their own way. What often, then occurred, was that a lone male wolf would encounter a lone female wolf in the wilds. If, as had now happened between Warrior and the big white female, the pair of wolves found that they liked and got along well with each other, they would form the beginnings of a pack with the male becoming the dominant male and the female the dominant female. Any offspring of this pair of wolves would then form the pack under the leadership of these two dominant wolves.

Warrior suddenly turned away from the white female, and to her chagrin, trotted off into the forest. Unsure of what was happening, she stood unmoving for a
moment before running after the now running Warrior.
Within a few moments she had managed to catch up with
him and was running by his side. As she came abreast of
him, Warrior turned his head as if to acknowledge her
presence. As he did so, the white wolf could easily see
what could only be described as a smile appear on his big
handsome face. This new romance and alliance between
Warrior and this strange white female was to be the beginning of a pack of big northern timber wolves whose
territory would eventually encompass all of Serenity Isl-
and.

Chapter 7

Snow

Warrior's extended absences from Tranquility Place had grown more and more frequent as the long warm days of summer grew shorter and the brightly coloured leaves of fall began to drop from the tree branches to the ground.

As the entire family was now busily collecting the delectable wild mushrooms, and the plentiful fall berries, they had very little time to pay much attention to Warrior's long absences until Caylen, one morning, as he and Shilah pulled in their long heavily laden salmon nets, said."I haven't seen Warrior now for at least three days. Have you seen him at all over the last few days, Shilah?" he asked.

"No, I have not seen him now for nearly a week, I did notice that he was here two days ago as I did see his tracks down by the creek." Shilah replied.

I wonder what could be keeping him away for so long." Caylen said.

"I have a pretty good idea." said Shilah."Beside Warrior's tracks at the creek I saw another set of tracks of a smaller wolf. I believe our Warrior may have found himself a girlfriend."

"I didn't think there were any other wolves on Serenity Island." Caylen said."I've never seen any tracks or sign here except Warrior's."

"This one probably swam over from the mainland to get out of the territory of some pack. The pack would kill a strange wolf in their territory. It's a long swim and the water is pretty cold but I don't know how else it could have gotten here unless it came across during the winter on the ice." Shilah said.

"Well, I guess we should be happy for Warrior." Caylen said."I hope he brings her home one day and introduces her to us."

***

For the next two weeks the Helms' household saw little of Warrior. The entire family group was now quite busy hunting, collecting and gathering, drying, smoking, preserving and otherwise preparing for the long cold winter months that would soon be upon them. Firewood, wild meats, mushrooms, berries, fish, geese and ducks were all part of their winter foodstuffs. These foods and supplies all required first, the obtaining and then the preparation and the storage in various forms to ensure that spoilage would not occur. Methods of preserving their winters supply of foodstuffs included canning, drying, salting, pickling and freezing.

For at least a full month, the preserving of these foodstuffs was to create a mouth-watering odor on the westerly breezes that would cause any passerby downwind within a country mile hungry enough to check out the delectable smells' origin.

Sihu had also asked Caylen to get her six laying hens, a huge white rooster, two pigs and two milking goats. Over the next few years, these birds and farm animals would reproduce and provide much needed eggs, meats, butter and milk for the foursome.

Sihu also began to prepare a large garden area in the clearing adjacent to Tranquility where she planted cold-climate crops such as cabbages carrots, potatoes, onions and peas. All of these additions required that Caylen and Shilah build barns and pens, erect fences and collect further food supplies to feed the poultry and animals.

Tranquility Place was now comprised of seven outbuildings and three fenced off areas in addition to the main house. The settlement now had the appearance of a beautiful, large country estate situated on a pretty, bridged, little year-round stream that ran down and into a small bay on the huge Atlin Lake. The bay contained the fifty foot long pier that rested on four rock-filled log cribs that in turn, rested on the bottom of the little bay.

Beside the pier on the beach, Caylen had constructed a long slide of wooden rollers on which he could winch his motor launch up so as to keep it safe from the crushing ice during the long winter months.

By the end of October, all was ready for the winter freeze. After one last shopping trip across the lake to the Atlin General store, Caylen and Shilah hauled the launch high up onto the beach and winterized its gasoline engine.

"Well, " said Caylen to Shilah."I believe we are ready for whatever winter now hands us. All we can do now is wait for enough ice on the lake to hold us so that we can go ice fishing."

"Ice fishing?" said Shilah."Why would we wish to fish for ice? And how would we go about fishing for ice?"

Laughing, Caylen was explaining to Shilah what ice fishing was all about when Shilah suddenly whispered, "Caylen, look over by the mouth of the stream, just on the other side at the tree line, do you see what I see?"

Looking to where Shilah was pointing, what Caylen first saw was Warrior lying on the sandy stream shore about ten feet away from the forest's edge. Looking closer at the tree line, he suddenly saw clearly, what Shilah was pointing at."My God!" he said."She is a beauty!, I don't think I have ever seen a wolf that pure white before. She appears to be all white and nearly as tall as Warrior although she is much slimmer than he. Warrior has sure picked himself a beauty!"

"He has brought her home to introduce her to us." Shilah said."He will soon tell her to come much closer to us and he will then show her that we are not to be feared."

"We must go and tell Aponi and Sihu." Caylen said."They will be happy for Warrior. Do you think she will ever be tame enough to pet?"

"We must give her time." Shilah said."If she has ever had contact with a human before now, I am sure it was not pleasant for her so she may be reluctant to approach us."

Aponi managed to get a good look at Warrior's new-found friend just two days later. She was with Sihu gathering the last of the fall mushrooms in the tall spruce forest when suddenly Sihu whispered to her, pointing as she spoke.

"Aponi, look over there by that clump of cranberry bushes."

Aponi looked and then gasped at what she saw. Sitting side-by-side in front of the high bush cranberry bushes, was the big jet-black Warrior and a pure white wolf that was slimmer but nearly as tall as Warrior. The pair just sat, calmly gazing at the two women who stood, open mouthed, gaping at the sight before them.

"They are beautiful!" said Aponi."Sitting together like that they look as though they really belong to each other. I'm so happy for Warrior."

"We shall have to give her a name." said Sihu."We will name her and then shall call her by that name so that she will get used to her name and to us."

"I have the perfect name for her," said Aponi."We should call her 'Snow' because she is as white as any snow that I have seen."

"That is a good name but would it not be better if it were more feminine? What if we added the name 'Bird' to 'Snow' and called her 'Snow Bird ' or 'Chilam' which is the Hopi word for Snow Bird." replied Sihu.

"I like it!" exclaimed Aponi."Hello there, Snow Bird," she said as she moved towards the two wolves. Snow Bird permitted her to approach within about ten feet before she stood. Cocking her head to one side, the female wolf stood, listening intently as Aponi repeated her name over and over."Hello, Snow Bird, hi there, Snow Bird, it's okay, Snow Bird, I won't hurt you, how are you? Can I come closer, Snow?" she said, unconsciously shortening the name to just 'Snow'.

Snow waited beside Warrior until Aponi, holding out her hand in a greeting gesture and slowly moving closer, was about five feet away before she turned and moved away about twenty feet or so before stopping and again lying down, facing the two women.

With that, Warrior also rose and moving alongside her, slumped down and licked her face twice before laying his big black head across her two outstretched front legs.

"I think we have bothered her enough for the first day." said Aponi."Let's just continue picking mushrooms around here and see what she does."

Some five minutes later, Snow rose and with one look back at the two women trotted off into the forest with Warrior behind her.

***

Over the following weeks, Snow began to get quite accustomed to human company. While she never did enter the main house, she eventually began to sleep on the covered porch with Warrior.

Warrior, although he had never spent the entire night in the house, now would not stay inside and away from Snow for any length of time. Snow would only tolerate the presence of all the members of the household petting her for a moment or so before she would pull away, uttering a low growl of warning as she did so. The pair would sometimes leave the area for a hunt but they were always back at Tranquility Place for the night, announcing their homecoming with a series of eerie wolf howls.

Chapter 8

A Precious Gift

It was late in November on a extremely cold clear night about eleven o'clock. Caylen and Aponi had stepped out onto the porch to enjoy the colorful display of Northern Lights that was dancing across the Northern skies. This display was presented almost every clear night but on this night the colours were exceptionally vivid and clear. As they stood, Caylen's arm around Aponi's shoulder, they spied in the northwestern sky, what appeared to be a shooting star coming towards them from the north. As it grew closer they could tell that it was not only moving towards them at a great speed, but also that it was rapidly losing altitude. They continued to watch in utter amazement as it neared and then suddenly plunged through the thick ice into the cold depths of the lake about a mile out from where they stood. They continued to watch as the thick ice and cold lake's water boiled out of the immense hole. The noise created by the door of the house striking the wall as Shilah and Sihu joined them broke their trancelike state causing them to turn and say, almost together.

"Did you see that?"

"See what? All we know is that we heard a loud whooshing sound and then what sounded to us like a tree falling into the house!" exclaimed Shilah."What on earth was it?"

"We're not sure but it looked like a meteor." said Caylen.

"A message from the Great Spirit!" exclaimed Si-hu."He is sending us a message."

"I really don't think that is what it was." said Caylen."Meteors are quite common and often hit the earth although this particular one was very large which is quite unusual. We shall go out on the ice tomorrow and look for any pieces that might have broken off and are still on the ice."

***

The next morning found Caylen and Shilah gingerly walking about the huge hole in the lake ice. The meteor had created a hole of about two hundred feet in diameter and had thrown huge chunks of ice out and over the surrounding lake ice. They found nothing that would help them identify or even indicate the composition of whatever it was that had shot out of the nighttime sky.

"I shall come back to-morrow and use a lake trout to have a look down there to see if I can find whatever is there." said Caylen.

***

Caylen was just beginning to stir the following day when he heard Sihu call out from the big kitchen."Caylen, Shilah, Aponi! Come quickly, hurry, you must see this!"

Easily sensing her concern, Caylen, Aponi and Sihu entered the kitchen at nearly the same time, dressed in their bathrobes.

"What is it, Sihu? What is it you want?" asked Aponi.

"Just look out the window over by the bridge." said Sihu.

"Oh, heaven protect us!" exclaimed Aponi as she looked out at what had grabbed Sihu's attention.

Caylen and Shilah also gasped in concern at what they saw. Standing in a row along the far bank of the frozen stream were nine furry, naked, humanoid creatures of varying sizes. The largest, quite obviously a male and the leader of the group, stood about seven feet tall and must have weighed close to three hundred and fifty pounds. Of the remainder, three were also males but were somewhat smaller. The remaining three large creatures were female who were holding two children in their arms, one of which was quite small and appeared to be covered with a fur robe.

"They are evil forest monsters and they have come to kill us!" whispered Sihu in abject terror.

"It is the Matah Kagmi." said Shilah."I think that if they wished to kill us that we would now be with the Great Spirit and not standing here looking at them."

"I agree," said Caylen."I shall go out and speak to them and try to find out why they have come to us."

"But how will you speak with them?" Aponi asked."Surely they do not speak as we."

"I shall try hand signs at first and if that does not work I shall try to enter their minds with my thoughts."

It took Caylen only a few moments to pull on his winter clothes and walk outside and over to where the nine creatures stood patiently waiting in the cold dawn.

Holding both arms forward and outspread in a peaceful gesture, Caylen slowly walked to within about five feet of the largest creature before saying, Hello, friend."

Holding out his right hand in a open fashion he patted himself on his chest and repeated, "me friend, me friend." Receiving no reaction whatsoever, he repeated himself, "me friend, me friend." Again, no reaction save for a deep grunt from one of the smaller males.

Suddenly, to the horror of the watching trio of Aponi, Sihu and Shilah, who had now gotten ready his rifle, the big male grabbed the small fur wrapped child from the female who had been holding it and held it out towards Caylen.

Unsure of how to react to the big creature's sudden strange offering, Caylen stepped back and away from the big male. In response, the creature moved forward towards him and thrust the fur wrapped child at him again.

"Now what is he trying to do?" Caylen asked himself."Surely he is not trying to give me one of his children. I suppose I had better try to see if I can get into his mind. I don't think they are human even though the look a little like us."

At this closeness to the creatures, Caylen could see that their entire bodies were covered with a thick warm fur that appeared to be about three inches long and comprised of a dense undercoat with long lighter toned guard hairs. Their faces were quite similar to the faces of gorillas but were also covered with short thick fur. They all appeared clean and quite well-groomed but they did have a very noticeable strong, unpleasant odor about them.

When Caylen sent a small mind thought over to the big male, his reaction was instantaneous."Aagooooooouummmmmm, aagooooooouummmmmm" he bellowed loudly as he stepped back.

"Aagooooooouummmmmmm, aagooooooouummmmm" yelled all the others in response.

"Well, I guess he really must have felt that."Caylen thought."I will try again but with a little less power." With that, he sent a soft, gentle mind probe at the big male, saying to him, "I greet you, my friend. What is it that you wish of me,? We wish you no harm."

To Caylen's utter astonishment, the creature responded almost immediately with his own mind.

"You speak as we, the Matah Kagmi speak. I have never heard your kind speak as we. Your kind only speak in such a way that harms our ears. Your kind only speaks in that evil manner or with the long thunder sticks that throw much pain at the Matah Kagmi."

"I am different than most of our kind." Caylen responded with his thoughts."I, my mate and my friends here wish to be your friends and only wish to share, in peace, this place with you and your kind. We also would thank you for protecting our friends from the evil ones who came to this place during the warm times."

"We, the Matah Kagmi, know your hearts just as we knew the hearts of the ones that we destroyed. The Matah Kagmi will not permit evil to live on this land. We wish you and your friends no harm." the creature said.

"What may we do for you?" asked Caylen."What is the reason for this sudden visit?"

"Before the snows came, one of the Matah Kagmi was fishing in a stream near the lake when he saw two of your kind in a floating log. The log turned over and the two of your kind were destroyed by the cold waters. The Matah Kagml, however, did manage to keep this little one from being destroyed. As she is not of our kind, we think that our life might soon destroy her. The Gods have also sent us a sign from the over world. That sign, a bright light that raced across the sky and disappeared into the lake was a message from the Gods to us about this child. We wish, therefore, for you to take her into your cave as one of your own."

"We do not call our place a cave, we call our cave a home. I and my mate would be glad to accept your gift of that little one. I shall, in return, leave you many gifts in this very place so you may get them before the next sunrise." Caylen said as he took the tiny fur-wrapped baby girl from the creature.

In the next instant, all of the creatures turned and without a sound, vanished back into the thick forest.

Caylen uncovered the face of the tiny child he now held in his arms. Expecting to see a small dark complexioned child of Native ancestry, he was astonished to behold the pink-cheeked, blonde-haired pixie-like face of a beautiful, healthy baby girl who was quite obviously of the white race. Walking back to the house he wondered to himself.

"Now what am I supposed to do with this baby. We will probably never know who her parents were, her name or where she came from. I wonder what Aponi and Sihu will say when they see what the Matah Kagmi have bestowed on us. This is some kind of present!"

"What did they give you?" asked Shilah."It must have been quite a important gift to bring what was probably the entire tribe down out of the mountains."

"Is it a bunch of animal skins?" asked Aponi, as all they could see was what appeared to be a small roll of fur in Caylens arms.

"Were you able to communicate with them?"asked Sihu.

"Hold on, you guys!" exclaimed Caylen."Yes, I was able to communicate with them, and yes it is a very, very important gift to both the Matah Kagmi and to us and no, it is not animal skins."

"Gurgle, gurgle, goo, goo, " said the tightly-wrapped baby.

"Caylen, what on earth do you have there?" asked Aponi.

"Well, I am going to put it down here on the sofa and then I will unwrap it so we can all have a good look at it." said Caylen.

With that he carefully placed the tiny little girl on the sofa and unrolled the soft furs from her and then, stepping back, said."Okay, everybody have a good look and then tell me what you think of the Matah Kagmi's gift to us."

"Ohhh my gosh!" exclaimed Aponi and Sihu almost in unison.

"She is a very pretty child," Shilah stated in a matter of fact, quite calm manner.

"She is not just pretty, " said Aponi."She is beautiful!. She is the most beautiful baby I have ever seen!. Just look at those eyelashes, they are nearly an inch long!"

"My, look at how pink her cheeks are and how she is looking around at us all. She looks very healthy. They must have looked after her quite well. Where did they get her? She looks to be only about four or five months old."

Caylen spent the next hour explaining to the others exactly what he knew about the girl. When he finished telling them what the Matah Kagmi had told him, he said, "We now have to figure out what we are going to do with her. I will get word out to Bill so he can try to find out who she is and if she has any relatives that will take her.

"The first thing we must do," said Sihu, "is to get some clothes on this child and feed her. Shilah, open a can of that condensed milk while I put together a bottle that she can feed from. Aponi, go and get some of those old bath towels. We can turn them into diapers. Shilah, after you get the milk you must go out and collect as much of that nice soft reindeer moss as you can to use as a lining for her diapers."

It was apparent to all that Sihu had almost immediately decided to assume the role of mother to the orphaned baby. It was also quite apparent that neither Aponi, Shilah or Caylen really knew just what to do next.

"Well, don't just stand there, get busy!. This child needs to be cared for now!" said Sihu."Caylen, you can help Shilah gather moss. We will need tons of it before this child will be fully toilet trained."

"What shall we call her?" asked Aponi."Do you think we will be able to keep her?"

"Do we want to keep her?" asked Caylen."I'm sure Bill and Mom can find a good home for her in Whitehorse."

"This child is going nowhere!" said Sihu."She will be the daughter of Shilah and Sihu and shall be taken into our hearts as if she were of our flesh and was born of us. That is my final word on this matter. I shall name her in three days as is the custom of our people."

"Well, I guess that pretty much settles it. It looks like we now have a fifth member of our family and that you, Aponi, now have a new sister! I will still have to report this to Bill but I am doubtful that he will be able to find out anything about her or her parents. They were probably prospectors who got caught in a storm and drowned. Who knows how long they may have been out in the wilds or where they might have come from."

"How is it that you were able to speak with the Matah Kagmi?" asked Aponi."I thought you were not able to speak with those that you occupy."

"Well, first of all, I am unable to occupy humans. I am permitted to occupy and control any creature except for humans. I do not think that it was I who initiated mind speech with them. I think that is how they communicate with each other. I think that they entered my mind with theirs and that permitted me to speak to them with my mind."

***

It was during the morning meal three days later when Sihu left the breakfast table to return after a moment holding the girl child in her arms."It is now the third day of this girl Childs arrival in our home and in our hearts. I have given much thought to giving this child such a name that is of our people and also of the white eyes. This name I have chosen will have the meaning 'Beautifull Water' in the white man's tongue. The translation of 'Beautiful Water' is the name that this child shall, from this day forth, be called." Holding the baby at arm's length, Sihu chanted,

> *"Oh Great Spirit Qaletaka, Sacred Guardian of the people, place your hands upon this child to forever know and protect her. Watch over this little one and forever recognize her by the name I am now about to bestow upon her. Thank You, Oh Great One for your Blessing on this small child that now and forever shall be known as 'Talisa'.*

"That was beautiful, Mom," said Aponi."I think that is a beautiful name, too. Don't you agree, Caylen?"

"I love it." said Caylen."It rolls nicely off one's tongue."

"I also think it is a fine name." Shilah said."Now may I please hold my little daughter Talisa for a few minutes?"

Chapter 9

Alien Encounter

Later that morning, following the naming ceremony of Talisa, Caylen and Shilah discussed at length the big meteor they had seen splash into the lake through the ice.

"I was going to take over a lake trout and swim down to see what it looks like." said Caylen.

"We could go out on the ice today and try that." said Shilah."The hole should be solidly frozen over by now. it has been quite cold the last few nights."

That afternoon Shilah and Caylen walked out over the frozen lake to where the big hole, although now frozen over, was still readily visible. The large chunks of thick ice that had been thrown up by the impact of the object also quite clearly delineated the big circle of freshly frozen lake ice.

It took Caylen only a moment or two of probing with his mind to locate a fairly large lake trout that he knew would be capable of descending great depths into the lake if required. In a instant he was in full control of the big fish and rapidly descending into the ever darkening icy depths. He estimated that he had gone down about three hundred feet when he began to see something far below. As he continued down, the shape became clearer in the dark waters. It appeared to be grey in colour, a rounded shape thicker in the mid section than outer edges that he estimated were about ten feet thick. He approximated it to be about one hundred feet in diameter and about fifty feet thick at its thickest point.

Caylen circled the object three times, searching for any details that might explain its presence or identify it. Its uniform shape indicated to him that it was not a meteor or asteroid but probably a ship of some kind. Seeing nothing but the craft's dull, smooth, gunmetal surface, he decided finally that he was not about to discover anything further so he left the fish and returned to his own self on the ice where he was standing with Shilah.

"Well it surely isn't a meteor," he said."It is shaped like a huge round saucer that is thick in the middle and thinner at the outside edge. I would say that it is about one hundred feet in diameter and about fifty feet thick in the middle. It looks like it is made of some kind of smooth metal."

They had turned and were about to walk back to shore when something caused them to stop and turn around and look back.

"What was that?" Shilah asked."Did you feel that?"

"Yes, I did." Caylen answered."It felt like something shaking the ice."

Suddenly, to their utter astonishment, a bright ray of light about three feet in diameter burst through the ice in almost the exact center of the newly-frozen area. The ice, where the light had penetrated, melted instantly with the thick beam of light continuing up into the sky and beyond. It continued to project upwards without any sound whatsoever for about four minutes before suddenly disappearing.

"What on earth was that?" Caylen finally said.

"I don't know but it sure makes me want to get to shore fast." said Shilah."I don't think I want to know what caused that light or how it melted the ice as fast as it did." he added."I really think that we should get to shore as soon as we can." Shilah said, turning and heading off at a fast trot. He had only gone about twenty feet or so, when not hearing Caylen behind him, he stopped and turned to see what Caylen was doing.

"Caylen!, where are you?" he yelled.

Caylen was nowhere to be seen.

"Caylen!" he yelled again, moving back towards the big bare spot. Receiving no response and not knowing what else to do, Shilah turned and walked slowly back to shore, turning every few steps to scan the ice for any sign of Caylen. *What am I going to tell the others*, he thought. *I can't tell them that he just vanished. Maybe I will say that he took off down the lake for a look-see and will be back later.*

Caylen, about to take off after Shilah who was headed towards shore felt tingling going through his body. In the next instant his vision went totally dark for just a second. He could feel himself moving but had absolutely no control over the moving. A second later he found himself standing in a small, well-lit room that held only a large chair that appeared to be constructed of a white shiny material. The floor and ceiling seemed to be of a grayish metal-like substance. All four walls were translucent-like, but impossible to see through. They contained no visible doorways or visible light sources.

Caylen walked about the small room studying the walls, floor and ceiling for any clues that might reveal to him where he was or how he had gotten there. After a few minutes of finding nothing that would tell him where he was, he finally sat in the chair and just waited. An instant later, he felt and saw arm and leg bands come out of the chair and wrap themselves around his wrists and ankles. A moment later a cold bowl-like object settled down onto his head. He tried to rise up out of the big chair but found that he was securely held and unable to move.

"Do not be afraid, Caylen Helms." A voice suddenly said."We mean you no harm but we must examine you through those things that now hold you. Our examination shall cause you no discomfort and shall take only a few minutes of your time after which we shall release you."

"Why have you brought me to this place?" Caylen asked."And where have you brought me?"

"We shall answer all of your questions in good time. First we must tell you that you need not speak to us with your voice. You need only to say your speech in your mind for us to hear and understand you. Our minds are in your mind. Just as you are able to place a part of your mind into the minds of the creatures that occupy your lands, we are able to occupy your mind in a like manner."

If you mean me no harm then why did you do this to me? How did you do this thing, and just who are you? Caylen thought.

"We are called 'Travelers'. Where you are now in is our ship. We have traveled to your planet from a far-away planet that is our home. We first came to your planet earth over seventy thousand years ago. At that time your people were still living much as your Matah Kagmi live today. We return here about every ten thousand years to evaluate your evolutionary progress and to enhance your progress if we decide you are worthy. We have been doing this thing to the peoples of over five hundred such planets for as long as they have been populated by intelligent beings." said a thought reply."

Why can I not see you? Caylen thought. *And what do you mean by 'enhance' us?*

"When we first came to your world, your people were as the Matah Kagmi but without even the Matah Kagmi's limited intelligence. We examined those that we found here and determined that with some help from us that they would evolve into intelligent beings and would be compassionate, useful people who would populate this world, eventually moving out onto other worlds as we have done. We took some of those that we found and placed in them the power of reasoning, compassion for all things, the will to survive and the wish for knowledge. All of those things we gave freely to your ancestors those many years past. You are now what you are because of those long ago gifts from us," said the thought."You cannot see us because we do not permit such liberties. We are not as you and our countenances might terrify you."

You have not said why you have now brought me here. thought Caylen. *Where am I and how long do you intend to keep me here?*

"You are on the ship that you viewed through the eyes of that fish that your mind entered. This ship is but a small replica of our mother ship that now circles your earth high above. You observed our message to our mother ship as you stood on the lake ice. We use light as a means of communication between ships and as a means of powering our ships."

But why am I here? thought Caylen once more.

"You were brought here because we have seen your powers. You are only one of a very few of your kind to possess such powers. You are one of the first on this world to have such powers. These powers that you have, will, one day, be possessed by all of your people and will be as common then as ordinary speech is today. We are now here to move you and the three others on this planet who have powers similar to yours, to the next level so that your descendants, as will all of the peoples of this earth, one day possess the powers that we will soon bestow upon you."

What is it you are going to do to me? thought Caylen.

"We will first, as we said earlier, examine you thoroughly. We shall then release you from the chair in which you now sit and then we shall continue our talk. Now we ask that you sit quietly for a few of your minutes." said the thought.

Caylen sat quietly for a few moments until the clamps and the headpiece suddenly released their hold on him. As he rose the thoughts again spoke in his mind."We shall now, give you the power to speak to all others in the way that we are now speaking. The spoken word will one day be no longer in use by any of your people."

What else are you planning? thought Caylen.

"We shall also give you the power to move earthly objects with your thoughts. This power shall not be limited to just simple objects but may be expanded by yourself as your powers strengthen to include many other things."

What do you mean by 'other things'? thought Caylen.

"That is for you to decide." the being thought."We will not give you or tell you all. There is much for you to learn and to evolve into by yourself."

What you are doing sounds like a massive experiment to me. You said you are doing similar things on over five hundred other worlds. Are you saying that there are other worlds such as ours? thought Caylen.

"Have you such thoughts and such an ego that you would think that you are alone in this Universe?. Do you not see the countless suns in the night skies? We, the 'Travelers' have been wandering through these suns for eons and are still discovering new worlds and new beings each time we embark on a journey."

Are you Gods? thought Caylen.

"No, we are not Gods. We are sentient beings just as yourself who have evolved over the centuries so that we no longer have use for a physical body. Our kind long ago decided to be a benevolent people and use our knowledge and powers to assist others. There are many people's on many worlds, including your own, who have believed incorrectly, that we are Gods. We have been called many names and worshipped as Gods by many. We do not deny that some of our kind have allowed some beings to worship them. We do not deny that some of our kind have broken our lawful commandments by allowing other beings to worship them as Gods."

You have commandments that you follow? Caylen thought.

"Just as you do. Our commandments are quite similar to your own. Our commandments are also our laws and must be followed by all of our kind. Our commandments are as follows:

> **No being shall knowingly take the life of another being.**

> **No being shall knowingly take that which belongs to another being.**

> **No being shall knowingly dishonor another being.**

> **All beings shall willingly give their knowledge to those less fortunate.**

> **All beings shall deny the existence of all false Gods.**

> **No being shall permit another to believe that they are a God.**

> **No being shall impose his or her will upon any other being.**

"Those are our Commandments. You are now free to return to your people. Our mission on your world is now complete. We must go now to the next world."

I thought you were going to give me the power to move objects, thought Caylen as he stood, free of the chair's bindings.

"That has already been done, Caylen Helms. Go now and use wisely these gifts that we have bestowed upon you."

Can you tell me why you chose me for these gifts? thought Caylen.

"We will only say that you were chosen for many reasons. The most important reason is that you have decided to travel through your life on the harder trail."

What do you mean, the harder trail?

"Life's journey is as a trail. Some trails are difficult, with many hills and obstacles and take one through life to a higher plane of being. Only a few such as yourself choose this difficult trail. Most beings choose one of the other trails that are much easier to travel. The level trail simply winds one about and around through life's obstacles, presenting only a few hardships or challenges. The other much easier trail that is chosen by many, leads one through life on a downhill grade, presenting few if any challenges. It is the challenges that a being faces in his life that permit him to grow and to evolve into what your peoples will one day become."

And just what will we evolve into? thought Caylen.

"Who amongst us can see into the future? You ask what we cannot answer. Now we must return you to your living place but before we do so we must inform you that the ones you call the Matah Kagmi are also a part of our great experiment of the evolution with various creatures and are the primary reason for our visit to your earth at this time."

Can I see what you look like before you send me back? thought Caylen.

Caylen's last question was met only with silence. Suddenly, on the wall in front of him, he could clearly see the wrinkled old countenance of Sania, his mentor and the Sacred Hopi Priest that had long ago befriended him and led him on his vision quest in the deep northern forests of Canada.

"Sania, my brother!, is that really you? Caylen gasped.

"It is I, my son, my Mato Honl, my Brave Wolf. These beings have asked that the Great Spirit Qaletaka permit me to speak to you on this, one of the most important days of your life. These beings will no longer speak with you. They have asked me to stare at their images and relate to you their appearances. I tell you now that they do not exist as you and other beings exist. They are but a puff of smoke, a wisp of mist, a intelligence contained in a machine no larger than a soup can. They have asked that I tell you these truths before they and I depart for our respective worlds. Goodbye now, my son. I go to be with the Great Spirit once more."

In the next instant Caylen found himself standing back on the lake ice. About two hundred feet away, walking towards the shore was Shilah."Shilah!" he called out.

Shilah turned and seeing Caylen standing on the ice, ran back to grab him by the arms."Where have you been?" he demanded."You just disappeared a few minutes ago and now you just as suddenly reappear!, where did you go?"

"I cannot tell you right now, you would not believe me anyway." Caylen replied.

As the pair walked slowly back to the lakeshore they suddenly heard a loud rumbling roar and crashing as the big spaceship broke through the ice and shot off into the afternoon sky, Within a very few seconds it was gone, leaving no indication that it had ever been present other than the large hole in the big lake's thick ice.

Caylen thought back on what the aliens said to him. In particular he gave some long thought to the part where they said that there were others on the earth with powers similar to his. *I wonder who they are and where they are,* he thought. *I wonder if I will ever meet one of them. What if some of them are evil?. I can just imagine the harm someone with my powers could do if he or she was evil hearted.*

Chapter 10

Northern Winter

Caylen and Shilah decided to not tell Aponi and Sihu what had occurred out on the ice. Shilah also respected Caylen's wishes to not discuss what had happened to him under the ice and did not ask again. They told Aponi and Sihu that they could find no signs of whatever it was that had crashed through the thick ice. Caylen felt that he needed some time to fully understand what had happened to him before he could properly explain it to the others in a believable manner.

As the winter's days grew shorter and the nights much longer, the temperatures continued to fall lower and lower. During the last week of December the thermometer hanging on the woodshed wall recorded a nighttime temperature of between fifty and sixty degrees below zero. The sound of tree trunks in the surrounding forest constantly exploding after freezing solid caused the families many a sleepless night. The beautiful, awesome spectacle of lights in the night skies was visible nearly every night as the colorful, ever-changing Northern Lights flashed back and forth. However, the extreme cold would only permit a viewing for a few minutes before tingling cheeks forced a return to the warm interior of the big house.

As the long nights became ever colder, Warrior's friend, Snow, finally began to accept food from the hands of the four humans. She had observed Warrior's interaction with the humans and when she saw that they never caused him any harm whatsoever, she finally permitted them to scratch the pleasure spot behind her big white ears.

She really enjoyed the foods that the humans placed out for Warrior and her. Her life up to that point had been either a feast or a famine. She had plenty to eat immediately following a kill but she also suffered many days of extreme hunger when she was unable to make a kill. At the top of the forest food chain, wolves were quite capable of bringing down a fourteen hundred pound moose. They were also equally capable of catching the big salmon that swam in the autumn streams. As carnivores, they were, of necessity, opportunists and would gulp down mice, rabbits or any other of the edible forest creatures that they could catch. Wild fruits and berries, while not their favorite foods, were also on their menus at various times of the year. Carrion, also not their favorite food was readily consumed by the opportunist wolves when food was scarce.

Snow's new life with her newfound friend Warrior was now causing her to reconsider her life. Survival no longer depended upon her ability to chase down and kill some big ruminant who could easily, during a takedown, inflict serious injuries to her. A serious injury to a top predator like a wolf was usually a death warrant as injuries could mean that they would no longer be able to hunt. She found that her new life was essentially a life of ease with everything she needed in order to survive being provided to her. In return, it seemed that all that was required of her was for her to be friendly with the humans. In addition, she was discovering that handling the terrible cold of winter was much easier when one had a warm place in which to bed down. Having the warm body of a handsome big male wolf beside her was another good feature of her new life that she was enjoying more and more each day. As the long cold winter days passed she and Warrior spent less and less time roaming the forests in search of food.

***

It was only a few days following Caylens meeting with the aliens when he decided to try out the powers that they said he had been given. His first attempt was to try to communicate with Warrior without speaking. He thought at first that he would try out this supposed gift on Aponi but then reconsidered, thinking it would be best to not frighten her.

Warrior and Snow were lying in their favourite place just to the right of the front door when he made his first attempt. **Warrior, bring me a stick of firewood,** he thought, projecting that thought to Warrior. He had scarcely finished the thought when Warrior looked up and over at him, rose and strolled over to the pile of wood by the big fireplace. Grasping a large stick in his big jaws, he carried it over and dropped it on the floor in front of Caylen before sitting down in front of him.

"Warrior, what on earth are you doing?" asked Aponi who had observed the entire incident."Did you see what Warrior just did, Caylen?. I wonder what made him do that."

Sensing a opportunity, Caylen projected a silent thought to Aponi. **I asked him to do it.**

For a few moments, Aponi did not react to Caylens sudden intrusion into her mind."I must be going deaf," she said."I did not hear you say anything to him."

That's because I did not say anything to him. I am also not saying anything aloud with my voice to you right now. I am thinking it and am directing my thoughts to you.

Aponi looked in a very strange manner at Caylen and said, "I think perhaps you had best explain in detail, just what it was that you just said to me and just how you said it to me."

Caylen spent the next two hours telling Aponi what had happened to him while he was on the aliens' ship.

At first, Aponi found it all quite difficult to comprehend but after a few demonstrations of his speaking to her with his thoughts and then understanding her mental thoughts, she said, "I'm not sure I like this new power that you have. Now you will know everything that I am thinking. I will have no privacy at all. Another thing, how close do you have to be to a person before you can communicate with them with your mind?"

"I cannot tell what anyone's actual thoughts are unless they want me to." Caylen replied."I can only hear in my mind the replies you are thinking in response to my questions or any thoughts that you specifically direct at me. I don't know how far away from someone I can be before it will stop working as you are the only one other than Warrior that I have tried it on. I will direct a question at Mom in Whitehorse and see if she responds.

Don't be frightened, Mom, but this is Caylen speaking to you. How are you feeling and what is Bill doing right now? Caylen thought.

"Caylen, what are you doing here?. Is Aponi with you?. Where are you? I can hear you as plain as day. Are you hiding somewhere?". Lora's reply was almost instantaneous and plainly heard in Caylen's mind.

"I can't explain it right now, Mom, but I am speaking to you through my mind. I'm not actually saying these words, I am just thinking them and directing them to you in my mind from here at home.

"Oh, my gosh! What next! Does this mean I can send my thoughts to you whenever I want to?" Lora asked.

I don't think it works quite that way Mom. I think that a mental conversation can only be initiated by my-

self. You can only speak to me with your mind once I have initiated a conversation and as long as I permit you to. Once I shut you off, any further talk has to be again, initiated by me. I will give you all the details the next time I see you and Bill. We will try to get out to see you guys next month as long if the ice holds. Aponi says to say Hi, Mom. Well, got to go for now but will talk to you and Bill more tomorrow.

"The aliens also said that they gave me another power that I have not tried out yet." Caylen said to Aponi.

"I'm not sure I want to hear what it was." said Aponi."All this is beginning to frighten me more than just a little."

"Well then, I won't tell you what it is, I will try to show you."Caylen replied, as he focused his thoughts on the piece of firewood that Warrior had dropped at his feet. In a few seconds, the piece of wood lifted completely up from where it lay and floated across the room to the fireplace where Caylen laid it on the hearth.

"Caylen, did you just do that?" Aponi asked.

"Yes I did." Caylen answered."I am not sure as to just what I can move as that was the first time I tried that power out. I don't know my limits on it yet. I will have to experiment more to find out."

"I don't think we should tell Sihu or Shilah just yet about your new powers." Aponi said."They might get frightened."

"I agree." Caylen replied."We shall wait a while before we tell them and Mom any more about my latest powers. I am just a little frightened of them myself."

***

The northern winter brought February in with a furiously cold storm. The wind howled and moaned out of the north for seven days straight with the nighttime temperature falling below fifty degrees below zero. Warrior and Snow ventured outside the house for only the time necessary to perform their toiletries. The cold nights were filled with the rifle like sounds of trees bursting open as their cores froze solid and exploded into solid shards of timber. The night skies literally crackled aloud as the Northern Lights danced and displayed their brilliant colours across the northern skies. Venturing outside the warm interior of the big house even for a few minutes meant risking frostbite to one's ears and cheeks.

It was mid-February before Mother Nature relented and decided to favor the foursome with a spell of beautiful mild but clear weather. Aponi and Caylen decided, with the onset of the mild weather, to take the motorized ice sled up and across the lake to Atlin where they hired a local musher to take them over Atlin Lake to Tagish Lake and then up to Carcross from where they rode the railway to Whitehorse. The trip took them a total of five days. Five days and nights of camping under the Northern Lights. Five nights of warming themselves around a roaring night fire with spectacular overhead vistas flashing and dancing about in the nighttime skies for their enjoyment.

***

Bill and Lora welcomed them with open arms. Lora was especially happy to see them as she was expecting the birth of her and Bill's child momentarily.

Bill and Lora also brought news from the south that was also good to hear. The Elders of the third Mesa had written back that they welcomed the gift of a portion of the gold find and were sending four strong young trustworthy men to work the placer mine. They expected that they would be arriving at ice out time, which was normally about the end of May.

"We have some really interesting news for you two." Caylen said to Bill and his mother."You will probably not believe me so I will show you." he added.

"Well, after you sent me your thoughts last month, I am ready to believe just about anything you tell me." said Lora."Although I'm not really sure that Bill believes in your new power. He has been telling me that it's all been just a night dream."

Well, Bill, I can assure you that it is for real and not just a dream, Caylen thought as he projected his words to both Bill and Lora.

"Now do you believe me?"asked Lora.

"Believe what?" asked Bill."I just heard you say that it was for real and not just a dream. That does not mean it's for real."

"But Caylen did not say anything just now." Lora said."He just thought it and you heard him."

"That's impossible!" Bill exclaimed.

"You go outside for a moment and I will demonstrate it again." Caylen said.

***

It did not take long after Bill had gone out for Caylen to convince him that he could initiate and carry on a conversation with someone without actually speaking. After Bill rejoined them he asked."How close do you need to be to someone in order to 'mind-speak' with them?"

"I really don't think there is any limit to the distance." replied Caylen."I 'mind-spoke' to Mom last month from home and it was as though she was standing right beside me."

"Can I initiate a 'mind-talk' with you?"asked Bill.

"No, it must be initiated by me before anyone can speak to me with their mind," replied Caylen.

"Well, that will really be useful," said Bill."It's like having a two-way radio implanted in your head with only you knowing what frequency you are broadcasting on."

"That's a good way of describing it." Caylen replied."Now I have to tell you just how I received this power. If you had trouble believing in my 'mind-speaking' you're really going to have a hard time with this story."

It took Caylen hours to explain his alien encounter to Bill and his mother. It was only after a few demonstrations of his 'mental' speech and of showing them how he could move objects that they finally had to believe him.

"Did they let you know where they came from?" asked Lora.

"Did you get to see what they looked like?" asked Bill.

"Can you speak to someone who does not speak English?" asked Lora.

"Hey!, hold on a minute. I can only answer one question at a time," Caylen said."First of all, they only told me that they were from another planet that was far away. No, I did not see them but I was told that they were no longer physical beings such as we are. Apparently they exist only as a energy that contains intelligence. With regards speaking to other with my mind, I do not actually speak to them. I just think what I am trying to say and they understand my thoughts. It is the same with me. I know what they are thinking in their minds no matter what language they speak."

"Well, all of these powers should prove more than useful to someone in the law enforcement business." Bill said.

"Yes, I would think so." said Caylen."There is one other thing that they said to me but I have not figured out just exactly what it meant yet."

"And what was that?" Lora asked.

"They said that my power to move objects could be expanded to other things as I grew stronger in its use." Caylen replied."I really don't know what they meant by that, maybe they meant that I would eventually be able to move larger things."

"I am at times almost afraid of him," Aponi said, referring to Caylen."He has so many different powers that some of my people would say he was either a God or a devil."

"Well, I am neither," said Caylen."And I hope you don't say such things to your mother or Shilah."

"Of course I don't, but I do know that both of them are more than a little afraid of you." Aponi replied."Did you two know that our family on Serenity Island has now grown by one beautiful little girl and one beautiful snow-white lady?"

"Whatever do you mean?" said Lora.

Aponi spent the next few hours telling Bill and Lora all the details of how their family had grown with the addition of the female wolf Snow and the gift of the beautiful little white girl Talisa from the Matah Kagmi.

"Whoever her parents were, they must have been drowned or they would have reported her missing." Bill said.

"Well, according to the Matah Kagml, they both drowned." said Caylen.

"We have not had any reports of anyone missing." Bill said."What are you going to do with her?"

"I believe that decision has already been made by Sihu and Shilah." Aponi said."It would take extreme force from everyone in the entire North to get her away from Mom now."

"I believe if no one comes forth to claim her after a certain period of time they can legally adopt her." Bill said, "I will make a few quiet inquiries about it."

"What about you, Mom? When is your big day? When do I become a big brother?"

"I would venture to say that from the way I feel right now that you might become big brother at any moment. I think perhaps we should be getting ourselves overtop the hospital as quickly as we can." Lora replied.

"Oh my gosh!"exclaimed Bill."I will go start the car and load up your suitcase. Would you mind helping your mother out, Caylen?"

***

At eleven twenty-three that night, Lora delivered to Bill a eight-pound, three-ounce healthy and very vocal blonde sister for Caylen. As Bill proudly handed out cigars to anyone who would accept, he revealed to Caylen some details of a mysterious case that he had been informed of by his superiors in Whitehorse.

"Apparently there is something really odd occurring in southern Alberta and northern Montana. A large pack of wolves has been roaming back and forth across the Canada-USA border killing off a lot of cattle and sheep. What is even more peculiar is that they are not eating their kills as would a normal pack of wolves. For the most part they are only eating the hearts and livers of their kills. In addition to that they seem to be concentrating on only a certain number of ranches and leaving many others that might be nearby, completely untouched. They have been at it now for nearly a year and have accounted for over two hundred cattle, seventy-four sheep and seven horses on just five ranches."

"That sounds really odd."Caylen said."But what are they asking of us? Sounds more like a job for a wolf trapper or conservation man."

"Well, that's just it," said Bill."They have had three different professional hunters and five conservation men on the case for six months now and they have only one dead wolf to show for all their efforts. In fact they think the one wolf that they got was a stray and not one of the pack that is causing all the killings in the area."

"Are they asking for my help?" Caylen asked.

"Not in so many words." Bill replied."They asked me to tell you and see what your reaction would be. I told them I would go, but that I couldn't go until I was sure that Lora and the baby would be okay."

"Well, it sure sounds like a interesting situation but what does a pack of renegade wolves have to do with the Mounted Police? As I said, it sounds like a job for a good trapper." said Caylen.

"The entire thing is weird," Bill replied."Some of the local ranchers are blaming the local native Indian tribe. They are claiming that their medicine man takes on the form of a timber wolf and is leading the pack."

"Why would they be thinking that?" asked Caylen.

"Apparently the natives have been trying to get the Government to expand their reservation boundaries out and expropriate about twenty thousand acres of private ranchlands. You can imagine the surrounding ranchers reaction to such a demand. They are definitely not happy and are quite adamant that the tribe is behind the killings. They have been threatening to take matters into their own hands unless the authorities do something. There has been talk of a vigilante group forming but so far nothing serious has occurred."

"And what does the tribal medicine man have to say about all the goings on?" Caylen asked.

"That's the odd part of all this." Bill said."He claims that the leader of the wolf pack is a wolf that has been possessed by an evil spirit. All that does is re-enforce the ranchers claims about the medicine man being the wolf. Things are nearly at the boiling point. The local authorities are concerned that things will soon erupt unless something is done. What is now making things worse is that two teen-aged sons of one of the ranchers are claiming that they were chased by the wolf pack when they were riding their ponies back from school and that they only escaped being killed by riding into a old hay barn."

"Well, it certainly sounds like it would be an interesting case to investigate." Caylen said."I will discuss it with Aponi tonight and let you know tomorrow if she will permit me to investigate it."

"Ha!, she's got you that well trained already!" Bill said."Well, you're doing better than me. Your mother only took about six months to convince me that I had better do what she asked or else!"

"Yes, but Mom has had some previous experience and Aponi is still only just a beginner." Caylen laughed."I think I can still convince her to let me go."

Chapter 11

Police Work

Winter had released its icy grip on the desolate prairie landscape when Caylen and Warrior finally stepped down onto the railway station's wooden platform in Calgary. The long car trip from Calgary to the little Village of Cardston in southern Alberta permitted him plenty of time and the opportunity to observe the terrain and to begin to comprehend the size of some of the areas cattle ranches.

A ranch of thirty thousand acres in this area was considered the minimum size required for a family to make a reasonable income from the sale each year of the lean, grass-fed range beef cattle. Cardston, a village of about four hundred souls, was about fourteen miles north of the Montana border. Law enforcement in the area consisted of one Northwest Police Constable on the Canadian side of the border and one Deputy US Marshall on the American side. The Deputy US Marshall was stationed at the little village of Browning located about thirty miles due south of the Canadian Border and about forty miles southeast of Cardston. The big reservation of the Blackfeet Indian tribe occupied most of the land to the west, the north and the south of the village of Browning and was policed by a few undisciplined and untrained tribal warriors who ranged over the huge reservation on horseback.

Caylen drove the old rented Ford coupe up and down the wide streets of Cardston twice, looking about for some kind of sign that said "Police ". The little village appeared to be completely deserted except for one old man sitting in a chair on the wide wooden platform of what appeared to be a general store. The old man's grizzled head turning to follow Caylens progress as he drove slowly by was the only motion visible to the pair as they chugged to and fro through the village. Unable to see anything that even faintly resembled a police station, Caylen, after driving through the entire village two times, finally pulled over in front of where the old man sat. Shutting off the car's engine and rolling down his window, he asked, "Say, Mr., would you happen to know where I could find the police constable?"

The old man stared at Caylen for a moment before rising up out of his chair and walking over to the car. Peering through the car's rear window, he could see what appeared to him to be a giant black timber wolf grinning at him through the dusty glass.

"That beast sure do look like a timber wolf, ceptin i'se never seen one that was that big. Is he dangerous?" he asked, not replying to Caylens question.

"What you see is my pet and he is a fully grown mature Arctic wolf that I got when he was just a pup. I raised and trained him so he will do pretty much anything I ask him to do." Caylen said."Now do you know where I can find the Constable?"

"Constable Sykes be in that there building over there." the old man replied, pointing at a weathered old building just across the dusty road."I'd be watchin' over that there wolf dog pretty close if'n I was you. Lots of folks round here is mighty touchy bout wolves right now. Lots of folks would shoot that animal on sight, no question." he added.

Caylen, leaving the car where it was, got out, saying to the old man, "I have to speak to the Constable about something so I am going to leave my pet wolf in the car for now. Would you mind keeping an eye on him and make sure no-one bothers him."

"No problem," replied the old man."Ain't no-body round here ceptin me fer most of the days anyhows. Do he bite?"

"No, he would never bite anyone unless they were to hurt him or unless I told him to." Caylen said, turning and walking across the road to the building the old man had indicated. Rapping loudly on the door he heard someone inside say, "Enter."

Entering the small dingy room, Caylen observed a young man wearing the scarlet uniform of the Northwest Mounted Police sitting behind a desk that was littered with papers and photo's. As he entered, the Constable rose from his chair and said,

"Good day to you, Sir. My name is Constable John Sykes. What can I do for you?"

It took Caylen about twenty minutes to explain to the Constable that he was there at the request of his superiors to assist the Constable in his investigation of the cattle killings. Constable Tom Sykes spent the next hour giving Caylen all the details of what was occurring and had occurred over the past six months. He also told Caylen that he had been informed by the Calgary office of the Northwest Mounted Police that they would be sending a "Special Constable "to assist him in his investigation of the cattle killings.

"I questioned the two boys who claimed to have been chased into a hay barn by the wolf pack, but I am not sure they are telling the truth. I think that they saw the pack in the distance and just wanted to embellish their stories a little by including a chase. That way they kept everyone interested in their story."

"Do you think you could take me out on horseback over some of the affected ranches and show me around a little?. I would like to meet some of the bigger ranchers as well as the Blackfoot Chief. And I will need some accommodations for myself and my partner."

"You didn't say you had a partner." said the Constable."Where is he? My sear gent in Calgary told me that you had a lot of experience dealing with wolves up in the North but he said nothing about your partner."

"Well, my partner has also got a lot of experience dealing with the big timber wolves up North. In fact he has more experience in that area than I or anyone else has, he' s waiting out in my car. Would you like to come out and meet him?" Caylen asked as he went to the door.

As he exited the Constables office, Caylen could see a number of men armed with thirty-thirty Winchester lever-action carbines milling about his car. Also seeing the rowdy group, Constable Sykes shouted out, "You men! Get away from this man's car! What in hell do you think you doing? Those guys are all local ranchers who have had wolf problems." he said quietly to Caylen.

"It's okay, Tom, I'll handle this." Caylen said."Do you men see something in my car that bothers you?. By the way, my name is Constable Caylen Helms and i am here to assist Constable Sykes in his investigation of the cattle killings that have been going on around here. Would you gentlemen like to introduce yourselves to me before I introduce you to my partner in the car?"

What appeared to be the informal leader of the group of men stepped forward towards Caylen and the Constable in quite a belligerent manner, saying, "Be that critter in yer car here a wolf? If it is, then my advice to you, mister, is to git in yer car and git to hell out of here before someone here decides to shoot that animal right where he sits!"

"That 'critter' in my car is definitely a wolf, mister, and if drag your sorry butt over to the Constable's lockup, throw you in his jail then I will draw up the necessary papers that will ensure you stand trial for the attempted murder of my assistant. And I can also assure you that it will only be 'attempted murder' because your shooting arm will be broken in at least two places before you ever get a chance to fire your weapon." Caylen replied in a low, even voice.

"Back off, Jim," said Constable Sykes."You men calm down now and introduce yourselves to Special Constable Helms of the Northwest Mounted Police. Constable Helms and his wolf dog partner are here to help me catch that wolf pack that have been killing your cattle."

The tall man named Jim responded, "And just how is he going to catch them?. Is he going to send his trained wolf out to invite them over for supper so's he can shoots them?"

"Something like that," Caylen replied."Now I would like to meet all of you guys, one at a time. I will assume that you are all local ranchers who have had problems with this wolf pack. Constable Sykes, why don't you introduce me to each of these men so they can tell me in their own words what has been happening on their ranches."

Constable Sykes introduced, in turn, the six men who, as it turned out, had just returned from a long fruitless hunt on horseback for the renegade wolf pack.

"All we found were three more young steers with their hearts and livers gone. One of them that we found this morning was still warm. We put the dogs on them but all they would do is sit, howl and run around in circles. It was as if they were afraid to track the wolves."

"It is a evil spirit that has put the fear into the dogs." said the old man from his chair where he had been listening to what was being said.

"Shut your mouth, old man. Why don't you go back out to the reservation and look after your Indian squaw and her papoose. This is all being caused by that cursed medicine man of yours."

"The ranchers are claiming that the Blackfoot medicine man has taken over and possessed the leader of the wolf pack. They claim that he is leading the pack and killing all the cattle so as to discourage the ranchers from trying to influence the politicians into voting against the expansion of the reserve. They say that no-one has seen the medicine man since the killings have begun. They also say that the only way to stop the killings is to kill the medicine man." said Constable Sykes.

"The killings have nothing to do with the Blackfeet or their medicine man. The pack is being led by a grey wolf from outside who has killed the old leader of the pack and taken over as the boss wolf. This wolf has been possessed by an evil spirit and is not what he appears to be." said the old man.

"And just how do you know all this? Have you been reading those Zane Grey books again, you old fool?" asked one of the ranchers.

"I have spoken with our medicine man. He says that there are evil things on the lands and that their will soon be much wailing and cutting of hair in the lodges unless this evil leaves our lands. The women are much afraid and the men will not leave the lodges without their weapons. There is much fear." said the old man.

"If that the case, you old fool, then why are you here and not back hiding in your teepee with your squaw where you belong?" said one of the ranchers.

"My wife has gone, three moons past, to be with the Great Spirit. I am now preparing myself to go on a vision quest and speak with the Great Qaletaka to ask him if he will permit me to join her." replied the old man.

"Old Joe here is three-quarters Blackfoot," said Constable Sykes."He married into the local tribe years ago but his wife passed away last week. He often comes into town and sits here watching what goes on. I think he acts as the tribe's news source, keeping the elders informed about what's happening here in town."

"Perhaps you could take me out to your reservation and introduce me to your elders so that I might learn more about this pack of wolves and the evil that is upon the lands." said Caylen.

"You don't needs to go out there to learn nothin'." said one of the ranchers."They ain't nothin they kin tells you that will helps youse. All they does is sit about their fires wailing and howlin like they was animals."

"What I do, and how I conduct this investigation is none of your business." said Caylen."Everything that you men are saying and the way you are behaving makes me suspicious of you and your intentions. Now I am going to ask each of you your names and what your personal involvement is in all this. I will also want to know, if you are a rancher, the details of any losses you have had. Constable Sykes, would you please ensure that all of these men stay in town until I question them. Joe, would you take me out to meet your peoples after breakfast tomorrow?"

"Will you buy me my morning meal first?" asked the old man.

"Of course I will." said Caylen."I shall pick you up here at eight a.m. and we shall eat a big breakfast before we leave for your reserve."

***

It took Caylen the remainder of the day to meet and question the six ranchers present. As it turned out, the six men owned the majority of the local ranches. Two of the largest ranchers according to Constable Sykes were not present even though they had claimed to have lost a large number of cattle to the wolf pack.

Caylens tally at the end of the day of the acreage of land owned by the six men present totaled nearly three hundred thousand acres to the south and east of the Alberta village of Cardston in Canada and the Montana Village of Browning in the USA. Constable Sykes then informed Caylen that the two ranchers not present owned the largest ranches in the area and that together their land totaled over three hundred and thirty thousand acres. These two ranches abutted and lay directly to the east of the Blackfoot reserve boundaries and would become part of the Reserve should the Government approve a expansion of the reserve in an easterly direction.

"Have they lost many cattle to the wolves?" Caylen asked.

"They have reported some forty-five steers taken over the past four months." Constable Sykes replied."As a matter of fact, it was the two Carlin boys who reported being chased by the pack on their way home from school just two months ago. George Carlin owns the biggest cattle ranch within a hundred miles of here."

"Then why would they not be participating in this wolf hunt?" Caylen asked."It would seem that they would stand to lose the most if the Reserve was expanded."

"They have told the other ranchers that they will take care of the wolves on their own and that no-one, not even the US Government, will ever take their land away from them. They have also threatened to kill the Blackfoot medicine-man if they ever catch up with him. They are saying that he has called upon the evil spirit of darkness to possess the wolf pack leader and that he is the one responsible for all the killings."

"Does anyone believe all that garbage?" Caylen asked.

"Well, the natives are saying that there is some truth in that rumor but that their medicine-man has nothing to do with it."

"And just what are the natives saying?" Caylen asked."I believe you said earlier that their medicine-man claims that the wolf pack's leader is possessed by an evil spirit."

"That right, but the ranchers, especially the two larger ones, have a lot of influence over the others and the smaller ranchers tend to go along with whatever the big ranchers say." said the Constable.

"And what do you think?" asked Caylen.

"All I know for certain is that there are cattle being killed by what is presumed to be a pack of wolves and that whatever it is that is killing these cattle is eating only the hearts and livers of their prey. I cannot, at this time, prove anything other than that." said Constable Sykes."What do you want to do next?"

"I really need to speak to the tribe's medicine-man, the two boys who claim to have been chased by the pack and the other two ranchers." Caylen said."What do you know about old Indian Joe out there? Do you think he going to be straight with me?"

"He used to be a scout with the US Army. He always had a good reputation with them, according to Army records. He claims that he has seen over eighty snows and that he was with Sitting Bull at the Battle of the Little Bighorn when the Lakota and the Cheyenne massacred Custer and the seventh Calvary. After the massacre he says that he then left Sitting Bull and came up here to live with and marry into the local Blackfoot tribe. I would tend to believe anything he says, keeping in mind that he is influenced to a large degree by native lore, native history and native superstitions. I do know from experience that one cannot always believe what is written in our history books about what goes on or what went on in the North American Indians' past."

"Well, we shall see what happens when I go out with him. Now, Tom, where can I get a good meal and a comfortable bed for the night?"

***

Quite some time later, following a delicious meal of a freshly roasted beef rib roast at a small local cafe, Caylen, comfortably housed in the village's only hotel, reflected on the information that he had gleaned from the old native, the six ranchers and the Constable. What he had not revealed to the Constable was the fact that he had used his powers to ascertain that not only were all of the men telling the truth, or believed they were telling the truth, but all of the men displayed auras that revealed them to be good men. Each of them displayed a yellow, an orange or shades of those colours in their auras. The colours were, as Caylen recalled from the teachings of Komall, some of the colours displayed by only good men. The only person who displayed a different coloured aura had been the old native man called Indian Joe who's aura was quite purple. This was, Caylen reasoned, because the old man was still mourning his wife's recent death.

"If all of these men are telling the truth about what is going on around here, I think that we may have a real puzzler of a problem." Caylen said to Warrior, who lay, looking at him in a quizzical manner with his big head cocked over slightly to one side."I don't dare send you out to snoop around just yet because if I do some rancher will surely take a potshot at you." he added."We shall have to wait and see what happens tomorrow when we interview the Blackfeet medicine-man." He said to himself as he nodded off.

***

Caylen and Warrior exited the hotel onto the narrow boardwalk just as the morning sun peaked over the eastern horizon. To his surprise, the old native man known to the villages residents as Indian Joe was sitting on the edge of the wooden sidewalk just outside the hotel's door.

"Good morning!"exclaimed Caylen."I did not expect to see you here this early. The sun is barely up yet. Did you spend the night here in town?"

"A true Blackfoot warrior would never sleep in the white man's bed as long as there was a sage brush plant to lay upon and a buffalo skin to lay under." said the old man."It is time now to eat the white man's morning meal. I will admit that the white man's fried ham and eggs with hot coffee lies much better on a man's stomach than does a meal of cold pemmican and cold water."

"Well," said Caylen, "let's see if the cafe is open.

***

About an hour later, as the two men sipped on their third cup of scalding coffee, Caylen said, "I know your real name is not Indian Joe so would you permit me to call you by your true name?. My Hopi name is Mato Honi or Brave Wolf. You may call me by whichever name you so chose. My wolf's true name is Cheveyo or Spirit Warrior and from the way he has acted, I believe that he likes you."

"I have known from the first moment of our meeting that you and your wolf friend were not what you appeared to be." said the old man."Your powers are quite apparent to one such as myself who has lived to see over eighty-seven snows. While I do not know the nature or strength of your powers, it is clear that you do possess much strength in your essence."

"You are correct in your thoughts, old man, but I wish for the moment at least to not reveal the powers that I possess. Know only that I have learned much from my spirit Father, the Great Hopi Whakan Powwaw called Sania by his people."

"I, and every true Blackfoot elder knows of the legends of the Great Hopi man, the Whakan Powwaw called Sania, but is it not just that, a legend?"

"I can assure you that Sania was indeed a man, a great man who took me as his son and blessed me in the eyes of Qaletaka, The Great Spirit and The Sacred Guardian of the People.". Caylen said."He then instructed me in the ways of his people and asked that Qaletaka bestow upon me many things that I wish to not reveal at this time."

"I respect these wishes of yours and would be honored if you would address me by my true name. My Blackfoot name that was given me by the Great Spirit during my Vision Quest many years past is Peta or Golden Eagle."

"Then from this moment forth, I shall address you by the name Peta." Said Caylen."Now, Peta, let us visit with your elders and request a meeting with your medicine-Man."

***

It was late morning when Caylen, Peta and Warrior drove into the Blackfoot village. The village, located just over the US border, consisted of about thirty or so wooden shacks in various stages of disrepair and of various sizes ranging from about ten feet by twelve feet to some that were at least fifty feet long and thirty feet wide. Caylen could see, interspersed amid the homes, the occasional sweat lodge but a only a very few tepees.

"There are some of us who try to live as our fathers did. We choose the old ways whenever possible. We try to teach our young in the language and in the ways of our fathers but the white eyes' school tells them to forget the old ways and that they should learn only from the white man's writings. Some of our children refuse to even undergo the rituals of manhood. Some even refuse to go to the sacred mountain on a vision quest to allow their essence to meet with their ancestors and the Great Spirit as did their fathers and their fathers before them." Peta explained.

"Since the going of the buffalo, the Blackfoot have become a lost people. We survive only with the cattle and the sheep and goats that the white man provides. Our hunters are no longer skilled in the ways of the hunter. They return from the hunt with only small animals that provide little to their lodges. Even the Sun Dance that is now happening has few followers who will participate." he added.

"What must I do if I am to gain the trust of your Shaman and your elders?" Caylen asked.

"If you are to be truly believed by those who you wish to speak, you must first participate in the ritual of the Sun Dance. Only if you complete this ceremony without complaint will the Elders and the Shaman agree to speak with you."Peta said.

"Well, I will do whatever is necessary to talk with these people." Caylen said."What must I do to enter this Sun Dance of which you speak?"

"I will take you into my lodge this day and begin preparations for this ritual. You must first cleanse both the inside and the outside of your body and your mind of all things, consuming nothing save water until the ceremony is complete. You must then, before the ceremony, permit the Shaman to prepare your flesh for the trial of the Sun Dance." said Peta.

"I will do whatever is required of me." Caylen answered as the old man bade him stop in front of a brightly painted tepee.

Chapter 12

Trial by Pain

Peta welcomed Caylen into his tepee and bade him remove all his clothing so that he could accompany him to a sweat lodge. Peta then, as Caylen was preparing himself, went to advise the elders that a outsider wished to undergo the ritual known by the Blackfoot people as the Sun Dance so that he could speak to the tribal elders and the tribe's shaman. Caylen, a little concerned for the welfare of Warrior during this ceremony, received assurance from Peta that Warrior could remain in his tepee until the ceremony was concluded.

"Just how long will this ritual take?" Caylen asked, totally unaware of just what he was about to participate in.

"It shall be concluded no later than the setting of two full suns." Peta replied."I have received the approval of the elders and of the tribal medicine-man for you to undertake this ceremony. Are you certain that you wish to participate in this ancient rite?. It can be a painful ordeal if you have not properly prepared yourself."

"Let us proceed." Caylen replied."If this is what I must do to hear words of truth from your people, then this is what I must do."

Caylen spent the next four hours sitting, nearly naked on a buffalo skin in the sweltering hot and humid sweat lodge beside Peta's tepee. While he had observed other tribal members going about their daily chores, none of them had greeted him or even acknowledged his presence in their community.

"Peta, why do your people act as though I do not exist? They do not even look at me."

"The people all know that you are about to participate in our most religious ceremony. It is forbidden that anyone other than myself as your sponsor and the medicine-man speak to you until you have undergone, without complaint, the Sun Dance ceremony." Peta replied."Now I must take you to our Sacred place so that you may think about your past and your future. If you have pleased the God Natos, Natos may permit you to speak directly to him. If he should permit this talk, you must never reveal your talk or his words to any living creature, man or beast."

Without saying anything more, Peta led Caylen, who was still naked save for a loin cloth that barely covered himself, out of the sweat lodge and out of the village. Caylen followed behind Peta along a indistinct trail to where it led out onto a narrow point of land that overlooked a wide gully through which flowed a fast-running stream of crystal-clear water. At the very end of the point of land, a wooden platform constructed on poles stood.

"You must sit on the floor of this place until the medicine-man sends his assistants for you. This will take place before the rising of the next sun. You will remain at this Sacred place so that you may, should they so desire and permit, converse with the Gods. You should also know that once you sit upon this Sacred place that you will have no choice but to complete this ceremony to its conclusion. You should also know that should you fail to complete this ceremony, that no person of this village will ever speak to you and that you will be forced by our warriors to leave our lands to never again return."

With that statement, Peta turned and strode off back in the direction of the village.

With a last look about, Caylen relieved himself and clambered up and onto the little platform where he found a small square of what appeared to be buffalo skin. Folding it into a smaller square, approximately twelve inches to a side, he placed it in what he estimated was the center of the platform before sitting himself, with crossed legs upon it. Recalling his only other such experience of many years prior, he settled himself down as comfortable as possible, expecting a long session of waiting for the unexpected to occur.

***

It was a long hot day with absolutely nothing of any consequence interrupting Caylen's contemplations on the platform. The only disturbance during the entire day was when a ragged grey coyote came trotting up along the faint trail from behind the sacred platform .The animal, seemingly more interested in the faint scent of the many deer mice that were present on the grassy slopes, failed to detect Caylen's presence until it was under the platform where he sat, motionless. The first indication he had of the coyote's presence was when he heard the sharp yip that it made when it realized that man, his worst enemy was only about two feet above him. As Caylen watched in amusement, the startled animal raced back in the direction it had come from, stopping once to look back to where Caylen sat watching him.

***

The moon was nearly directly overhead in the night sky when the first incident of note occurred. Caylen estimated that it was about midnight when the great
horned owl swooped silently down out of the black sky to perch on the edge of the platform where he sat, nearly asleep.

"You should not be trying to sleep, young man. You are here at this sacred place to converse with the Gods, should they wish to do so. Do you think the Gods would wish to speak to one who is asleep?" the owl said to an astonished and suddenly wide-awake Caylen.

"Why do you look so surprised?" the owl asked."Do you not speak to other creatures such as yourself with your thoughts just as I now speak to you?"

"Well, yes, I do." replied Caylen."But I speak to them. I have never heard a creature of the forest such as yourself other than the Matah Kagmi speak to me as you do now."

"Do you think that all creatures save mankind lack the ability or the intelligence to communicate with other creatures? If you think that, then you have much to learn. Do you understand the speech of the Blackfoot people when they speak in their tongue? Of course you do not. Why therefore do you think that one such as yourself would understand my language when I speak it in my tongue? I am quite sure that should I speak in my tongue that all your ears would hear would be a sound that would appear to your ears to be 'hoo, hoo'. Is that not so, my young Mato Honi?"

"Why do you address me by the name my blood-brother and my adopted father gave to me many snows past?" asked Caylen, now beginning to suspect that he was hearing the speech of a very dear old friend.

"Your suspicions are quite correct, my son. You are speaking mind thoughts with I, your blood brother and your adopted father. It is I, Sania. I have been sent by the Great Qaletaka, Sacred Guardian of the people to reveal to you many things that are of great importance to you." said the Owl's thoughts.

"I have missed you, old friend. Your voice and your words are like music to my soul. Are you not pleased with my life as I have lived it?. Do you know of my union with the beautiful Aponi, daughter of your daughter's daughter?"

"How would I not know of such an event?. I, Sania, knew that you would wed my young Aponi even before you were aware of her very existence." Sania replied."Even before I summoned you to me in the forest I knew of your union-to-be with my Aponi. I also know that your union is a happy union and that it has been blessed by the Great Qaletaka."

"Why is it that you have sought me out, my brother?" asked Caylen."Am I in danger here?. Is Aponi and her mother ill?"

"I have come to you to warn you that there is much evil on this land. Neither the Blackfoot people or their medicine-man has full knowledge of this evil. It is an evil unlike any evil seen by these peoples before this time. This evil will possess animals and people and cause them do many evil things to others. This evil will, if given the chance, kill my brother Caylen as one would kill a bothersome flea. Only through great care and caution will you be able to defeat this terrible creature who's evil essence has permeated this land."

Are you able to tell me who is behind this evil?" asked Caylen.

"I am forbidden to tell you more." said the owl."All I can tell you is to beware of any strangers who pretend to be your friend before having true knowledge of you, who you are and of the powers you possess. Now I must leave you, my son. May the Great Qaletaka keep you from harm. I wish not for your beautiful Aponi to have to cut off her hair and slash her arms in mourning for you should you fail in this mission that you have chosen." With that, the big owl spread his wings and floated silently off into the dark night.

Caylen remained awake for the remainder of the night. The eastern sky was just beginning to lighten when the two natives arrived and led him, without speaking, back to the tepee of the Blackfoot medicine-man who stood in the early morning darkness just outside the door of his home awaiting Caylen's arrival.

"Are you prepared for this ritual, young Mato Honi? Do you still wish to undergo this ancient ceremony that will, if you complete it successfully, make you as one with my people?"

"I am prepared. I wish to complete this Sun Dance and become as one with your people." replied Caylen."And please tell me how you know of my Hopi name?"

"I know many things about the young Mato Honi who comes into my village seeking knowledge of the evil that is present on these lands. Now, you should consume, with this water, this root that I give to you. You must consume all of it as it will make this ceremony much easier for you to withstand. There will be great pain for you if you do not take this now." said the medicine-man as he began rubbing a red watery substance on Caylen's bare chest.

"I shall complete your ceremony without the use of this medicine." said Caylen."Pain does not frighten me as it does most men. Pain is often a most welcome sensation as it can often heighten a man's awareness of his physical being."

"You speak as would a Blackfoot warrior who is about to go into battle with a mortal enemy." said the medicine-man."Prepare yourself now for what I am about to do." With that, the shaman, grasping part of Caylen's left breast chest muscle, drove a small bone dagger completely through the portion of chest muscle he held pinched between his fingers. As he withdrew the dagger, one of the other men inserted through the severed muscle, a small rounded peg that was about six inches long. Once the stick was inserted so that it was centered in the cut, the medicine-man, his hand red now with Caylen's blood, smacked his chest where the stick protruded, with his flat, open hand.

Gasping at the sudden pain, Caylen was about to speak when the old shaman repeated, on his right breast muscle, a similar piercing and the insertion of another wooden peg.

Holding Caylen by his arms, the two warriors, followed by the shaman, led Caylen through the village to where a large pole stood. Caylen could see through the hazy red of pain that blanketed his eyes, what appeared to be the entire tribe, standing silently in a great circle about the pole. The pole itself stood about thirty feet long with its base firmly embedded in the hard prairie soil. What appeared to be the dripping head of a freshly slaughtered steer was impaled on the pole's tip. Long braided rawhide ropes hung loosely from where they were secured near the pole's top, just under the impaled steers head.

Reaching the pole, the shaman took one of the dangling ropes, looping and tying it quickly around both ends of one of the wooden pegs that pierced Caylens chest. He then repeated this action with another rope on the second peg as the two assistants moved away.

"Now what do I do?"Caylen asked the shaman through his pain.

"I shall now leave you to release yourself from these ropes that hold you. You must free yourself without help from another or the use of your hands. You have only the weight of your body as your means of release." said the shaman."If you should fail to find your release in this manner before the setting of this day's sun, you will be released by myself but you will be driven in shame from this village and forbidden to ever return. All male members of the Blackfoot people who wish to join the society of the warriors of the Blackfoot people must successfully complete this ritual so that the people may see the bravery as the boy becomes a man and the man becomes a warrior. Now I shall leave you and with the others, watch and await as this trial of pain either permits or fails to permit you to call yourself a Blackfoot warrior and a honored member of the Warrior society." With that, the shaman joined the circle of spectators who stood quietly by, awaiting Caylen's success or failure to his trial of pain. Caylen stood quietly for just a few moments looking about at the mass of silent spectators who stood in a circle about the pole to which he was tethered. Finally deciding that he had better try something he backed away from the tall pole until the rawhide ropes attached to the wooden pegs in his chest tightened and pulled on his severed chest muscles. The pain in his chest grew proportionately with the tension that he placed on the pegs. Slacking off slightly to ease his pain, Caylen thought to himself, *What have I gotten myself into?, I wonder if Sania knew I was going to have to go through this ordeal. What am I thinking? Of course he knew and of course he would not tell me. I am glad now that he didn't tell me as I don't know if I would have gone through with it had I known what I was going to have to do. Now, I have to get out of these ropes and apparently the only way I can do it is to tear or break these pegs out of my chest using my body weight to rip my own flesh apart.*

Leaning back again, he increased the tension on the ropes until, looking down at his bloody chest, he could see his flesh stretched tightly against the wooden pegs."Perhaps I should have taken that man up on his offer of a pain medication." he said to himself through clenched teeth as he placed even more tension on his severed muscles. *The only way that I am going to be able to do this without bringing shame upon myself is to utilize some of the powers that I possess.* He thought. *Now which of my powers would be the best for this situation. Perhaps I could detach myself and get out of my physical self on my life thread until I can rip myself free. Or maybe I can use my mind to unfasten these ropes and free myself that way.*

As he contemplated his situation and tried to think of a way out that would cause the least amount of pain to himself, Caylen suddenly recalled something that the Aliens said to him just before they left the earth.

"Life is a journey down many trails that each one of us embarks upon. Life is a trail that each one of us must take, in many ways, alone. We may decide that the trail we wish to follow through life will be the easy trail or we may decide that it will be the more difficult trail. It is by taking the harder trail that we evolve onto a higher plane of being. You, alone, have chosen to travel life's journey via the more difficult and complicated trail that will present you with many challenges and cause much hardship and pain in your life."

As the morning sun finally broke over the eastern horizon, Caylen, without further ado, moved back even further against the terrible pain. Steeling himself against the fire that stabbed into his very soul, he jerked his body back, using the full weight of his body until he finally felt a searing, tearing sensation in his breast. With one final step he suddenly fell back onto the hard-packed soil of the Blackfoot Warriors proving grounds, free of the raw-hide ropes that had tethered him to the ceremonial pole. Quickly getting to his feet, Caylen felt the hands of someone helping him over to where he could sit on a wooden bench that was strategically placed so that anyone sitting on it faced towards the east.

To Caylen's utter astonishment, he could see the mornings sun just becoming fully visible over the horizon to the east. *I'll be darned,* he thought. *It only took me about ten minutes to tear myself free. I wonder if that's a normal time for a aspiring warrior to take or does it usually take longer?* Looking about for the group of spectators that just a few minutes earlier circled the Sun Dance pole, he could see that the majority of them had departed the area and gone about their business.

"You will make a fine member of our Warrior society, Mato Honi. You have completed the Sun Dance in the shortest time ever seen by the people. You have been blessed by the Gods. The people are well pleased and will now, this very day, prepare a feast to welcome you as a Warrior to our village and to our lands." said the old medicine-man as he washed and dressed the gaping wounds in Caylens chest."You will be welcomed here on Blackfoot territory for as long as you wish to stay. You are now one of us and shall be forever treated as if you were born a full-blood Blackfoot man and a warrior."

***

The feasting and dancing went on that night until well after midnight. With plenty of food and homemade beer consumed, the tribe's people filled Caylen's ears and mind with plenty of information pertaining to tribal life as well as the cattle killings of late. During the long festive evening Caylen found himself, on two occasions, offered a young Indian maiden in marriage. After declining, with thanks these two offers, he was then approached by a handsome widow who indicated to Caylen that should he be willing, he could move into her tepee where he would be welcomed by her and her four children. After again explaining that he was already married with a wife awaiting his return, he was, at last, given up on by all the single women of the village. He spent the next three days recovering from his Sun Dance ceremony. The old medicine-man applied a reddish liquid to his wounds three times a day after sewing tightly closed the tears in Caylens chest.

Caylen, now having much time on his hands, spent these days talking to the villagers about the killings and gathering as much information from them as he was able. He soon determined that the Blackfoot people knew little of value about the killings. The old man speculated that a malevolent and evil spirit had appeared on the land and occupied the wolf pack's dominant male and was now leading the pack on their deadly forays after the ranchers cattle.

On the third day, Caylen rose before dawn and mounted the painted mustang the tribe's chief had, the night before, presented to him as a gift to honor his successful completion of the Sun Dance warrior ceremony. You completed this ritual of pain faster than any warrior of the people can recall," the chief said."You are a warrior amongst warriors. Your feat of endurance and acceptance of pain during the ceremony shall be the source of stories told by the people of this village for many, many years to come. I wish now for you to accept the gift of this, my fastest pony, as my way of honoring your feat and as a welcome to my village and my people."

Caylen spent the entire day riding across the undulating landscape of the beautiful foothills of the Rocky Mountains. Warrior bounced along beside him as he rode, straying off a few feet on occasion when a gopher, startled by the approach of a horse and wolf, sounded the alarm and raced to the protection of his burrow. He saw nothing of interest during his ride save the occasional small gatherings of some rangy half-wild Indian cattle and some antelope that spotted them from afar and who just stood patiently watching until Caylen and Warrior were well past them.

Chapter 13

Meanwhile

Aponi found herself missing Caylen terribly. The days were bad enough but the long nights alone seemed to stretch on forever. She found herself welcoming the early morning noises that originated from the kitchen as Sihu and Shilah bustled about preparing breakfast and feeding the always-hungry Talisa. Her evening long-range mind discussions initiated by Caylen only served to make her miss his presence even more. The warm lengthening spring days kept her quite busy gathering the wild morel mushrooms that grew in profusion on the sloping forest floor and up the sides of the big Serenity Mountain. Aponi knew that the wild delectable morel mushroom, prepared in any fashion, was one of Caylens most favourite foods. She could usually fill her wicker basket twice over in one day's outing, washing them thoroughly in a salty brine before laying them out for the hot sun to dry. She would then bag them and store them away in the cold room for later consumption.

She quite frequently observed areas on the mountains grassy slopes where the grasses were laid flat. Caylen and Shilah had both warned her that these areas of flattened grasses were usually the result of the big northern brown bears having fed on the newly grown spring grass and then resting in the warm sun.

"You have nothing to fear from them as long as you do not startle them or come between a mother bear and her young." Caylen had said."If you sing and make lots of noise, they will hear you coming and will get out of your way pretty fast."

"You better be careful out there." Shilah now teased."Them big brown bears just love the taste of tender young Hopi ladies. Specially in the springtime."

"Shilah! Don't be trying to scare that girl!" Sihu retorted quietly for Shilah's ears only."She is sad enough with her man not being here. And besides, I have a feeling that it won't be to long before our Talisa has a little brother or sister to play with."

"Is the girl with child?" whispered Shilah."It's about time."

"You just keep quiet about it." Sihu replied quietly."I am certain that Aponi does not realize yet that she is with child. Her cheeks and the sudden change in her appetite tell me much about her condition."

"I don't know what you two are whispering about, but I really feel quite safe up on the mountain." Aponi said."Besides, Snow has been following me everywhere since Caylen and Warrior left. I think that perhaps Caylen, before he left, instructed her to stay with me wherever I go. I think that if a bear or anything else tried to attack me that they would have to deal with her first. Now, you two, I have packed myself a little lunch and am going to go back up Serenity to where I was yesterday. There were all kinds of big morels up the slope about a mile or so and I want to get as many as I can before the animals and bugs do."

"What animals are you talking about?"asked Shilah.

"I really don't know what is eating them but I am finding a lot of them that seem to have been broken off just above the ground." Aponi replied.

"You be careful up there." Shilah said."You must be getting close to where the Matah Kagmi live and forage. They might not be too happy to find someone harvesting what they think belongs to them in areas that they might think are theirs alone."

"I will," replied Aponi as she left the house."I should be back in time to help with supper, Mom."

***

It took Aponi nearly an hour to find her way to the little forest clearing on the north slope of Serenity Mountain. Snow maintained a pace that matched hers during her ascent, roving out to the left and right of Aponi as she climbed ever upwards. Finally reaching the little clearing where she had ended up at on the previous day, she sank down on the soft fragrant meadow grasses and wild mountain flowers to rest awhile before beginning her search for the elusive morels.

"I must be out of shape," she said to Snow who had flopped down a few feet from her."I used to be able to come up here without resting at all. Now it seems as though I have to stop and catch my breath every five minutes."

She rested for only a moment or two before rising and moving into the wooded area uphill of the clearing. In a unusual display of caution, Snow seemed to hesitate for just a moment before following her into the forest. Aponi immediately began to see the delicious grey/brown morel mushrooms on the cool, damp forest floor. She also noted that Snow appeared to be agitated about something and kept making a low whining sound as she kept attempting to block Aponi's forward movements.

"Snow!, what is the matter with you?. There is nothing here to bother us so why are you acting so strange?" she said aloud.

"Your wolf animal senses our presence and is trying to warn you to leave this place." said a voice inside her head.

Startled, Aponi jumped to her feet and looked about herself, not realizing that the voice she heard had originated from within her brain and was not audible to her or Snow's ears.

"Who are you, and where are you?. It is as though I can hear you clearly but I do not really hear your voice." she said aloud.

"We see you clearly and will now come forward to reveal ourselves to you. We did not wish to frighten you or your wolf dog. That is why we warned you of our presence before revealing ouselves to you. You must control your wolf dog before we reveal ourselves as she may think that she must attack us to protect you." said the voice in Aponi's head.

Snow was now leaning against Aponi and was making a continuous low growling sound. Aponi reached down to grasp her long white neck hair, saying as she did so, "Stay, Snow, stay girl, stay."When she next looked forward and up the mountain slope, she let out a involuntary gasp. Standing not twenty feet in front of her were three big, hairy, naked creatures.

"You are the Matah Kagmi!"she exclaimed aloud."You are the ones who brought to us the little girl child that we have named Talisa or Beautifull Water."

"Yes, that is what we are called and yes we are the ones who gave the little female child to you to raise as your own. You must not make further talk at us with your mouth. Your speech harms our ears and is unpleasant to us. You need only to speak to us with your thoughts as we speak to you. Your mind is as ours and is able to speak without sound. Your mate gave this gift to you after the ones called the 'Travelers' who came here from without, gave those same powers to him."

So, you are telling me that I can speak to others with my mind now and that I no longer have need of my voice? Aponi .thought

"That is not as it is." said the tallest of the three Matah Kagmi."You are able to hear and speak only with thoughts to others such as yourself who possess the same power. You are not able to initiate such speech on your own and must speak with your mouth to all others."

And what is it you wish of me? thought Aponi.

"You have been taking our food from this forest. We have come to ask that you take no more of the plants that you call morels from this place. We, the Matah Kagmi, need all of these plants that grow in these forests for our food. If you take our food from us we shall surely perish during the long freeze that you call winter." said the tallest of the three with his mind.

I did not know that you claimed this part of the forest as your own. Aponi replied with her mind. *I shall not again take food from any territory that you deem as yours. If you will describe your territory to me, I shall not return to those areas to collect food unless you invite me.*

"Our foraging areas are from the clearing where you last rested to the peaks of this mountain." said the mind of the middle-sized Matah Kagmi."We also go down to the creek and river mouths when the fishes enter those places. We are eaters of plants and water creatures only."

May I see your home? thought Aponl, thinking that such a tour would really be interesting to relate to Sihu, Shilah and Caylen.

"We are not comfortable with such a visit at this time." said the thoughts of the larger of the three."We live high on this mountain and we also do not think that you should attempt such a climb in your condition."

What do you mean, 'my condition', asked Aponi with her mind.

"A climb to our home is very difficult and should not be attempted by one who is with child." said the thoughts of the smaller of the three Matah Kagmi.

"Whatever are you talking about!" exclaimed Aponi aloud, not quite fully understanding what had just been said."I am in very good condition!"

"Yes, you appear to be in good condition for a female of your kind who is so obviously with child." thought the smaller Matah Kagmi."I am a female of our beings who has borne many young. I easily recognize another female who is as plainly with child as you are."

"Are you trying to say that I am going to have a baby?" Aponi exclaimed aloud.

"Yes, you are with child. And please do not use your mouth to speak as it harms our ears. You will, in about eight moons, give birth to a male child."

I don't know what to think or even if I believe you! thought Aponi.

"We do not speak to any creature of things that are untrue." thought the female."Now take the food that you have gathered and go from our lands. We mean you no harm and will, at another time, take you to our home so that you may see how we live."

I would like that. thought Aponi, her mind racing with the news that she had just received. *I must get back home and tell Mom, Shilah and Caylen the good news that you have given me.*

"We do not think that knowledge of your soon-to-be child will be news to the one who has become mother to the white-skinned child we gave to you many moons past." thought the female Matah Kagmi."That one also knows that you are with child."

***

When Aponi finally reached home that afternoon, she found Bill and Lora with their new daughter Georgina and five young men from her village on the Third Mesa awaiting her arrival.

"I think you know this bunch." Bill said."They are here to start mining our new claim. I have brought all the materials and supplies they will need to get started on removing the gold from that creek. I am going to stay with them for a couple of weeks to make sure they know what to do. By the way, Aponi, how is Caylen doing on his mystery investigation? Have you heard from him lately?"

"He speaks to me nearly every night." said Aponi."Lora, may I hold Georgina for a while. My, she has really grown. Is she healthy and eating well?"

"Well, for a girl that is less than four months old she is doing really well. She weighs over twelve pounds and seems to be trying to crawl at times. She is also starting to get her baby teeth and are they sharp!" said Lora."Here, take her for a while. She makes friends with everyone."

Aponi, in all the hustle and bustle with her sudden company decided to wait until after she shared the news of her pregnancy with Caylen before revealing that news with all the others.

After a sumptuous evening meal, as the entire group sat about the big stone fireplace reacquainting themselves, Bill announced that he would take the five young men to the mine site first thing in the morning, leaving Lora and Georgina at Serenity to visit and await his return.

He and the five men departed early the following morning, towing a barge loaded with supplies behind his boat.

Chapter 14

Evil

Caylen was overjoyed at the news from Aponi that he was to be the father of a son. *We will have lots of time to decide on a name for him,* he said with his mind voice. *Have you given any thought to a name for him, Aponi?* he asked.

I have not even had time to really think about any-thing since Bill and Lora arrived. As you say, though, we have lots of time. You should see Georgina, Caylen, she has to be the prettiest little girl that ever was! Aponi thought.

Caylen and Aponi talked back and forth for over two hours before Caylen finally broke off the mental conver-sation, saying, *I must get some sleep Aponi. I just arrived back in town and have to visit the two biggest ranchers to-morrow. The Constable is going to drive me down to meet the Deputy Sheriff of Browning on the US side of the border. Apparently their ranches extend across the border but their ranch houses are both on the US side. I will try to talk to you again tomorrow night.*

Caylen had decided to not tell Aponi of his Sun Dance ceremony until he returned home. He knew that she had enough to think about without having to worry about him any more than she already was.

***

After a good night's sleep and a big country style breakfast, Caylen and Warrior walked across the quiet main street of Cardston to the police station where he found Constable Sykes shuffling through a pile of wanted posters.

"Good morning, Caylen." he said."How did your trip out to the reserve go? Did you find anything out or were they all keeping quiet as usual?"

"No, I just made a few more friends. They really don't know anything more than we do. I did find that none of them trusts the ranchers in this area though. They told me not to believe anything that the ranchers tell me, especially the two that we are going to see today. They say that the planned reservation will almost completely engulf the open lands that they utilize for their summer range. They say also that some not too subtle threats have been made to some of the elders of the reserve, including a few shots having been fired at some of them."

"Well, I have not heard about the shots being fired at them. I certainly would have investigated those had I known." said the Constable.

"They are convinced that there are evil spirits about and that the spirits have possessed some, if not all of the wolves and that is what is causing the pack to do what they are doing."Caylen said, ' They really do believe that, and I know enough about the Native Indians' history and lore to realize that there usually is some connection to reality in what they say. They do not always think or speak in terms that we whites are able to comprehend, but just because we do not understand them or their beliefs does not mean that what they think or believe in is wrong."

Caylen soon decided that he would not reveal to Constable Sykes or anyone else that he had undergone the painful Sundance Ceremony. He was unsure of just how such information would be received.

"Well, let's get on the road." said the Constable. It's about a three hour drive over some pretty rough roads to the first ranch. It belongs to the Carlin family. They settled in this area nearly fifty years ago and had to fight a lot of Indians in the early years for their land. They lost quite a few of their ancestors in the Indian wars and still dislike the Indians and anything to do with them. They are the biggest of the two big ranches and stand to lose the most if the reservations are expanded. They run well over five thousand cattle, have about thirty or so cowhands, and probably have the most influence on the other ranchers and are likely the most responsible for whatever rumors are circulating at any given time. Old man Carlin is about seventy-five years old and likes to brag that he personally has killed over fifteen of 'them there damn Injuns' and would like to kill a few more before he dies."

"Is he still the family matriarch or do his sons run the place?" asked Caylen.

"He has two sons, William is the oldest and Hershall is the younger. They take care of the day to day operations on the ranch but the old man still makes all the important decisions. There are also the two sons of William who are still going to school. The only woman on the ranch is Hershall's wife and she is a real looker. Old lady Carlin died years ago and William's wife died giving birth. Hershall has been married now for about ten years but has no children. It is said that the old man says to everyone that Hershall is 'a damn fool idiot who doesn't know how to do anything - he can't even make himself a son'. I believe that given the chance, Hershall would pack up and leave but the old man won't give him anything, not even a horse of his own. It is also rumored that William is the one who is bedding Hershall's wife and that Hershall knows about his wife's infidelity but won't do anything about it because he is terrified of his father and William."

"Wow! "exclaimed Caylen."Sounds like a really nice family."

***

After about two hours of steady driving, Constable Sykes turned to Caylen and said."We have been on the Carlin ranch now for the last half hour or so. Those little herds of cattle we have been seeing all belong to him or to his friend Jack Fagan who owns the adjacent and next biggest ranch. Between the two of them, they own more land than all of the other ranchers combined and most of it is on the land that the Government is going to give to the Blackfoot Reservation."

"That sounds like a lot of motive for them to try to change the Government's mind about expanding the Reserve." said Caylen.

"Yes, it does," said Tom."But they are also losing cattle and then there is the fact that the two boys were chased by the pack of wolves."

"So they say." said Caylen."So they say."

Before long Caylen could see the indistinct shapes of a number of buildings on the horizon. Within a few minutes the buildings revealed themselves to be a large sprawling ranch house, a large hay barn, three bunkhouses and a number of other buildings of various shapes and sizes. Large wood-fenced corrals surrounded these outer buildings. One of the corrals contained about twenty or so horses that milled about in what appeared to Caylen to be an agitated state. There was also something else visible that caused Caylen to turn to Constable Sykes and ask, "What is that over the ranch buildings?"

What he could see, suspended over the entire area encompassed by the ranch house and its outbuildings, was a dark, nearly black cloud. It appeared to resemble a thunder cloud that was about to deluge the ranch with thunder, lightning and torrential rain.

"What are you referring to?" asked the Constable."I don't see anything but that big old vulture up there soaring around waiting for an easy meal."

Looking closely, Caylen spotted the vulture gliding around in circles, high above the black cloud that appeared to be motionless directly over the ranch buildings.

"Do you mean to say you cannot see that big black cloud?" he asked.

"What cloud?, there is not a cloud in sight." said Constable Sykes.

Hearing that, Caylen felt a sudden thrust of fear run through his entire body.

Sitting upright on the rear seat of the car, Warrior's low growling noises added to the feeling of dread that suddenly permeated the entire vehicle.

"Good God!" exclaimed Constable Sykes."Do you feel how it suddenly it got cold in here?" he asked as he drove up in front of the main house.

"Now I see that cloud," said the Constable."Where did it come from? Boy, it sure got cold fast." he added.

"Tom," Caylen said."I will explain everything to you later but I want you to stay in the car for now. I think you will be safe in here from whatever is about to happen. I want you to keep the car running and if anything really bad happens to me, get yourself out of here as fast as you can and don't come back!"

"What are you talking about?" asked Tom.

"There are evil spirits here." said Caylen."I have seen and felt evil before and I recognize the signs. There is so much evil in this place that even the sun's rays have been blocked from the earth. Dark spirits are here and may be in control of all things, human or animal that are present in this place."

As Caylen and Warrior exited the car, the ranch house door opened and a group of men, led by an old man with a cane, trooped out onto the large roofed porch that faced the parked car. When the last of the group had exited the house, the door closed and at least a dozen men, women and children stood before Caylen.

Before anyone could speak, the door re-opened and another man exited the house to stand slightly behind and off to one side of the main group. As this man came out the door, Caylen could feel the hair stiffen on the back of his neck. He could easily see that each and every person standing before him was displaying brownish or grey Auras except for the last man out, who's Aura was a solid jet black. He could sense the very air around him grow even colder as Warrior's growls grew louder as even he could now sense the evil that stood before them.

"Who be you? And what's you want here with that there wolf animal? Don't you knows that we kills any wolves we sees round here?" asked the old man, looking closely at Caylen and Warrior as he spoke.

"My name is Constable Helms and I am here to assist Constable Sykes in the investigation of the killings of the cattle that have been occurring around here." said Caylen.

"We don't need yer help." said the old man."I owns all these land as far as you kin see. Me friend Jack Fagan here owns all the rest twixt here and the Injun lands and we don't needs any help from you or anyone else fer that matter."

"Well, maybe you don't want or need our help, but the other smaller ranchers do and have asked us to investigate as they are losing a lot of animals to that pack of wolves." replied Caylen."Now if you would be so kind, would you please introduce all these people to me."

"I will do that and then I wants you offen of my lands. Youse are tresspassin and I wants you out of here." said the old man.

"This here people on my right be my friend Jack Fagan and his wife. Those two behind him be my foreman and the range boss. The bunch on me left side be my two sons, William, Hershall, Hershall's wife and William's two boys, Sammy and Billy."

"Are you the two boys that the wolf pack chased up a tree?" asked Caylen, looking at the two boys.

"Don't you be askin anything of anybody ceptin me." said the old man."I does all the talkin fer everyone here. Yes, they's the ones chased by them danged cow-killin beasts."

"Don't you carry rifles with you when you're out riding?" asked Caylen, ignoring what the old man had just said.

"Don't you say nuthin, boy." said the old man as one of the boys was about to answer Caylen."I's told you, copper, I's the one who does all the speakin round here."Now, I want's you to take that damn wolf and yer talkin and gets offen of my land. Yer tresspassin and yer not welcome here."

"Before I leave I have one last question fer you, Mr. Carlin. You have not introduced the gent who is standing off to one side there." said Caylen.

"That there gent be a bounty hunter that I's hired to git rid of them dang cow-killin wolves." said the old man."His name be Mr. Warg and he be from a place a long way from here. That man, he knows all there is to know bout wolves and sech."

"And just where did you say you were from, Mr. Warg?"Caylen asked, watching the man's face as he sent a light mind probe at him. In the next instant, Caylen felt a searing pain in his head and found himself falling helplessly to the hard-packed dirt. As he fell he could see Warrior leaping towards the man whose mental powers obviously far exceeded Caylen's own.

When he saw Caylen suddenly fall to the ground where he now lay, unmoving, the dumbfounded Constable Sykes leaped from the car, drawing his revolver as he did so.

"Warrior!, come back here." he yelled at the attacking wolf. Warrior, to his surprise, obeyed him immediately and walked back to lie beside Caylen who continued to lie unmoving on the hard packed earth.

Caylen could feel himself floating in the air. Opening his eyes, he could see below, his outstretched body on the ground with Warrior beside him. He could also see Constable Sykes waving his service revolver about and yelling at the group of people on the porch of the ranch house. After a few moments he could sense that he had been placed in the back seat of the car and that they were driving at a breakneck speed across the flat prairie landscape.

***

Totally unaware of what had just occurred, Constable Sykes had observed Caylen suddenly fall, unconscious to the ground. Seeing Warrior beginning to attack a man who was simply standing there made no sense to him at all.

Knowing that he must take control of the situation before it went completely out of control, the Constable drew his service revolver and leaping from the car, called off the lunging Warrior.

"Something seems to be wrong with yer partner, Tom." said old man Carlin."William! You and Hershall help Tom git that there man into his car so they's can gits themselves the hell out of here."

Chapter 15

Recovery

"Adahy!, Adahy!, Wake up. Do you not know your blood-brother? Do you not recognize me for who I am? Wake up, my son or you will surely cease to exist in the land of the living and will join me in this place where I now walk with the great Qaletaka."

Caylen slowly opened his eyes at the familiar sound of Sania's voice. For a few moments he lay, bewildered, as his mind slowly but surely began to function so that he could recall the events that led to his current state. His last recollection was of his mind probe towards the strange Mr. Warg and the searing pain that penetrated his head and sent him, unconscious to the ground. Now fully awake, Caylen rose to his feet to stand in front of his old friend and mentor.

"What has happened to me?" he asked."The last thing I remember was feeling a terrible pain in my head. Am I dead?, where am I?"

Looking around himself, all he could see were swirling white clouds and his old friend Sania who now looked like a young man. Beside him stood his old wolf pet Abhaya who also looked to be young again. As he looked about, the white cloud beneath his feet cleared so that he could see, far below, a black car racing across the flat prairie. Driving the car was Constable Tom Sykes. Sitting beside Constable Sykes was his pet Warrior while in the back seat, lay the obviously unconscious body of a man.

Looking closer, Caylen saw that the inert figure lying on the back seat was himself.

"You are not yet ready to join your blood-brother and the great Qaletaka in the land of the afterlife. You have much more to do before you are called to us. I have brought your essence to me so that I may warn you and advise you of the perils of your present mission. You will be very ill for three days and three nights. On the fourth day you shall awaken from your long sleep and shall be as you were."

"Do you know what happened to me?" asked Caylen."The last thing that I can recall is that I was sending a weak mind probe at that strange Mr. Warg. The next thing I knew was when I saw you looking down at me. It is good to see you again, my brother."

"I too am also pleased to again see my young brother. The Great Qaletaka has again favored me by permitting this meeting of our spirits. I also have knowledge of the young and beautiful Aponi's condition. I have knowledge that a certain young man who just happens to be my blood-brother and my adopted son is soon to have a son of his own spirit and his own blood." said Sania."Now," Sania continued."This Mr. Warg that you speak of. Are you not able to recognize who and what your Mr. Warg is?"

"All I know about Mr. Warg is that his aura is solid black and that he gets really angry when I try to read his thoughts." Caylen replied.

"You are very fortunate that your essence is still with your physical self," said Sania."Any mortal man who was not in possession of powers such as yours would have died instantly from Mr. Warg's mind thrust. You should know that your Mr. Warg is the spawn of an ancient and dark evil. He is a child of Satan himself and is permitted by the evil Lord Satan, the King of Darkness, to pursue his evil actions at his own discretion and without the guidance or approval of the King of Darkness."

"Is he then the Devil himself?" Caylen asked.

"No, he is not the King of Darkness. Had he been that one, your essence would now be with the Great Qaletaka and not just injured." said Sania."Mr. Warg is better known in the books of your peoples history as a "Hellhound "or a dog of hell. He possesses great powers and is able to transform himself into a huge, fearless wolf like creature at any moment. His powers are mighty as is his howl. His howl can be heard for great distances and he easily becomes the dominant male leading and influencing the wolves that roam your lands. The Hellhounds of history are well known for their cunning and their cruelty to others."

"How does one defeat such a creature who possesses these abilities and such powers?" asked Caylen.

"One such as yourself can never defeat a Hellhound. A Hellhound can only be sent back whence he came by the actions of those creatures who are known to yourself as the 'Travelers' or by Satan himself. You must seek the aid of the 'Travelers' if you wish to rid the land of Mr. Warg." said Sania."There is one other way to rid the land of such a creature. That way is to convince the King of Darkness himself to take action against a Hellhound and return him to whence he came."

"Wow!" said Caylen."Both of those methods of removal appear to me to be impossible."

"I know not that word." said Sania."The word impossible is not a word of my people."

"But I know of no way to contact either the 'Travelers' or Satan. I don't think that I would want to contact the King of Darkness anyway." said Caylen.

"If you desire, I may contact the 'Travelers' on your behalf." said Sania."They are still nearby and may agree to assist in banishing Mr. Warg back to the land of demons from whence he came."

"I would like that." Caylen replied."We must try to rid this world of evil such as he."

"Then I will do so. I know not if they will agree to help and I know not how they will help if they do so." said Sania, "You will know if they do decide in your favor as they will require you to participate in such a banishment. Now I must leave you, my son, my father is calling for me. Go now, and rest so that you may again be healthy and strong for the terrible battle you will soon face."

***

Caylen woke with a start when he felt Warrior's warm wet tongue licking his face."What on earth is going on?" he asked of the strange woman who stood by his bed."Who are you, where am I and what happened?"

"You are in the first aid station of Browning and I am nurse, Molly O'Brien," said the woman."You have been unconscious for three days now. How are you feeling?"

"I feel fine." said Caylen."Do you know what happened to me?" he asked.

"No, I have no idea what happened." said the nurse."Constable Sykes said that you just fell over unconscious as you were speaking to the owners of the big ranches."

With a rush, all the memories of the incident suddenly returned to Caylen. In addition, he could now recall his conversation with his dead friend Sania and that he, Sania was going to attempt to get the 'Travelers' to aid in Caylen's upcoming confrontation with Mr. Warg, the Hellhound from Middle Earth.

"I am really hungry, " said Caylen."I am going over to the cafeteria and order the biggest steak they have."

"Constable Sykes said that I was to let him know the minute you woke up." said the nurse.

"Tell him that I will be at the cafeteria." replied Caylen as he walked out onto the street.

***

Caylen took the remainder of the day to explain to Constable Sykes roughly what had occurred to him. He skipped over the part where Sania had explained about Mr. Warg and his association with Satan. He simply said that Mr. Warg was a disciple of Satan and that he possessed powers that he could use to kill mortal men and that he, Mr. Warg, was behind all of the cattle killings."It appears, " said Caylen, "that our Mr. Warg was hired by the Carlins and the Fagans to scare the Blackfoot tribe into not pursuing the addition to their reservation. It also seems that they may have gotten themselves into a mess that they cannot get out of. I think they are as frightened of our Mr. Warg as are the natives and they now don't know what to do."

"And just how do you all of a sudden know all of this?" asked Constable Sykes.

"I will tell you."Caylen replied."But you must swear that you will never reveal to anyone what I am about to tell and demonstrate to you. My superiors in both Ottawa and Whitehorse know these things as does my mother and my wife. Those are the only people alive who know of my abilities and what I am about to reveal."

"Well whatever it is it must be pretty good. I wondered why they sent me someone from as far away as Whitehorse when there are lots of qualified men in the Calgary area." said Tom."Let's go back to my office and you can tell me there."

***

It was nearly dawn of the following day before Caylen finished relating his story and demonstrating his pow-

- 152 -

ers to Constable Sykes, who said, "I would never, in a million years have figured all that out. Do you have a plan on how we can get rid of this Hellhound, or can we? If you are correct then his powers exceed yours and there is no way we can get rid of him. Can he be killed?"

"Tom, how do you kill someone who is already dead?" asked Caylen."This guy has been dead now since nearly the beginning of time. No, we cannot kill him in any way that we would kill a mortal man. Our Mr. Warg is not mortal so we will need to tackle this in a different way."

"Do you think these 'Travelers' will help you?" asked Tom.

"I really don't know," Caylen replied."I have not had any sign that they will or if they do, how they will help."

"Well, I think that we best be getting some rest." said Tom."It will be dawn soon and I need some rest."

"As do I," said Caylen."If you don't mind, Warrior and I will just nap in this cell until morning."

"No problem." said Tom."See you in a couple of hours."

***

It seemed to Caylen that he had just dozed off when he was awakened by the urgent whining of Warrior. When he was fully awake, he slid his legs off the narrow bunk and sat for a moment, gathering his thoughts. Looking towards the jail cell door he could see what appeared to be a swirling white cloud of smoke in the doorway. A moment later a thought entered his now fully-awake mind.

"We have given much thought to your friend's request of us." The voice said."**We Travelers do not normally interfere in mortal matters but this Hellhound, Mr. Warg, has chosen to enter the world of mortals to create havoc upon the land. This thing cannot be allowed to**

continue. *His interference in the scheme of events of your world may cause serious harm to the natural evolution of you earthlings. We cannot allow this so we have decided to offer you a means to banish this spawn of evil back to the dark world from whence he came."*

"What am I to do?" asked Caylen aloud.

"You need not speak with your tongue. As we told you on our visit, your thoughts are as loud and clear to us as though you were shouting. At high noon, two days from this day, we shall, for a period of only two hours of your time, relieve the Hellhound, Mr. Warg, of all his satanic powers save one. This being shall not be aware, during that time, that he has lost his powers and shall only possess one power and one power alone, for that time period. The power that we shall leave with him for that period will be the power required for him to return to the Dark World from where he came. You will have that time and that time alone, to convince this spawn of Satan to return himself to the lands whence he came."

"And how do I do that?" thought Caylen.

"We cannot reveal what we do not know." said the Traveler."*What we will say is that you will have all of your powers intact and that once this Hellhound returns to the dark side, he will be unable to return to your world for one thousand of your years."*

"Thank you for what you have done and for what you are about to do." said Caylen through his mind.

"We go now. What you do now is yours to decide. Remember that the Hellhound, Mr. Warg shall not be aware during those two hours that he has lost all his powers save one until he tries to use them. You may then have to advise him of his one remaining power so that he can use it if he so chooses."

"I shall remember what you have said." thought Caylen as the white cloud slowly vanished from sight.

Chapter 16

Battle

Caylen decided not to reveal to Constable Sykes that he had been visited by the Travelers. He simply said to him, "Now that I know what I am up against, I will force him to leave us and return to the dark world from whence he came, I shall do battle with him at the Carlin ranch at noon tomorrow. We must prepare for this battle as it will take all of my strength."

"What must we do to prepare?" asked the Constable.

"I would like you to get as many of the tribe's elders out there as you can to witness what may occur. I would also like you to get word to the Carlins and the Fagans that I will be there at noon tomorrow to finally resolve the cattle killings. I also want you to bring along a couple of armed officers to ensure that no-one interferes with what I will be doing. We may also be making some arrests so we will need a few pairs of wrist and leg manacles."

"You sound pretty confident that you will defeat this Devil." said Constable Sykes.

""I am not at all certain that I can make him leave us but we had better hope that I do or we will be in a lot of trouble." said Caylen."Just be prepared for whatever happens and please do not interfere unless I ask for help. I will probably also be using Warrior so be prepared for anything. I am certain that our Mr. Warg will not give up easily. Now if you will excuse me, I need to get some rest. I have a feeling that tomorrow will be a long day.

***

At eight a.m. the following morning, Caylen stepped out of the cafe where he had just finished an enormous breakfast of steak, eggs, hash browns, toast with jam and four cups of strong, steaming black coffee. Feeling totally refreshed and anxious to proceed, he beckoned to Warrior to follow him and then walked over to clamber into the school bus that Constable Sykes had borrowed from the village's school. Already waiting on board were all of the Elders of the Blackfoot tribe, the tribe's medicine man and the Chief of the tribe. Also seated at the front of the bus with Constable Sykes were three heavily armed deputy constables. Each one of the three men carried a holstered loaded English Webley revolver of .455 caliber as well as a thirty-thirty caliber Winchester lever-action rifle. Each man also carried over their shoulders, a fully loaded cartridge belt.

Caylen noted that the majority of the Blackfoot men were also armed with carbines of various calibers."Well, everyone, good morning!, I see were all loaded for bear!? exclaimed Caylen.

"Are you not armed as well?"asked the tribal medicine-man."Bullets will not harm the evil being that I am about to do battle with." said Caylen.

"I wanted armed men with me simply to stop the ranchers or their men from interfering with me when I confront our enemy. You were correct, old man," said Caylen to the old medicine-man, "when you proposed that a evil spirit was on the land and possessing the wolf pack's leader. You were absolutely correct, that is what has been occurring. The Carlins and the Fagans together, hired Mr. Warg to try to scare your tribe into giving up on your attempt to have the Government impeach their ranches so that your reservation would be larger. What they probably did not know was that Mr. Warg is a evil spawn of the Devil himself. Mr. Warg come here from the Middle Earth, the dark side. He is known as a Hellhound and he possesses powers that enable him to occupy the mind of the wolfpack's leader and control the pack's actions. It is he and he alone that is responsible for all the cattle killings that have occurred hereabouts over the past year."

"And just how do you propose to get rid of this creature if he is that powerful? asked one of the deputies."That all sounds like a lot of bull to me."

"I have information from a confidential source that this Hellhound will be stripped of all of his powers save one, for a two hour period, commencing at exactly noon today." replied Caylen."The only useable power he will have during that time will be the power to return himself to the dark side from where he came. This creature cannot be killed and cannot be kept as a prisoner. His powers, after that two hour period, will return to him. After that time period, he will be unstoppable and will be capable of killing all of us in an instant. That is why we must defeat him and force him to return to Satan's land. Once he does return to Satan's lands, this Hellhound will be unable to return to our world for one thousand years."

"And how are you going to make him go back to Hell?" asked the deputy.

"Speak to him no more of this matter, Mato Honi!" suddenly roared the old Blackfoot medicine-man."Do you not know, deputy, that it is dangerous for a man to speak aloud of such evils from the dark side?. If the evil one hears such speech, that evil one might be warned of what is to come. Let us speak no more of what is to occur this day."

Other than the occasional comment from the bus passengers, the remainder of the ride out to the ranch was uneventful. When they could finally see the ranch buildings it was nearly noon. As they grew closer, Caylen spoke again to the bus passengers.

"Now, what I want all of you to do is to just keep behind me during whatever happens here today. I want Constable Sykes and you deputies to make sure that none of the ranchers or the ranch hands are armed. You must also not interfere in anything that happens over the next two hours. You are here only to bear witness to what is about to occur. You will all probably see things today that no man has ever seen before or will ever see again. You and your children's children will be telling their children many stories of today's occurrences for generations to come, so observe and be silent during all that happens."

As the bus pulled into the ranch yard, Caylen could see about fifteen or so people milling about in front of the big house. He easily identified the Carlin and Fagan families standing together on the big veranda of the house with Mr. Warg standing alone just to their rear.

"We are all here, just as you asked and none of us are armed." said Mr. Carlin."Why do you now come to my home armed when you have asked us not to have our weapons with us?. Can we not trust each other even for a few hours?"

"I will speak for all of these men that are here today." said Caylen."We are here to cure this land of the evil that has come here from a faraway place. Before long you will all see this evil for yourself and shall know this evil for what it is. Now, I am about to send my wolf pet Warrior out over the land to bring back here to us what we are most afraid of. Do nothing but observe what is about to be." With that statement, Caylen signaled Warrior and with a small portion of his mind traveled with the big black wolf as he loped off across the prairie.

"Now, it is one minute after twelve and I would like to speak to your bounty hunter for a few minutes." said Caylen as he stepped forward.

Mr. Warg came forward to stand, facing Caylen, about three feet from him. He spoke softly for Caylens ears alone, smiling as he said, "Have you no fear?. Are you now prepared to die?. I shall not be as gentle with you as I was the last time you tried to use your puny, pitiful powers on me. Do you not know who I am, you stupid fool? You will soon be not of this world so prepare yourself to die and to leave this world forever, Caylen Helms."

Before the Hellhound could react or say anything further, Caylen stepped forward and with all of his strength struck him full on his face with his fist. The loud 'SMACK' could be heard by all as Mr. Warg's nose and jaw were totally shattered by the impact of Caylen's iron-hard fist. As Warg fell to the ground, everyone present could tell from the amount of blood that sprayed out from his face and from the terrible crunching sound that Mr. Warg's nose and jaw were both badly broken. His bloody nose lay skewed off to the left of centre and lay nearly flat against his cheek. His jaw appeared to be about a full inch to the left of where it should have been.

The silence was broken only by the thud of Mr. Warg's body striking the ground. To the amazement of all, his body appeared to simply bounce as he leapt to his feet to stand again before Caylen. This time when he spoke, no-one, not even Caylen, could understand what he said. Speaking in some unknown language that was only known to himself and to his underworld master, Mr. Warg then, in full view of all present, rearranged and straightened his nose and jaw with his hands, causing all the blood that covered his face to completely disappear from view.

"My God! Did you see that?" said one of the deputies.

"I don't believe what I just saw!" said another.

"There is a terrible evil here!? said the old medicineman."We shall all die here this day."

"No you won't!" said Caylen."I have just begun to give this spawn of hell what he deserves!" Using the full force of his levitation power, Caylen, for the next ten minutes lifted Mr. Warg high into the air and slammed him repeatedly onto the hard-packed soil of the ranch yard. Each and every time he was smashed to the ground, Mr. Warg simply bounced back up smiling, to stand before Caylen, straightening and resetting his broken limbs as easily as one would straighten ones clothes.

Caylen then, with his levitation powers, took from the corral gate, a long leather bullwhip. The twenty-foot long whip's snapping sound as its tip broke through the sound barrier was only interrupted by the smacking sound as it cut into the flesh of the evil being who was now standing, exposed to all and unable to respond in any way except to repair the damage being inflicted on his body. It seemed that the only power that Mr. Warg now possessed was the power to heal himself. He soon realized himself, that all of his powers, save the power to rejuvenate himself, were now gone. He could only relieve himself of the terrible pain that his flesh and blood body was now feeling by healing himself as best and as quickly as he could.

After about thirty or so minutes of brutal and bloody punishment, Mr. Warg stood subdued, silently waiting for whatever was to come next.

"You cannot kill me Caylen Helms. I am able to repair instantly, any damage you might do to this earthly body. I do not know what has become of my powers but my Master will never abandon me. I will surely kill you Caylen

Helms. I will kill you and then I will then kill your Aponi and your unborn child. I will tear your bodies into a thousand pieces and feed each piece, one at a time, to the vultures that fly over this land."

"I will tell you, you spawn of hell, you Hellhound of Satan, the only other power that you now possess is the power to return to the dark side. Unless you wish to be torn to pieces and to become wolf food, I would strongly suggest you use that power before your friends arrive here." said Caylen.

It was only after a minute or so of dead silence that the big group of ranchers, deputies and Blackfoot Indians beheld, racing towards them across the flat prairie, a pack of seven large timber wolves led by a giant jet-black wolf whose emerald green eyes sparkled brightly in the afternoon sun.

"I believe your friends are here." said Caylen."Perhaps you could ask them to help you."

The pack raced directly at Mr. Warg. The men could see the hot saliva dripping from their snarling jaws as they leapt at him, tearing great chunks of flesh from his body.

Screaming in pain, everyone present easily saw what happened next. In one instant, Mr. Warg, a Hellhound and a spawn of Satan himself, vanished from the centre of the snarling wolf pack. The wolves then turned and raced off across the flat countryside, finally realizing that they were in the midst of man, their worst enemy.

The silence that then fell over the two groups of men was total. No-one spoke for at least five minutes.

The first one to speak was the rancher Mr. Carlin."I swear, we did not know about him. He just told us that he was the best wolfer in these territories and that he would eventually get them all. We had no idea that he was the one behind all this."

"I'm pretty sure we will never see our Mr. Warg again." said Caylen."Now, let's go home, I'm really tired. I'm quite sure that the politicians will now be able to make the right decisions about whether to expand the reservation boundaries."

Chapter 17

Home Again

Caylen stopped at the Calgary detachment of the Northwest Mounted Police and filed his report with the Superintendant of that office. Unwilling to reveal exactly what had transpired, he simply stated that all of the evidence that he had discovered had brought him to the conclusion that a hired wolfer, a Mr. Warg, from parts unknown who owned a trained wolf was responsible for all the cattle deaths. He concluded his report by saying that the man's pet wolf, after a severe beating by Mr. Warg, had finally rebelled at his owners cruelty and turned on him, ripping out his throat and killing him instantly.

Constable Sykes, agreeing to maintain silence about what he had actually observed, also filed a report with his superiors that fully supported what Caylens said. "I am certain that after so many people witnessed what you did, that rumors and stories will be circulating about you for years. The natives are sure that you are a all powerful Medicine-Man sent by the Gods to rid the lands of a evil spirit. They will be telling stories about your deeds for generations." he said to Caylen as they shook hands goodbye.

Caylen arrived back in Whitehorse three days later to discover that Bill, Lora and his new sister were at Serenity to establish the Hopi men at their new mine and that Bill was still at the site of the mine.

***

Aponi waited only a few moments following Caylen's arrival home to fill him in on all the details of her encounter with the Matah Cagmi. She described in detail, her conversation with them and how they told her of her ability to speak to them with her mind. She told him of how they informed her of her being with child and the fact that they knew it was to be a son.

"I have no idea how they knew about my pregnancy, In fact I had no idea that i was even pregnant. Oh Caylen, I am so happy!" Aponi said."I have already told Lora and Bill. They are almost as happy as we are except for one thing."

"What is that?" Caylen asked.

"They said that you gave me that mind-speaking power just after the 'Travelers' gave it to you." Aponi replied.

"That is very interesting." Caylen said."I wonder if I can also give it to anyone else."

"I really can't say. All I know is what they told me. I never thought to ask them and they told me something else."

"What is that?" Caylen asked.

"They both said that they were not sure that they were ready to be called Grandpa and Grandma." Aponi said with a smile." But I'm quite sure that they were just joking with me."

"I'm sure they were." Caylen replied."You cannot imagine how happy this news makes me, Aponi. Just imagine, a son! We'll have to come up with a name that will make both sides of our families happy and not offend anyone."We shall also have to re-establish some kind of contact with the Matah Kagmi and try to get them to show us where they live. We must be really careful not to encroach onto their foraging areas without their permission." Caylen added. "It's also quite interesting that you can now initiate a 'mind conversation now'.

I don't know just how you gave it to me. Perhaps you can give it to anyone you wish." said Aponi.

"Well, they did say that my powers would strengthen and that they would evolve into other things." said Caylen. "The power to 'mind-speak' must have evolved to where I can now bestow it upon others. The only problem is that I don't know how I did it. I will have to experiment and see if I can give it to someone else. Maybe the Matah Kagmi can tell me the next time we see them."

***

Anxious to meet the Hopi men who were to work the mine, Caylen, after only a day's relaxation at home with his family, boarded his big boat and set off down the inside passage to the mine site. Arriving at the mouth of the gold-bearing stream late in the afternoon, he tied up his big launch to the beautiful sailboat that Bill had left anchored out in the sheltered, deeper water of the bay fed by the stream. Quickly unloading his little fourteen-foot cedar-strip canoe, he was soon ashore and walking upstream to locate Bill and the five Hopi men.

Caylen had only to walk about two hundred feet upstream before he encountered the group of men busily constructing a large log cabin on a small knoll about fifty feet to the north of the stream.

Bill immediately introduced each of the five men to Caylen. "Caylen, meet Honaw, Honaw means 'Bear' Bear is the informal leader of the group as he is the oldest. The man next to him is called Lapu or 'Cedar Bark'. Next is Istaqa or 'Coyote Man '. The shorter one beside Istaqa is Honani or 'Badger'. This last one is called Lansa or 'Lance'."

After the introductions were over, Caylen asked Bill to gather the five young Hopi men about the big campfire that they had been using since their arrival at the stream site.

"Welcome to your new home." he began. "This place will be your home until the north winds and the cold weather bring a stop to your mining ventures so make it's as comfortable as you can. We shall arrange for a supply boat to come here at least once every three weeks until the weather dictates that it is time for you to leave. We will then arrange for you to return to your homes on the Third Mesa should you so wish. If you wish to spend the winter here or in Whitehorse or at Tranquility Place with us, you may do so but only if you make yourselves aware of our winters. They can be colder than any of you can even imagine. For example, even the wooden trees that you see growing about in this place will freeze so hard that a iron axe will sometimes shatter in the cold when it strikes a frozen tree. Another, even more important thing that each of you must understand is the need to keep this place a secret. If word were to get out about the richness of this strike, you will find this place quickly overrun with prospectors. You will find that many of those prospectors are not honest men and will kill you for what you have. I cannot stress the need for secrecy enough. Bill and I will show you, before we leave, a few ways and means of keeping most prospectors away from this spot but the best way is by keeping quiet about it to anyone you meet and by keeping it well hidden from the lake. You do not want any prospectors who might be passing in boats to observe any signs of activity here as they will surely investigate what is going on. If they do investigate it will not be long before this place will be overrun with gold seekers."

Caylen continued to emphasize the need for security and just what the lack of security could mean. He and Bill then took the men down to the lake shore and showed them how to camouflage the mouth of the stream and

how to erase any signs of their presence from the shoreline.

"Now," said Caylen, "let's get back to work getting
you guys a comfortable place to live. As soon as we get
this cabin built, Bill and I will show you how you're going
to get the gold out of this stream. We are quite sure that
you and the entire village of Oraibi will be quite wealthy
by the first snows of this fall. You will, however, find that
Mother Earth does not always give up her riches easily.
You will, if you are to be successful in your gold seeking
endeavors, be exhausted each night when the sun disap-
pears behind those mountains. You must quickly learn to
pace your work and to get sufficient rest so that you may
begin work each morning well-rested with plenty of food
in your bellies."

***

It took the following two days for the seven men to
complete the construction of comfortable accommodations for the five Hopi men. With the cabin fully completed, Caylen and Bill spent the next day showing the
men gold panning methods and practicing, on the stream.
Once they were reasonably proficient in panning, they
then took two days to construct a long portable sluice
box with a wooden water supply trough that ran on wood
bracing up along the stream to a small waterfall. A strategically placed swiveling section of the upper end of the
supply trough ensured full control over the water's flow
to the sluiceway.

The day of panning confirmed to Caylen and Bill the
potential of the find. A estimate of the quantity and value
by Caylen at the end of the instructional day was quickly
relayed to the men. Addressing them, Caylen said."Do
you guys realize that in one day, with absolutely no experience, you have recovered over ninety-five ounces of
gold?. That much gold is worth about nine hundred and

fifty dollars. You each made about one hundred and ninety dollars today. Not bad for twelve hours of work, especially when you consider that five dollars a day is a really good wage! Now, if you think that's good, just wait until you see what one day's work on the sluicebox gives up."

The demonstration by Bill and Caylen of how the sluicebox worked was to be a real-eye opener for all the native men as well as Bill and Caylen.

"We shall first scrape the materials from the bottom of the stream nearest the lake and work upstream."Caylen said." The best places to take it from is at the bottom of any part of the stream where the water's rush has slowed. Those areas may not be the richest but will probably hold a lot of fine gold and the smaller nuggets. Scrape it out and pile it at the top of the sluice. Then handpick out any nuggets that you can see before running the remainder through the sluiceway. Bill and I will demonstrate this procedure so you can observe the process and ask any questions you might have."

Caylen and Bill, in early afternoon, had a pile of wet gravel about four feet high and about six feet across at the base. They had also, picked out about twenty ounces of nuggets of varying sizes. Diverting the intake pipe, Bill soon had a adequate supply of clear cold water running down and over the riffles of the sluiceway.

"Okay, now we just shovel the gravel we dug out into the top of the sluice and let the water take it down and out the other end," said Caylen as he and Bill began to shovel.

They had only shoveled about one-half of the gravel into the sluiceway when Bill shouted at Caylen."Hold up, Caylen, all of our riffles are full, we must not have enough slope on our sluiceway to keep the lighter gravel moving. Go and turn the water off so we can adjust the slope."

As the waters flow subsided, Bill spoke again."Holy smokes, Caylen! Do you see what I see?"

"If you are seeing one huge amount of yellow gold in this sluiceway then yes, that is exactly what I am seeing." Caylen responded.

The men took about an hour to clean out and collect the gold from the riffles of the sluiceway. Caylen estimated the take of gold to be approximately thirty pounds and a estimated value of four thousand two hundred dollars. As they still had about one half of the excavated gravel remaining, he decided to finish sluicing the pile before revealing to the Hopi men, what he and Bill had accomplished in just that one day.

Later that evening, as they all sat about the fire in front of the little cabin, Caylen again addressed the five natives, "Well, what do you guys think of our sluicebox?. How do you think it compares to the panning we did yesterday?"

"We thinks, from the gold we saw, that it be much better than panning." said one of the men.

"Much better would be a understatement," said Bill.

"Your tribe became about seven thousand dollars richer today."Caylen said."We took about seven hundred ounces of gold out of that stream today. As you can see the sluiceway produces much more for much less effort. Panning, though, is the best and fastest way to conduct exploratory sampling of an area. It is only once you have a established find that it is worthwhile building a sluiceway."

***

The following morning Caylen spoke at length with the five men about how they should proceed. He explained to them how the stream may have varied its course through the lower reaches and that some, if not all, of its older courses might contain even richer amounts of gold than its present course. He and Bill showed them how to dig and test exploratory test holes at regular distances from the present streams course, keeping records as they went. By conducting these tests they would soon discover the richest areas from which to excavate the gold-bearing gravels.

The men spent the next four days digging test holes and plotting the richest route that they surmised was the best to excavate for their first run. As it turned out, the richest test holes were nearly two hundred feet to the West of where the stream now ran. Their test holes in this area revealed almost immediately just how rich their find was. The very first test hole in this area revealed bedrock at about six feet down. It also gave up, in the bottom foot, just above the bedrock, twelve ounces of easily-spotted nuggets and ten ounces of finer gold in the first test pan.

Once the rough limits of the gold find were confirmed, Bill and Caylen took the five men on a short trip upstream, following the stream up the canyon about a mile or so to where it fell over a steep rocky rapids and exited a narrow fast-flowing gorge.

"I do not want you going past this point for any reason." said Caylen."I do not care if the richest areas are upstream of this point. You are not to venture past this spot. You may travel along the shores of the lake as far as you wish, but you shall not, for any reason, travel inland further than this point. This limitation to your travel distance extends around this entire island.

"But why do you limit our travel distance? Is there some reason for this?" asked one of the native men.

"There is a very good reason." Caylen replied."I have promised the beings that live in that mountain that I would not permit other beings to enter onto their lands without first seeking their permission."

"Why do you say 'beings'?" asked another of the men. "What do you mean when you say 'beings'?' Why do you not say men? Are these beings that you speak of not men as we are?"

"Oh, Oh." said Bill."Maybe you shouldn't have said anything at all about them, Caylen. You have gotten them worried now. Perhaps you had better tell them about the Matah Kagmi and hope for the best."

Caylen spent three hours trying to explain the Matah Kagmi to the five young men. Assuring them that they were in no danger as long as they stayed in the immediate area appeared to ease the men's concerns so Caylen and Bill retired to their respective boats for the night.

***

"Caylen! Caylen! Come ashore and see this," Bill shouted.

"What on earth is going on?, it's still dark out. What time is it?, What do you want, Bill?". Caylen asked, shaking the sleep from his eyes at Bill's insistent shouting.

"Come ashore, you will not believe this!" Bill replied. "This will really make your day!"

"I'm coming. just let me get my pants and shirt on. I'll be right there."

It was only a few minutes before Caylen saw what it was that Bill wanted him to see. Huddled together on the roof of the cabin were the five young Hopi men. They were all holding thick wool Hudson's Bay blankets over themselves for warmth. In addition, each man was peering about in the dark early dawn and was holding a rifle at the ready.

Roaring with laughter, Bill said."Well, Caylen, do you think that you really convinced them last night that the Matah Kagmi were harmless?"

"I don't think that those five guys think that this is funny, Bill." Caylen said as he stifled his laughter.

"Hey! You guys can come down off that roof now, Caylen and I will protect you from those wild Matah Kagmi." yelled Bill at the five terrified men.

***

Caylen and Bill spent the next few days showing the five men how to run the sluice way properly and how to bag and store the gold that they extracted from the rich streambeds. They decided to take back to Serenity all the gold that had so far been taken. This amounted to over twelve thousand dollars worth that Bill was to take to the bank in Whitehorse to deposit under the name of the company that the group had come up with.

"I believe that the name 'Serenity Mining Company' is a suitable name for our company."Caylen said after much discussion with Bill and the five men. "Now that you men are relatively comfortable here and at least accepting that the Matah Kagmi will not harm you, Bill and I will be returning home. I will, however, return in about three weeks with supplies for you and to take out whatever gold you have by then."

Chapter 18

War and Peace

Caylen and Aponi spent the following three weeks becoming re-acquainted, discussing Aponi's pregnancy, and just enjoying each other's company. Bill, Lora and Georgina sailed off on their return journey up the lake to Whitehorse taking the heavy bag of gold nuggets and dust to deposit in the Whitehorse bank.

"We will be back in late August," Lora replied to Aponi's query about when they would be back. "We really enjoy the trip down here. It is so relaxing and Bill gets a chance to catch some of those really big lake trout that live in the deep waters of Atlin Lake. Another thing, I want to see how you do as you progress with your pregnancy. By then you will be about five months along and getting quite large. Have you began to think of a name for him yet?"

"Well, I want to name him Caylen but Caylen wants to name him George after his dad with his middle name to be Sania." said Aponi.

"Oh, oh! " said Bill."I'm staying neutral on this naming game. I refuse to get in the middle. Either name sounds good to me!. I would even be okay with you naming him 'Faris' if you wanted to."

"Oh, be quiet, Bill. I would be very unhappy if Caylen named him Faris. You wouldn't do that, would you?" Lora exclaimed.

"He's just joking, Mom." Aponi said with a smile.

***

It was three weeks and two days later when Caylen set off down the lake to ensure all was well with the five Hopi miners. He first motored across the lake to Atlin to purchase sufficient supplies and to replenish the men's foodstuffs and equipment. He arrived at the site of the mine to see the five men crouched about a huge bonfire on the beach a few hundred feet from the mouth of the stream. All of the men carried their rifles and appeared at first sight to be extremely agitated, peering intently towards the thick forest that blanketed this part of the island.

"What is going on?" Caylen yelled, as he nudged the launch up to the sandy shore. Not waiting for a reply he jumped off the bow, taking a tie rope with him to secure the boat to a big log that had washed ashore during the last storm.

"Why are you fellows down here with your rifles?. Why are you not up working your sluiceway?"

"We are afraid." said Bear. "Lapu went up past the area that you marked to tell us how far upstream we could go. He found many big gold pieces there so we all went up and took many big pieces of gold from the stream. We knew we should not go that far but we thought that a few days up there would do no harm."

"So what happened to make you all so afraid?" Caylen asked.

"On the third day that we were up there we heard terrible sounds coming from the forest. We were very afraid and fired our rifles towards the sounds. The sounds then stopped and we returned to our cabin." Bear said."We decided not to go up that far again."

"Well, I am quite angry with all of you " said Caylen."What you have done is really inexcusable and may cause much difficulty for us. I should send you all back to the Third Mesa and tell your Elders that you have disgraced yourselves up here. Now tell me what happened next."

"Two nights past we heard much noise from outside of our cabin. We were very afraid and did not leave the cabin until the sun was high. When we went out we found our sluiceway destroyed, much of our supplies and tools gone. We looked about and found many tracks of some kind of large beast in the sand of the stream. We then became even more afraid so we came here to await your coming."

"So you have been here on the beach for two days and one night? Has anything else happened since you came down here?"

"Tell him of the sounds that we heard last night." said Coyote Man.

"What sounds did you hear?" asked Caylen.

"The most terrible sounds." said Bear. "It was a sound so terrible that we covered our ears to prevent the sounds."

"Aaah oooooga, Aaah oooooga," wailed Caylen, mimicking the noise made by the Matah Kagmi.

"That is it!, said Cedar Bark."That is the sound we heard coming from the night."

"Did you then do anything else?" Caylen asked.

In response the five men looked at each other and at Caylen, saying nothing to his latest query.

"I asked you a question!" Caylen said as he began to suspect and fear what the five men may have done. "I want you to tell me exactly what you did next and I want you to tell me now!"

"All we did was to fire our rifles at the sounds." said Lance."We wanted to frighten them so they would leave us. We do not think that any of our bullets struck them. It then became very quiet."

"And you heard nothing more?" asked Caylen.

"No, the next happening was when we heard the sound of your coming." said Bear.

"Well you had all better pray that none of your bullets has struck any of those 'beasts' as you call them. Those 'beasts' were the Matah Kagmi and they were only protecting what was theirs. Did I not tell you that you were not to go up past the point on the stream that I marked?. Did you not understand what I said? Did you not think I was serious when I said that you were to go no further upstream?" Caylen asked angrily. "You had better pray that I can contact them and try to straighten this mess up, cause if I can't we may as well all go home and just forget this gold. Now, I want you to come up to the cabin with me and get your personal belongings. I will take you all back to Tranquility Place to stay until I can get this mess straightened out."

The five men said nothing more until after they had gathered their meager belongings and were aboard Caylen's motor launch headed for Tranquility Place.

"I do not think that you will be able to convince these men to go back to that accused place." said Bear."It is the home of the devil himself."

"We shall see." said Caylen."I shall return and speak with them. You must tell the men that these creatures are not evil but simply different. I shall endeavor to make things right on your behalf so you may return and continue mining the gold. All those 'creatures' as you call them want is to be left alone and for us to recognize their territory. Remember that you are doing this for your people back on the Third Mesa. What you are doing here will make all their lives and their children's' lives much better for many, many snows."

"We shall speak to each other on what you have said." replied Bear. "I shall try to convince my brothers that you speak the truth and then I shall hear what they each have to say on this matter. We are greatly fearful of these creatures that you call the 'Matah Kagmi'."

***

Arriving back at his home later that day, Caylen and Shilah made the men comfortable in the big guest house.

"I shall go back tomorrow and try to make contact with the Matah Kagmi. I don't know if they will listen to me but I shall try to convince them that the men meant them no harm." he said to Aponi, Sihu and Shilah later that evening. "I can only hope that none of them were hit by all the shooting that bunch did."

"Oh, I hope that none of them were hurt." Aponi said."Do you think that they are the same family that we have seen on this side of the mountain?"

"I don't know for sure but I am confident that if not the same family that they are related and know of each other's group." Caylen replied.

***

Caylen returned with Warrior to the mine site the following day. Scouting about he easily ascertained from the signs left by the miners and the Matah Kagmi that what the miners had related to him of the incident was more or less accurate. He did find many empty rifle cartridges strewn about the areas where the miners had been hiding in fear of the Matah Kagmi.

"I think they may have fired off more bullets than they admitted to." Caylen commented to Warrior."I sure hope they did not hit any of them, perhaps I will use your nose to check around for any sign of fresh blood."

A good hour of sniffing about the edges of the campsite revealed only the strong musky odors of the Matah Kagmi on the forest's floor. Satisfied that none of the Matah Kagmi had been struck by a rifle bullet, Caylen sent a mind-probe up the steep mountain slopes, hoping to first encounter the creatures with his mind before initiating a face to face meeting. Receiving no response to his probe, Caylen hiked up the rushing stream shore to where it became quite obvious he was at the site where the Hopi men had taken the many large nuggets. The site was nearly one half of a mile upstream from the trees that Caylen had marked as the upper limits that the men were to obey. He could plainly see many more gleaming pieces of gold on the stream's rocky bottom.

"This find might even be richer than my first mine was," he said to Warrior, who was happily rushing back and forth in and along the rushing water chasing the many grayling that seemed to be teasing him with their short dashes towards the stream's shore."I wonder if the Matah Kagmi realize just what they have here and what it could mean to them."

Having finished that comment, Caylen could sense the beginnings of an idea forming in his mind."This just might work, Warrior, especially if I can convince them of the benefits it could mean for them. I will have to discuss it with the others and think on it some more before I talk to the Matah Kagmi of it."

Returning to the main camp, Caylen made himself and Warrior a evening meal that both he and the big wolf finished off just as the sun slid behind the snow-capped peaks to their west.

"Aagooooouummmmmm, aagooooooouummmmmm,' the eerie howling brought Caylen fully awake. Peering off past the nearly-out campfire into the dark night, he could see nothing. "Where are they, Warrior? Show me where they are, boy."

"Aagoooooooouummmmmmm," the howl sounded much closer now. Realizing that he should attempt to make contact with them before they grew too close so that they would know of his presence he sent out a mild, friendly mind-probe that was quickly answered.

"Who are you? Are you one of those who take the food and the yellow stones from our land?. Are you the one who used the long iron rods that roar and spit fire and throws the stones at us?" came the thought to Caylen.

No, I am not one of those creatures. I am one who is here to try to make things right with your people. I and others of my tribe are well known to the ones such as yourselves who live on the far side of the big hill. Do you know of these people?

"The ones you speak of are the children of our father's brother. They left us many snows past to begin a second group of our kind. This move was made because the food at this place was not able to supply all of our kind during the cold and snow times. Many of our kind were made ill and weak because of this lack of food. We have found that the forest and the waters will supply us with only enough foods for those of us that now are. We will soon have to send some of our kind to live elsewhere. If we do not do this many of our kind will surely perish during the coming snow time."

I know of your struggles to find and store foods for those of your kind. Caylen responded with his thoughts. *If you will come down out of the forests, we shall see one another and I will show you many ways that may be new to you that will provide you with more foods for the cold times*

"Are the others who take our food and the yellow stones now with you? We fear that they will try again to destroy us."

They are no longer here. They will only be allowed to return to this place when they have learned to obey the laws that I have told them of. They will no longer take your food and the yellow stones from your places. They shall soon meet with those of your kind and will also help to provide your kind with more foods. There is much for your people and for our people to learn about each other's ways.

"We shall now show ourselves to your eyes. We know, from your words to us and from the words of our brothers who live on the other side that your words and your hearts are true. We also find that we are able to speak our thoughts to you. When we tried to speak to the others, they did not reply. Why is it that you are able to do so while they could not?"

It is because the Great Spirit has blessed me and given me this power as well as many other powers that I cannot speak to you of at this time. Caylen thought.

Caylen met with the Matah Kagmi for the remainder of that day as well as the next. He told them of, and showed them of ways and means that they could catch fish at any time instead of waiting for the fall spawning runs. He showed them how to preserve fish through smoking and salting.

I shall soon leave but I will return with much more of this material called salt. Salt is very useful in the preservation of fish. It also adds much to the flavors of any foods. I shall bring back many of the steel barbs that you can use to capture fish in the big waters at any time. I will also return with tools and foods that will permit you to grow in the forest clearings, food stuffs that will allow your people to not feel hunger and to do well during the cold times.

"Your thoughts tell us that you wish from us, something in return for these things that you have told us of." the Matah Kagmi thought.

Yes, I do. thought Caylen. *I want the Matah Kagmi to permit those others of my kind to return and take the yellow stones from the earth as they were doing. They will not enter the areas that are yours ever again. They will also wish to meet with your kind and give you many things that you might find useful.*

"We shall do as you ask. We shall also give to your people more of the yellow stones that they dig for. Our kind has taken many of the larger yellow stones from the earth to our sleeping places. We have done so for many snows. We have much of these stones to give in return for the things you will give to us."

I wish to do all of these things for you within the next moon, but I must first discuss it with others of my kind before beginning. These things that I wish to do may have a great effect on your lives and for your future." Caylen thought in return. *I must now return to my home to discuss the many things we have, this day, mused upon.* With that thought Caylen closed his mind to any further communication with the Matah Kagmi. Returning to his launch he cast off and headed back to Tranquility Place.

Chapter 19

New Beginnings

What do you think, Bill? asked Caylen with his thoughts. He had explained in detail to everyone in his family his ideas regarding the teaching, the supplying and the trading of goods with the Matah Kagmi with mixed results. Aponi and Sihu thought his ideas were well thought out and would serve everyone including the Matah Kagmi well. Shilah, on the other hand, wondered if their interference in the lifestyles and habits of the Matah Kagmi was really in their best interest. He was now explaining his plans to Bill and Lora in order to get their opinions.

"I think it is a marvelous plan, Caylen." Lora thought. "You will not only help them to evolve but if they trade their gold for supplies, you will have taken the first step in introducing them to our ways."

"What would the 'Travelers' have to say about this if they knew?" asked Bill.

For some reason I think that they probably know of my plan and that if they really disagreed that they would not permit it. Caylen thought in return.

"Well, if you go ahead with it, I don't think you should expect too much from them in return any too soon."Lora thought."They will have a lot to absorb."

From what I have seen and observed about them I think that they are quite intelligent and will grasp whatever I show or tell them quite quickly, Caylen thought.

Caylen spent the following day cruising across the lake to Atlin where he immediately went to the general store. He purchased nearly the entire stock of the store's gardening tools, fishing lures and lines, bags and bags of salt, vegetable seeds, knives and candies. He considered getting boxes of matches and candles but after thinking more on the subject of fire, ended up purchasing a supply of flints and steel. He figured that showing the Matah Kagmi how to start a fire with these objects would benefit them much more than simply giving them matches. Returning to Tranquility that evening, Caylen explained to Aponi that he was going back to meet with the Matah Kagmi to give them much of the supplies that he had purchased. He explained to her that he was also going to spend some time with them in a effort to teach the purpose and uses of the items that he was going to give them. Informing the five Hopi men of his intentions, he instructed them to do as Shilah instructed until his return.

"I may not be back for a week or two so I want you to keep these guys busy until I get back. Have them go out and collect dry wood for next winter. They can also cut it up into useful sizes for our heaters and cookstoves. Perhaps you can even get across to them that the Matah Kagmi are not evil and that they could be very useful allies to them when we take them back to work the mine."

"I shall try but they are very afraid of the Matah Kagmi. I am unsure of whom they are more afraid of, you or them." replied Shilah.

"I will try to return within a week or so, Aponi."Caylen told her as he and Warrior boarded his boat the following morning."In any event, I shall keep you informed of my progress each night with my thoughts."

***

Three hours later Caylen stepped ashore at the mouth of the gold-bearing stream to utter silence. The only sound that was audible was the gurgling of the stream as it tumbled down over the rocky creek bed and into the big lake. He unloaded the canoe of all the trade goods that he had purchased for the Matah Kagmi. All in all, he figured that he probably had at least two more loads of goods aboard the launch but decided it was best to leave it on board for the time being.

"I wonder if they are nearby." he said to no-one in particular. A moment later a loud thought entered his mind.

"You have returned. You are the one who spoke to us of many things just four darkness's ago. You are the one who removed the five beings such as yourself who take the yellow stones from our earth and our waters. You are the one who promised us many things that would permit us to live in a easier way. Are you now here to give those things to us?"

Yes. I have returned just as I said I would. Caylen thought in return. *And I have brought many things from my land just as I promised. If you will come out of the forest I shall show these things to you. I will also show you what these many things are used for and then I shall instruct you in the use of them.You will be pleased at the way these things shall make your life so much easier and better for you.*

"We shall show ouselves to you but we will not come onto the open shore. We have learned that it is unwise to go onto places where other beings such as yourself might observe our forms. We have seen your kind many times when they observe us. They always send the stones at us from their long sticks. These stones come at us with fire and loud noises that hurt our ears. One of those stones once struck my mother's brother in the middle of his body. His life fluids came from his body for two dark-nesses. He was in much pain before his essence finally left him and his body became cold. We shall come to the place where the other beings constructed their cave." thought the Matah Kagmi. "We shall meet you and see what you have brought to us from your places."

Caylen and Warrior soon had all of the items he had brought with him laid out on the grassy meadow behind the cabin. He could see four of the male Matah Kagmi and two smaller females waiting patiently just outside the forest wall by the side of the creek. He had brought up two fifty pound bags of salt, flints and irons, knives, wool blankets, axes, a variety of sizes of cooking pots, hun-dreds of yards of heavy fishing lines and a assortment of fish hooks.

Come closer, my friends and see what I have for you These things you see here are only some of what I have for you. Come, and I shall show you what purpose each of these objects has and then I will show you how to use them.

For the remainder of that day, Caylen showed each of the items to the Matah Kagmi. The items that held the most interest to the males were the fishing lines and hooks. Each of them in turn drew blood from his fingers as they examined the hooks while Caylen patiently ex-plained their use.

It is simple. he thought as he knotted a hook to one of the lines. *You take one of these iron hooks and tie it to the line like this. Then you take a small fish or a piece of meat and imbed the hook in it. You then hurl it out into the lake as far as you can and then you just wait for a big fish to eat what you have placed on the hook.*

"But why do you throw all that out into the waters?. Surely you would not just throw it all out into the water. If a big fish did eat the smaller one and get the sharp iron in its mouth it would just swim away into the deep waters taking the line and the sharp steel away forever." thought the biggest of the males.

"Yes, all would be gone!" exclaimed one of the females. "I could make much better use of the sharp steel and the strong ropes. It seems that it would be quite wasteful to just throw it all out into the lake. Why would we do this?"

Oh, oh! thought Caylen to himself. *I didn't tell them to hang onto the other end or to tie it to something. The best way is to show them. We shall prepare more of these lines and then I shall show you how to use them. You shall watch everything that I do and then you shall do what I have done.* he thought.

He spent the following hours instructing the Matah Kagmi how to tie and bait a hook. He then showed them how to tie a rock on the line for weight. The next step, throwing the baited hook out into the lake brought quite a few questions that caused Caylen to smile in amusement to himself.

"How can the big fish see in the deep waters?. Is it not dark at the bottom of the waters?"

"Why would the fish wish to impale themselves on the iron barb? Would they not simply remove the dead fish or the meat from the iron barb before they ate it?"

"Would not the fish who impales himself on the iron barb inform other fish of the dangers in consuming something that was impaled on a iron barb?"

The sun was beginning to set as the group of Matah Kagmi and Caylen finished tying off the last of the set lines to the flexible mountain ash that grew in abundance along the lakeshore.

Go now and return with the rising sun and we shall examine our set lines to see what we have caught. Caylen thought. *I will then show you how to prepare the fish so that they will stay good to eat for many suns. You will also learn how to make the fish taste much better no matter how you eat them.*

***

Caylen took most of the following morning preparing the seven large lake trout they had caught for smoking. He first filleted them after having to first show the Matah Kagmi what a knife was, how to hold them and how to use them. This instruction took the better part of two hours and resulted in more than a few nicked and bloody fingers before they finally figured out how to use them without cutting themselves. He then had to explain what salt was and how to prepare a suitable brine to marinate the fillets in prior to smoking or drying.

It took Caylen a additional eight days to show and teach the Matah Kagmi all that they needed to know in order to get the most benefit from all he had brought them. It was easily apparent that the males were most impressed with the knives and the axes while the female Matah Kagmi were happiest with the salt, the flints and steel fire starters and the pots.

I have many other things to give you. thought Caylen. *I will return after three suns with the five beings like myself so that they can find more of the yellow stones. They will not ever again enter your lands and they also shall bring other things for you that might be useful to you.*

"We have taken some of the yellow stones from our sleeping places and have placed them on the sand close to your floating log. They are yours as a gift of our thanks for these many things that you have done for us. No longer will our children suffer the pains that come from too little food. No longer will our mates cry out in pain when our children wither and their essences leave their tiny bodies to be with the Great Ones. You may bring the other beings to this place when you return. We shall meet with them and trade the yellow stones for other things that they might wish to trade."

Caylen, when he returned to where he had left his canoe was astonished to find, piled neatly beside it, a huge stack of gold nuggets. As he loaded his gift from the Matah Kagmi aboard the launch he estimated its total weight at over six hundred pounds.

"Oh, my gosh!" he exclaimed to Warrior. "I had no idea! There is about ninety thousand dollars worth of gold in this pile. I wonder just how much they have stashed away in their caves."

Chapter 20

Tragedy

Caylen placed all of the gold in the big vault that was in the lower part of Tranquility Place. "Just a little petty cash to keep handy." he said to Aponi after relating all the details of his encounters with the Matah Kagmi."We can use it to purchase other things for their use."

"Do you think that they will be able to adapt themselves and utilize all these things that you are giving to them? They must be overwhelmed with that stuff." said Shilah. "I can remember my father telling me how all the modern things that our people got from the white man affected our people. Many of them just could not readily adapt to using all those luxuries. Many of them just threw themselves into the river rather than succumb to the white man's ways. It was just too much too fast for them to adapt to and accept."

"No, I am quite sure that they will be okay." replied Caylen. "They sure seemed appreciative of everything I gave and showed them."

***

The following day Caylen met with the five Hopi miners, briefing them on what he had accomplished with the Matah Kagmi. He stressed to the men the importance of remaining calm in the presence of the creatures and that they should not expect them to respond to their speech vocally if at all. He was unsure if the Matah Kagmi would even show themselves to the Hopi Men but he did say to them, "Leave a few trade goods out on the grass at the edge of the forest. You may be surprised at what you find in return." He was careful to warn the men to not leave anything for the Matah Kagmi other than what he had already given them as he knew they, the Matah Kagml, would have no knowledge of how to use anything that they had not been shown how to use.

"I will be back in one week to see how things are going. All you guys have to remember is to not go up-stream past the point that I marked."

Caylen dropped the five men along with numerous fishing lures and lines, knives, bags of salt and axes for them to leave for the Matah Kagmi. He was quite sure that the creatures would take the trade goods and leave gold in their place. He did not tell the men of the gold the Matah Kagmi had left for him as he did not want them to necessarily expect anything in return for the trade goods.

He was about mid-way on his return trip, cruising slowly along the Eastern shore of Serenity Island when his engine suddenly and without warning stopped, leaving him becalmed on the waveless lake.

"Now what?"Caylen muttered to Warrior who just looked at him with his gleaming emerald eyes as if to say, "Why are you asking me? I don't know anything about boat motors."

He had just raised the wooden hatch that covered the engine well when he suddenly heard a very familiar voice.

"Mato Honl, my brother, what is it you have done? Why have you interfered in the lives of the Matah Kagmi? Why have you done this terrible thing?"

Sania, my brother, is that you? Why have you come to me? Am I in danger from the Matah Kagmi? What is it that brings the Great Whakan Powwaw, Sania from the side of Qaletaka, The Great Spirit, and The Sacred Guardian of the People?

"My son, Brave Wolf. I have come to inform you that the 'Travelers' will not be pleased with what you have done with the creatures called the Matah Kagmi. They are still, at this time, in their great ship high above the earth that is your home and once was mine. They have seen your actions and your attempts to better the lives of the Matah Kagmi. They are, even as I speak, assessing what you have done and the possible repercussions of your actions on the lives and the future of the Matah Kagmi on your island. You must cease your giving and your teachings at once. You have no idea what you have done or what they, the 'Travelers', might do in response to your interference in what they consider one of their experiments."

But I meant no wrong my Brother. What I did and what I am intending to do for the Matah Kagmi will only benefit their lives and make their future much better for them. Why would the 'Travelers' be angry with me for helping the Matah Kagmi in this way? Caylen asked.

"It is because the Matah Kagmi were placed on this world many eons ago as an experiment. The 'Travelers' did this in such a way so that they could observe and monitor the evolvement of the Matah Kagmi over the years. They wish to see if the Matah Kagmi are able to learn new ways without help from other beings such as ourselves. Your interference in the ways of the Matah Kagmi will not be taken lightly by the Travelers. You may have unknowingly destroyed all their research and their plans for this group of Matah Kagmi by what you have done."

What can I do to make things right? Caylen asked. *I really don't want the 'Travelers' angry with me."*

"I do not think that you can now undue what you have done. The matter now rests in their hands." Sania said. "You must cease your interference at once and pray to the Great Spirit for the safety of the Matah Kagmi that you have contaminated with you good intentions. I go now, my brother, the Great Qaletaka calls to me."

Speak to him, my father, I wished no harm to any being. I only sought to better the lives of the Matah Kagmi.

"Your intentions are of no consequence. Your deeds have now been done and can never be undone. All is now in the hands of the 'Travelers'. I once more say goodbye to my brother, Brave Wolf "

***

Caylen replaced the engine cover and returned to the boats controls where he restarted the engine, turned the boat around and headed back at the boat's best speed to the mine site.

"Bring all those trade goods back to me." he yelled at the men who were still packing their supplies up to their cabin."I want it all back on board now! I do not want you to trade anything more with the Matah Kagmi." he told the men."I don't even want you to approach them or attempt to communicate with them in any way."

"But why have you now changed your ideas?" Honaw asked."It was only this morning that you told us to trade all these things to the Matah Kagmi."

"As I left here my Spirit Guardian told me that the Great Spirit was displeased with me and wished me to not do as I had planned. He said that to give the Matah Kagmi these things was wrong and that we must not continue. He said that we would place great dangers on the Matah Kagmi if we continued to give them our tools and trinkets." Caylen replied. He knew that he could not tell the men the exact truth about what had occurred but felt that the 'near truth' was much better than a outright lie.

"We shall do as you say, Mato Honi. We do not wish to make war with these creatures of the forest. The Matah Kagmi are not those who we wish to do battle with. They are very big and very strong. It would take many bullets to slay one of them and it would take a man much braver than I to attempt to count coup on them."

"I shall leave as soon as we get this stuff loaded but I shall return in one week to collect whatever gold you have accumulated and to see how things are going." Caylen said as he made room for the trade goods that the men were returning.

***

Caylen had been back at Tranquility Place for only two days when he and the entire household were startled by a loud rumbling and shaking just as they were finishing their evening meal.

"What on earth was that!" Aponi shouted over the rumbles as she caught a dish that was about to fall from the table.

The rumbling and shaking lasted about a minute before it stopped almost as quickly as it had begun. A few seconds later it began again but only lasted for a few seconds.

"The Gods are angry at us, they are shaking the very earth to show us their displeasure." said Sihu.

"We are all about to die!" exclaimed Shilah as Talisa began crying.

"Don't be so foolish, you guys. That was an earthquake and it is now over. Everyone look around in here and make sure that it caused no damage to Tranquility. I shall go out and make sure everything is okay outside and in the other buildings." Caylen said aloud in a effort to calm everyone down.

About twenty minutes later everyone reported their findings of damage to Caylen.

"Well, it appears that the only damage that we could find were the two cracked windows and three broken dinner plates. Shilah can replace the windows tomorrow with the spare glass in the workshop. I shall go back down to the mine site tomorrow and check on how the guys made out down there."Caylen said.

***

Caylen arrived at the mine site in late morning to find the five men busily working the sluiceway. They reported no damage to any of the mine buildings or workings but did say that the rumbling and noise seemed to be quite close and sounded like it had originated from just up the mountain side to the north of the mine.

Fearing for the family group of Matah Kagmi that lived on that part of the mountain, Caylen, accompanied by Warrior hiked up the stream to the edge of the area claimed by the Matah Kagmi. Spying a large pile of something at the edge of the stream he walked up to it and was amazed at what he saw.

"Well, I'll be darned!" he said to Warrior when he realized what the pile of material was. "They must have packed all their gold down here in the expectation of trading it for goods. I shall send out a mind probe and see if i can get a response."

He had no sooner projected a thought out and up the mountain when all his surroundings went totally black for an instant. When he could finally see again he could only see a swirling mist that appeared to completely envelope himself and the area surrounding him. No walls or floor were visible yet he felt as though he was on solid footing. As he looked about, wondering where he was, a thought suddenly came into his mind.

"We meet again Caylen Helms. We the Travelers are those that spoke with you once before this time. We have brought you before us to reveal to you the wrongs that you have done and the consequences of your wrongdoings."

I greet you Travelers and welcome your teachings and your explanation of any wrongdoings that I may have done. Caylen thought.

"We are greatly displeased with your recent interference with the Matah Kagmi that live on the mountain near your gold mine. We have brought you here to explain to you what you have done and what the consequences of your actions will have."

I intended nothing wrong. What I did was for the benefit of the Matah Kagmi in every way. I wished to make their lives easier and to eventually help them to integrate into the human society. I mean no harm to them." Caylen thought.

"You have already done irreversible harm to the Matah Kagmi. You have given them tools and other things that might appear very basic and simple to you but are, to the Matah Kagml, very complicated and very advanced. Their concept of what you have done for them makes them think that you are some kind of supreme being and possibly a god. There is no way for you or ourselves to now undo these things that you have done. This group of the Matah Kagmi are now contaminated and are useless in our experiment."

I did not realize that what I was doing was so wrong. I only wished to better their lives. thought Caylen.

"Do you not recall that we informed you on our previous visit that the Matah Kagmi were a part of our present experiment in the evolution of various creatures of your planet?"

Yes, I do remember you telling me that but you said nothing to me about not interfering by giving to them and teaching them. Caylen thought.

"We incorrectly assumed that you would realize that your interfering in their evolutionary process would

compromise and skew the results of our experiment with them. Any resulting evolutionary changes to this group will no longer be valid or of any consequence. The further potential is that this group of Matah Kagmi may now contaminate neighboring groups. If this were to happen our experiment would further be skewed." the Travelers replied.

I sincerely regret all that I have done to hamper your experiments. What can we do about it now? asked Caylen.

"The problem has already been resolved. The problems you have created no longer exists."

What do you mean, 'no longer exists'? Caylen thought, beginning to feel just a little apprehensive.

"We have caused this entire group of Matah Kagmi to cease to exist. This means that the problem with our experiment no longer exists." came the reply.

You mean that you killed that entire family? Caylen exclaimed.

"We, the Travelers do not kill any creatures or living beings. Our laws do not permit us to kill. We simply caused them to cease their existence on your world."

How could you just cease their existence and then say that you did not kill them? exclaimed Caylen in anger and frustration.

"We feel your anger and your sorrow for these Matah Kagmi, Caylen Helms, but the reason that they were made to cease their existence was entirely of your doing and not ours. You, and you alone must bear and accept that responsibility. We will now return you to the place we took you from."

Chapter 21

Population Increases

Caylen remained at the mine site only one more day. When he was returned to the streamside by the Travelers, he called out to Warrior and the pair headed upstream. His heart heavy in his breast he continued to send out mind-probes to no avail. As the pair climbed higher and higher up the mountainside he could detect more and more frequent signs of the Matah Kagmi where they had passed in their quests for food. When he at last came to the freshly-fallen rocks, he began to realize what had happened. The scattered boulders and broken slabs of granite soon gave way to an enormous pile of rocks, trees soils and other forest debris. Confirmation of his suspicions became final when he suddenly spotted, projecting out from under a massive boulder, the crushed and broken lower arm of one of the Matah Kagmi. As a final irony and the thing that finally brought Caylen sobbing, to a halt in his search, was the sight of the steel trade knife that was still tightly clenched in the creature's broken and bloody hand.

He sat quietly on a broken slab of granite with Warrior by his side until dawn of the following day. Leaving everything as it was he then returned to the mine and the five Hopi miners. After explaining that the entire group of Matah Kagmi had been killed by the avalanche, he took the men up to the pile of gold and had them load it all on his launch.

"I would estimate that we have about twenty four hundred pounds of gold here. That will bring us another three to four hundred thousand dollars. The village of Orabi is now quite wealthy. I will have the village's share sent to them when I next visit Whitehorse." he told the men.

***

"Caylen, have you seen Snow lately?" Aponi asked."And I also haven't seen Warrior since early yesterday." she added.

"No, I haven't seen either of them." Caylen replied, still sad after his recent encounter with the Travelers and the deaths of the family group of the Matah Kagmi. "They're probably out somewhere, chasing a moose or a caribou. They will come home when they get hungry."

***

Warrior and Snow had pretty much given up on the killing of any of the larger forest animals. They would still take the odd hare or mouse but only chased the larger moose and caribou for sport and exercise. Besides, Snow was becoming quite heavy as she entered the last few days of her pregnancy. As a result and to the chagrin of Warrior, she was forced to rest quite often and seemed to lose interest rapidly in any chase. What she did seem quite interested in was quite puzzling to Warrior who, as was usual, only wanted to rush about the forest exploring and sniffing at anything and everything.

Snow, with a considerable amount of her wild self still controlling her actions knew that something was about to happen to her. Her instincts told her that she needed to find a secluded and easily protected den for what was about to occur. She observed and checked out many potential den sites on her and Warriors romps through the forest but none seemed to suit her pressing needs. Unable finally to wait any longer, she finally chose to prepare a nest of sorts in a old abandoned fox den that a red fox had dug into the soft sand of the creek embankment just a few hundred feet from Tranquility Place.

Warrior looked on with a puzzled expression on his face as she cleaned out and enlarged the old den to her satisfaction. When he attempted to enter the den with her, Snow tuned and snarled a quite plain "stay out" message at him. For the first time in months Warrior was forced to spend the next few nights alone in his bed on the front porch of Tranquility place.

***

It was well before the morning sun peered over the Eastern mountains when Warrior heard the low keening whimper coming from the den that Snow had occupied. He had sensed that something important was happening to Snow so he had, late the night before, left his comfortable blanket on the porch to stay by the entrance to the den in which she lay. Following about an hour of Snow's whimpering and the occasional yelp, the den suddenly became quiet. It remained so for more than two hours.

Warrior had just nodded off and was blissfully dreaming of running through the forest on the trail of some frightened caribou who's scent indicated that he was terrified for his life when he was rudely awakened by the soft nuzzle of Snow's muzzle at his neck. Raising himself up and stretching the night's tightness from his legs, he sensed that Snow now wanted him to enter her den. Warrior did so, finding that he had to crawl along the sandy, sweet-smelling tunnel until it suddenly opened up into a much larger cavity that contained a number of tiny black and white creatures that crept about on the floor of the cavity emitting little mewing sounds and smelling like rich creamy mother's milk.

Hastily beating a retreat out of the area, Warrior found, sitting just outside her den, a tired mother wolf who sat eagerly awaiting the approval of her mate for the nine healthy little wolf puppies to whom she had just given birth.

***

It was nearly two weeks later before the nine little wolf puppies began to venture outside the den. The entrance to the old fox den was easily visible from the verandah of Tranquility Place. Shilah had often seen Snow going in and out as she readied the den for the birthing of her pups. Even though she had never given birth prior to this, she instinctively knew that the event was about to occur and that she must make preparations for the birthing. Privacy and the security of her unborn babies was of the utmost importance to her in her choice of locations. The old fox den, while needing some improvements, provided all the privacy that she required. The proximity of the den relative to Tranquility Place provided much security in that any wild creature that might be a danger to her babies would hesitate to venture this close to where humans resided. She also knew that the presence of Warrior would also provide a deterrent to any of the forests deadly creatures.

The largest of the wolf pups. a miniature male replica of Warrior, was solid black in colour with his father's emerald eyes. The only feature that differed him from Warrior was a small perfectly formed, four-pointed white star that was centered exactly between his tiny pointed ears. The next larger of the puppies was a pure white miniature female replica of Snow. This pretty little daughter also had a perfectly formed, small four-pointed black star centered exactly between her tiny little ears. The little white female had also inherited her father's emerald eyes.   The remaining pups were of mixed black and white shades with no outstanding features other than the fact that they all possessed their fathers emerald eyes.

***

Caylen, Aponi, Shilah and Sihu were having their evening tea on the verandah with Talisa crawling about and trying to stand with the help of the railing that kept her from toppling off and onto the grassy yard.

"Say, folks, would you look over by that old fox den." Shilah suddenly said. "Is that what I think it is?"

"Well, I'll be darned." Caylen said."Warrior, you old devil. It looks like you've gone and got yourself quite a family there."

"Warrior, devil." mimicked Talisa, pointing at the family group of wolves with the chubby little forefinger of her right hand.

Sitting on the mound of sand directly below the entrance to the den was the entire family of wolves. On the extreme left sat Warrior with what appeared to be a proud silly grin on his face. To his immediate right sat his miniature replica son with his little eyes glowing brightly in the late afternoon sun. To his right, in what seemed to the family like a perfect line, sat seven other mixed coloured puppies. On their immediate right, sitting beside her mother, was the perfect little miniature replica of Snow.

***

Within a week the entire family of wolves was quite at home on the large veranda of Tranquility. Aponi set out an old blanket for Snow to lie on as she nursed her hungry brood. Talisa was overjoyed at having the nine little puppies on the veranda to play with although the little replicas of Warrior and Snow seemed a bit standoffish towards her many attempts at enticing them to join in the many childlike games that she managed to think up for them.

"Ball," she repeated over and over to the frisky little animals until they began to recognize that she was about to throw the little rubber ball across the veranda deck for them. When she did so it was pandemonium for a few moments as the seven pups raced each other in their attempts to be the first one to reach the ball. As all these games proceeded, the little replicas of Warrior and Snow would raise their little heads and observe all that transpired. They never did, however, participate in the chase.

Chapter 22

A Few Years Later

"What on earth are you two doing?" Aponi yelled. She could see her five-year old son Hawk and her three-year old daughter Spirit standing on the big front yard seemingly staring up at the bright morning sky.

"We're playing with that seagull up there." Hawk replied.

"Playin wit dat gull." mimed Spirit.

"Talisa," Aponi said, "would you please see what those two are talking about. It sounded like they said that they were playing with a seagull! And while you're out there, see if you can see Caylen and Shilah anywhere. If you do see them, tell them that Sihu has our morning tea ready."

The five years since Aponi had given birth to Caylen's son had passed quickly. Life on Serenity Island had became a idyllic, dreamlike existence for the family group with everyone thriving and growing more and more in love with the big island and their Eden-like existence.

The arrival of their beautiful daughter Spirit was celebrated by all, especially little two-year old Hawk who immediately assumed the big brother role, seemingly able to communicate with Spirit almost immediately following her birth.

Caylen had been called upon a few times by the Whitehorse Police Force to assist in the investigation of a few local, minor offences that he soon easily resolved without travel to any far away locations. The birth of Caylen and Aponi's children had been quite easy for Aponi with no complications whatsoever. Life was good.

"They are out there making that poor gull do loops and dives." The seven and a half year old Talisa reported. "And Uncle Caylen and Dad are out pulling the net. It looks like they have a good catch."

"Whatever do you mean, they are making the gull do loops and dives?" asked Aponi.

"Hawk just points his finger at the gull and it dives or loops over." Talisa said. "He must be controlling it with his mind just like Uncle Caylen does."

"Oh, my God!" exclaimed Aponi. "How long has he been able to do that?"

"I don't know, Aunt Aponi, but I have also seen him making the dogs do some funny things for a few weeks now."

"O wow! Just wait until Caylen hears this." exclaimed Aponi to Sihu."Hawk must have inherited the power from him. I wonder if he has the rest of Caylen's powers, too? I wonder if Spirit has them.

"They must be counseled on the use of the powers they have." Sihu said."We must not permit others to see that they possess such power. Evil men would give much to have the possessor of such powers in their control."

"You tell those two that I want them to leave that seagull alone and to get in here right now!" Aponi exclaimed.

***

Caylen and Sihu finished processing their catch of lake whitefish about two hours later. As they entered the big house after cleaning up they observed Spirit and Hawk sitting quietly at the kitchen table.

"Hey! How come you two are being so quiet?" asked Caylen.

"Hawk was making the seagull do all kinds of funny things with his finger." Talisa said."The seagull didn't like it cause he was squawking real loud all the time."

"We think that he may have some of your powers and that he was controlling the gull." Aponi added. "I thought that I should bring both of them in until you had a talk with them. Maybe you can find out just what Hawk and Spirit are capable of."

Caylen took Hawk out on the porch where he could speak to him without the others hearing what was said before questioning him. Neither Hawk or Spirit had ever seen Caylen use his powers. They did not know, or even suspect that he possessed any extraordinary powers as he had always strived to keep that knowledge from them.

"Okay, young man, just how long have you been able to make birds do whatever you want?"he asked.

"I can make animals do things, too." replied Hawk."I have been able to do it for quite a while. I can't remember when I first found out I could do it. Can I show you, Dad?"

"No, you don't have to show me. Can you do anything else with your thoughts?"

"I can tell Spirit things without talking."Hawk replied. "And she can sometimes tell me things, too. We speak back and forth sometimes after we have gone to bed. Can you and Mom do that, Poppa?. Can everyone?"

"What do you think Hawk?" Caylen asked."Do you think that everyone can do it or do you think that just you and Spirit can?" Caylen thought it best to ascertain if his children knew that the powers that they had discovered on their own were natural and common to everyone or if they knew that they were different.

"Well, I tried to speak to Georgina when Grandma and Grandpa Thompkins visited us last month but all she did was to look at me kind of funny. The same thing happened when I tried to talk to Talisa with my thoughts so I kind of figured from the way they looked at me that they could probably hear me but that they did not know how to reply." Hawk said. "So I never tried it again with them. I kind of thought after that happened that maybe Spirit and myself were the only ones that could do it."

"Do you know if Spirit can control birds and animals like you do? Have you ever seen her do it?" Caylen asked.

"No, I have never seen her do it." replied Hawk.

"Are you able to do anything else with your thoughts?" asked Caylen.

"I've never tried to do anything else, Poppa. I kind of figured that not everyone can do those things with their thoughts but I don't know how I can tell if they can or can't."

"Well, you're right that not everyone can do the things that you have been doing. I am going to tell you something now that you must never ever tell anyone outside of the people who live here, your Grandpa Bill and Grandma Lora. You must never let anyone else know what you can do or they might try to harm you. And you must not use or show your powers to your sister again until she has figured them out for herself." Caylen said. "Now I am going to tell you a story. This story is my story and how I got those same powers and many more. This story is about my and your Grandma's life before we moved here and before your Mom and myself got married. Everything I am going to tell you is true and really happened. You should not talk to anyone about what I am about to tell you other than your Mom, your Aunt Sihu, your Uncle Shilah and you Grandparents. Do not tell your sister either as she is much to young yet to understand it all just yet."

***

Caylen then, over the next four hours, related to young Hawk his own life story, starting with his father's death in the great war. He told him of Fariss and their life together in the little forest hut. He told him of Wildflower and her death. He related the story of how the big wolf had come to him with the gift of Warrior. He told him of his life with Sania and how he had received his powers from the Great Qaletaka. He explained Faris's and Sania's deaths and how Sania still on occasion talked to him. He told him of his meetings with the 'Travelers' and what they had revealed to him and about the additional powers they had granted him.

Aponi interrupted them only once to bring them a sandwich and a glass of milk, saying nothing.

***

Finishing his story, Caylen said to his young son who now sat quietly in awe, trying to absorb in his young mind all that he had just been told."Now young man, you know just about all there is to know about your dad's life up to now. I want you to think about everything that I have told you tonight and we will talk again to-morrow. I also want you to remember that you should never reveal to anyone that you and I and your sister have these powers. Now I think I heard your Mom say that our supper was ready and waiting."

***

Caylen spent the next few weeks teaching Hawk how to use his powers properly. It was quickly apparent to him that Hawks only abilities were the power to control animals, birds and fish that were within his range of vision and the power to speak with his mind to those who had the same ability. When Hawk asked about Caylen's own abilities, Caylen told him that he would only reveal his own powers to Hawk when he, Hawk, had mastered completely the powers that he already possessed. He did not tell Hawk anything about his other abilities nor did he ask or tell Hawk about any other possible abilities that he, Hawk might possess.

"And I want you to stop mind-communicating with Spirit for now. If she tries to initiate a talk I want you to ignore her. She is just too young to understand that she has a wonderful gift that few others have and that inappropriate uses of it could get her into trouble. Have you ever seen her try to control animals or birds yet?"

"No, Poppa, the only thing that she can do is to speak to me with her thoughts." Hawk answered.

"Okay. Now, young man, I also want you to stop controlling the birds and animals unless I am with you. Do you understand?" Caylen said."I don't want you to use any of your powers at all from now on unless I am with you and have given you permission."

"Okay, Poppa." said Hawk."But what should I do if Spirit tries to talk to me with her mind?"

"You just ignore her and pretend that you can't hear her. She will soon quit trying."Caylen answered."She is much too young to be able to handle even the most basic powers. I will teach her about them when she gets a little older."

Chapter 23

Evil Plans

Caylen's first gold mine had finally given out. Kosumi and Loknl, the two native brothers of Wildflower reported at the shareholders annual meeting in Whitehorse that the previous year's take had been barely sufficient to meet the mine's payroll. They recommended, with Bill and Caylen concurring, that they clean up the site, restore and replant the disturbed areas and then vacate the mine site, leaving it to return to its natural, original wild state.

A review of the mine's take from its finding by Caylen until its closing some eight years later showed that it had earned profits for the four partners of over thirty-four million dollars after expenses. Caylen's bank manager informed him that his and Aponi's savings account balance was slightly more than fourteen million dollars. This account had been kept separate from their account that reflected the earnings of their newest mine on Serenity Island. This mine had proven to be even richer than the original mine and had, to-date, given up over twenty-seven million dollars. This second mine had added more than ten million dollars to Caylen and Aponi's accounts giving them a total savings of over thirty-seven million dollars and making them the richest mine owners in the whole of the Northlands.

Exploratory work at the Serenity Mine site revealed that the undeveloped areas upstream probably held another forty to fifty million dollars worth of gold waiting to be unearthed.

It was impossible in the gold mining community for a good find to be kept from the public. Within a year of Caylen recording his first claim, the surrounding areas were awash with hopeful prospectors who panned every available stream within fifty miles of Caylens mine. Some minor finds were made but nothing of any real significance was ever recorded in the Whitehorse recording office.

Caylen's newest find also drew much interest from the ever-hungry prospectors, but because the mine was contained entirely on Serenity Island which was owned by Caylen who also held the mineral rights to the island, they could do nothing. News of the richness of this new find and the accompanying stories of the extremely rich, strange young man who lived in the huge log house on the big island with his beautiful Hopi wife spread across the Northern Territories like wildfire. Many curious adventurers made the long water trip to the island to see for themselves just where and how these seemingly eccentric wealthy family lived. Those who landed at Tranquility Harbour were welcomed, fed and sent on their way, having satisfied themselves that most of the stories that they had heard about the Helms were in fact just that - stories with little if any truth in them. The one truth that was quite obvious to any visitor, however, was that Caylen's family was in fact, very prosperous and very wealthy. The huge house, its many outbuildings, guest houses, gardens, smokehouses and drying sheds left little doubt of that fact. The large custom-built yacht and the sleek mahogany speedboat tied to the pier further confirmed the wealth of the islands residents.

It was quite common for sightseers to cruise back and forth in front of the big house in hopes of seeing some of the home's residents. Sightseerers were not however, encouraged to remain in the vicinity of the mining area on the south end of the island. The mining crew now, six years into its operation, numbered twelve actual miners, four security guards, a cook and two general handymen. The security guards patrolled both by land and water, quickly discouraging any sightseerers who ventured into the area.

***

The old gasoline powered fishing boat had been cruising back and forth in front of Serenity for three days. It had arrived a week earlier but had left after one day of slowly drifting about less than one-half mile offshore.

Shilah, ever on watch, reported that he had seen three bearded men on board watching the house and its surroundings intently and constantly through binoculars. "They just don't look like the average sightseers." he said to Caylen."They don't come too close but they are always watching us through binoculars or telescopes. I just feel that something is wrong. Maybe we should take the speedboat out and ask them what they want."

"Well, we can't stop them from watching us and we can't make them leave without threatening them, so I guess we are just going to have to ignore them and hope they leave soon." Caylen replied as he studied the three men through his powerful telescope. "I don't think they are up to anything good as I can see dark auras about their heads." he added.

***

"That should be jest 'bout 'nough watching." said the bearded leader of the three men on the old fishing boat. "We has a pretty good idea of the layout of their place and jest what their daily routines are so we's can go now and plans our next move."

"When are we going to make our attempt?" asked one of the other men.

"Well, I tink he will be goin on down to the mine pretty soon so that would be the best times fer a clean job. We knows the kids go's out to play every afternoon for a couple of hours and we knows that one of their favourite places to play is on that there beach a few hundred yards south and out of sight of the big house. The only man around of any consequence will be that there old injun. We's should be able to handle him real easy." said the leader."We's will go down about halfways to the south end of the island and waits there to see when Helms goes down to the mine and then we will comes back up and do our jobs at the house. We's is goin to be really rich very soon and Mr. Caylen Helms is going to be a whole lot poorer."

The leader of the three men had recruited his two helpers after carefully considering their personal qualifications and speaking at length with each of the two men. They both appeared to be well experienced in criminal acts. They had each spent quite some time in prison for their crimes and would now go to extreme lengths to avoid repeating any further jail time. They also knew the northern woods and lakes quite well and had spent the last few years in fruitless prospecting throughout the northern forests and lakes. It had taken the bearded leader many years of observing and patiently investigating Caylen Helms. He was also well aware of Caylen's association with the Royal Canadian Mounted Police and of his many successes in apprehending the accused in the cases he took on. He had even heard some rumors of some weird goings on in a case where Caylen Helms had gone into northern Montana to investigate a case where wolves had been selectively killing cattle.

The bearded leader was also quite familiar with the areas where Caylen had previously lived with his mother and Fariss Lubak. He had investigated the Carcross area and after speaking with some of the local natives, determined that Caylen and another policeman had chased down Fariss and that Fariss had, according to police reports, apparently fallen to his death in an area of the north that was thought to have been occupied be a evil forest spirit known as a Wendigo. He had also discovered that the rich gold discovery on the little lake was owned by Caylen and another couple who proved to be Caylen's mother and the policeman who had been with Caylen when he chased down Fariss Lubak.

***

It was only three days later when Caylen announced that his monthly trip to the mine site was overdue. "I'll not be gone for long," he said to Aponi. "I just have to run some supplies down and pick up the gold. I will probably run it over to the bank in Atlin and bring back some fresh fruit for us if I can find any."

"Well, you keep in touch every night. You know how I enjoy trading mind-thoughts with you when you are away. I just wish that I could initiate them like you can instead of having to wait for you to begin them." Aponi said.

"I will," Caylen replied. "Now let me have your shopping list before I go and remember that Bill, Mom and Georgina are flying down for a visit next week."

"That's right," Aponi said. "I nearly forgot. Has Bill gotten his pilot's license yet or does he still hire someone to fly them around?"

"I'm not sure. He said he only needed a few more hours to qualify. I hope he gets it. That Fokker seaplane is sure a beauty and is really powerful. It can land and take off on some really small lakes."

A few minutes later, after warming up the twin engines on the big cruiser, Caylen with Warrior beside him, eased the big boat out of Tranquility harbor and onto the main lake. As he turned Southward he looked over and saw Hawk and Spirit waving goodbye from the little sandy beach where they loved to play.

"Warrior, will you look at that! I must be the luckiest man alive. I have the world's most beautiful wife, the two greatest kids on this earth, the best friends, the greatest dog ever, the best fishing and hunting and all the money I will ever need. What more could any man want out of life!"

Setting the engine controls on half speed, Caylen did not notice the old wood fishing boat that was anchored in the little bay about five miles down from Serenity Place. If he had looked back however, he would have seen the old boat pull out and head north at top speed.

Chapter 24

Tragedy

It took the old fishing boat with the three men a few minutes to reach the north end of Serenity island. As they neared Tranquility Harbour they could see Hawk, Spirit and Talisa on the sandy beach of their little hideaway cove, running happily about with Snow and her nine now fully-grown pups.

"There they are!. They are all alone except for the dogs and we can take care of them if they give us any trouble. They also have that older girl with them " said one of the men.

"Okay, I will gits in close to shore and then I's will wade ashore and talk nice to Helms' kids and see if I can git them to come aboard and go for a little ride. You's two stay on board with your rifles ready in case of trouble. Keep the guns out of sight lessen you needs to use them but make damn sure you don't hits me or either of the kids. If I turns and wave at you I wants you to kill all those damn wolf dogs as fast as you's can. Thems two kids is going to make us our fortune as long as we's can keeps them alive." said the bearded leader.

"What about the other kid?" asked one of the men. "What are we going to do about her?"

"I donts give a damn 'bout her." said the leader. "If she gits in the way's jest shoots her dead."

The old boats bow was soon nudging the shore at the south end of the beach. As the bearded leader

jumped into the shallow water, Hawk and Spirit and Talisa watched with interest.

"How's would you two kids like to go's out for a little
boat ride?" he asked in a pleasant tone. "We's will take
you'se up and drops you off at your dock. We heard your
Mom callin you as we came by there a few minutes ago."
As he came nearer the three children, Snow edged up to
the side of Spirit and began a low growl. Hearing her
growls, the other wolf dogs bounded up to stand by her
with the big black replica of Warrior standing in front of
the group.

"Why is yer dogs bein so unfriendly?" asked the bearded
leader. "We don't means any harm to thems or to you's.
If you's don't want a boat ride then we's will just leaves
you's all here and gits on our way."

"They just don't like strangers coming on our land."
Talisa said. "So you guys just get off our beach before I sic
them on you. We don't want to ride on your stinky old
boat. We have a really nice big boat that we can go out
on any time we want. Now I think you had better go before I call my poppa."

"Yes! "Hawk said."This is our island and you had better get going! "

"Git goin! "mimed Spirit.

"Well! That's no ways to be treatin a visitor." the
leader said as he turned back to wave at the two men still
on the boat.

It took only a moment for the two men on the boat
to grab their lever-action rifles and began firing at Snow
and her offspring. Snow was the first to go down, killed
instantly by the mushrooming heavy caliber bullet. In less
than a minute later, all the remaining wolf dogs were
dead or badly wounded.

Hawk, Spirit and Talisa simply stood, open mouthed,
in shock at what had just occurred. The big bearded lead-

er then grabbed Hawk and Spirit around their waists and quickly waded back out to the waiting boat where he handed them up to the other men before clambering aboard himself.

"You let Hawk and Spirit go!" screamed Talisa in abject helpless horror at was occurring in front of her innocent young eyes.

"Okay, we's gots them. Now let's gets us the hell out of here." The leader said as he slammed the boat into reverse, backing it out into the deeper water before moving the controls to the forward position to propel the old boat out onto the main lake.

***

Shilah and Sihu, working in the big vegetable garden heard the rapid flurry of shots from the big rifles as the pack of wolf dogs were fired on.

"What on earth was that!" Sihu exclaimed." It sounded like it came from the kids' play area."

"Momma, Poppa! "screamed Talisa as she raced back up the path to the main house.

"What is it, child? What is going on and where are Hawk and Spirit? You know you're not supposed to leave them out there alone." Sihu cried.

"They killed Snow and all the other dogs! " screamed Talisa as she came closer. "They took Hawk and Spirit on their boat!"

"What on earth are you talking about?" asked Shilah. "What do you mean, they took Hawk and Spirit?. Come on, Sihu, we had better check on them and see just what is going on. Talisa, you tell Aunt Aponi to come on down to the kids' beach. That where we will be."

***

It was a beautiful day as Caylen motored south along the eastern shoreline of Serenity Island with Warrior lying by his side. As they cruised along at half-throttle enjoying the great scenery, Warrior suddenly rose from where he was lying and rushed to the rear of the boat. Throttling back after seeing this sudden unwarranted move by the big animal, Caylen was then astonished to see Warrior lay back his big head and give out the most ungodly howl that he had ever heard. To his amazement Warrior then leaped off the rear of the boat and into the water where he quickly swam to the islands shore and raced off to the North towards Tranquility Place.

"Warrior! Warrior! Come back here." he yelled to no avail. Sending a mind-command out he found to his utter astonishment that for some reason he could not make his thoughts enter Warrior.

"Well!, I'll be darned if I know what got into him but I had better scoot back home and see if he goes there." he said as he swung the boat around and headed north.

***

Shilah and Sihu could not believe what they were seeing. Dead and dying wolf dogs lay everywhere about the small beach. There was no sign of Hawk or Spirit, so then they quickly determined that there was nothing that could be done for Snow and the rest of the executed animals that lay dead and dying in the widening pools of their life's blood as it flowed from the terrible wounds in their bodies.

"I don't see Black Cloud." Shilah said looking about. And where are the children?"

"Hawk! Spirit! Where are you?, Come out here right now!".

"Ohhh my God!. What has happened?" Aponi screamed as she entered the little clearing and observed the carnage that lay before her.

"Take Talisa away from all this, Aponi." Shilah said. "She does not need to see any more than she already has. Now, you must try to calm yourself. It appears from what Talisa has told us that a boat with three men on it came in and one of them tried to get Hawk and Spirit to go on board. When they refused and sicced the dogs on them the men on the boat shot them all, grabbed the kids and took off."

"Ohh, what are we going to do! Caylen won't be back until at least tomorrow. Ohhh, my poor babies. What can we do?" Aponi wailed in anguish.

"The first thing we have to do is to calm down. I will take the speedboat out and see if I can spot them, but first I want to get my rifle. Sihu, see if you can find Black Cloud. Sometimes a wounded animal will crawl off and hide."

Shilah ran back to the house to find Aponi already there, sitting on the porch holding the crying Talisa in her arms.

"It's my fault." Talisa wailed."I should have grabbed Hawk and Spirit and ran away as soon as they came ashore."

"It's not your fault, Talisa."Aponi was saying. "You could not have known what was going to happen. You tried to stop them by siccing the dogs on them"

This statement about the wolf dogs caused Talisa to sob even more. "I should not have done that either!" she cried. "That's what made those bad men shoot them all. Are any of them okay, Aunt Talisa?"

"We did not see Black Cloud so your Uncle Shilah thinks he may have been just wounded and crawled away somewhere. We shall have to go and look for him." Aponi responded.

***

Shilah grabbed his hunting rifle and raced down to the pier where the sleek polished-mahogany speedboat was tied up. Starting the two big powerful engines to warm them up, he soon had the boat untied and headed out of Tranquility harbor. Not knowing what direction the men had taken he decided that his best course of action was to make a big, high speed circle and see if he could spot any other watercraft. As about three-quarters of an hour had elapsed since the kidnapping had taken place, he knew that it was unlikely that he would be able, even with the powerful speedboat, to overtake the kidnappers without knowing what direction they had taken. From what Talisa had said, it was probable that the kidnappers were aboard a fast powerful boat and could easily, by now, be twenty or thirty miles away.

***

Sihu checked Snow and her litter carefully to ascertain if any of the poor animals were still alive. Finding them all dead from their terrible wounds, she dragged them all together and started back up the trail to the house. She had only gone a few feet when she heard, coming from the thick bushes on her right, a low whimpering. Pushing aside the bush she saw Black Cloud lying on his side licking his shoulder. Sihu could see the gaping gouge where the heavy bullet had torn its way through the animal's muscular shoulder and exited on the same side. It appeared to have stopped bleeding, at least for the moment. Sihu quickly untied from her waist, the long cotton sash that she always wore and wrapped it tightly around the open wound.

"This will have to do for now." she said to the now calm wolf. When we get you back to the house I will have to clean it up and sew it shut or it will get infected and we will lose you too.

***

Caylen, now less than twenty minutes away from Tranquility, sent out a mind-message to Aponi. *Aponi, is everything okay back there? Warrior starting acting funny all of a sudden and then he jumped overboard, swam to shore and headed off towards home at the run. I'm headed home right now and should be there in about ten or fifteen minutes.*

"Oh Caylen, you must hurry. It looks like Hawk and Spirit may have been kidnapped. I'm really scared so please hurry. The kidnappers shot and killed Snow and all her pups except for Black Cloud who is badly wounded. Sihu is sewing him up but she does not know if she can save him. Please hurry!"

Caylen, after hearing this news, slammed the engines into its fastest speed, sending the big boat into a high-speed planing-mode across the quiet waters of Atlin Lake.

In a few minutes, he was tying the boat to the pier and running up to the house where Aponi stood waiting on the porch. The badly frightened Aponi shakingly blurted out the events as she knew them, explaining that Shilah was out on the lake in the speedboat at the present.

"He's been gone for almost an hour now." she said. "Can you ask him if he has seen anything?. Oh Caylen, I'm so frightened. What are we going to do?"

"We're going to get our kids back safe and sound and those men are going to regret that they were ever born." Caylen responded, tight lipped.

***

"I have seen nothing." Shilah's thoughts returned to Caylen."I have made a big circle about twenty miles or so in diameter and am on my way back. I am checking all the bays and inlets as I return in case they ducked into one of them to hide. I should be back in about an hour."

"I'm going to see if I can contact Bill and Mom and see if he can get down here with his plane today instead of tomorrow." Caylen thought back. *"We could really use it now."*

***

"Of course we can come now." Bill responded. "I'll bring Lora and Georgina down, too. It sounds like Aponi and you can use a lot of support right now. I will bring some medical supplies also that Sihu can use on Black Cloud. Are all the other dogs dead?. Snow, too?"

"We are not sure that Black Cloud will make it but we are hoping. I don't know how Warrior is going to react when he realizes that Snow is gone but I'm certain it won't be pleasant." Caylen thought back.

***

As Shilah passed the little bay where the slaughter of the animals and the kidnapping had taken place he could see the big black shape of Warrior standing beside the dead, stiffening, still white carcass of his beloved mate and long time companion. As he watched, Shilah saw Warrior lay back his big head and give out the loudest and the most eeriest howl that he had ever heard. Even over the sound of the big engines, the terrible wailing howl sent shivers running up and down his spine.

I would not want to be the ones who killed her if Warrior ever catches up with them. he thought as he pulled up to the dock in front of Tranquility.

Chapter 25

The Search

Bill, Lora and Georgina arrived just as the sun was setting over the big western mountain range. They could hear the high-pitched sound of the big radial engine long before the Fokker seaplane came into view giving Caylen plenty of time to get down to the dock before Bill taxied into Tranquility Harbour.

"I see that you must have gotten your license." Caylen said to Bill as Bill clambered out of the seaplane and onto its float where he assisted Lora and Georgina out of the plane and onto the dock.

"Yes, got it about three weeks ago and have been up nearly every day for a couple of hours." Bill replied."Do you want to go up for a quick look around before it gets to dark to fly?"

"Okay, let's get going. Mom, would you tell Aponi that we won't be gone long."Caylen said.

A few minutes later Caylen was scanning the big lake for any sign of the kidnappers. Knowing only that the boat they were looking for was an old lake fishing boat with three men aboard they assumed that it had to be a reasonably good-sized craft. Forty-five minutes of scanning the lake from a altitude of three thousand feet revealed only a lone prospector paddling his canoe along the western shore of Atlin Lake a few miles south of the passageway that led through to Graham Inlet and the big Tagish Lake. Growing darkness then forced them to return and land in Tranquility Harbour and home for the night.

***

Bill and Caylen, after comforting Aponi and the still sobbing Talisa, grabbed a bite to eat and discussed their next move.

"We need to question Talisa in detail and try to get her to recall even the smallest of things that occurred before and during the kidnapping. We have to also make sure that she understands that what happened was not her fault and that she did nothing wrong. She has to be made to believe that there was nothing she could have done." Caylen said to Bill.

"Yes, I agree." Bill responded. "It's easy to see that she feels really guilty about it all. Oh, here is Shilah back from burying the dogs. Did you get them all buried, Shilah?"

"All except Snow." Shilah replied. "Warrior would not let me touch her. I will go back in the morning and try again. He had licked the big bullet wound in her chest clean of all the blood and was lying close beside her with his head across her chest. When I came up to him he raised his head, looked directly at me. I could swear that I could see tears in his eyes and that he was crying."

"I must go to him right now and comfort him." Caylen said. "I don't want him to suffer like he is. I can feel the pain that he is suffering and it is terrible."

Caylen then went to where Warrior lay beside his beloved Snow. As he approached, Caylen could see Warrior watching him intently as he neared. He could also see, in the deepening twilight, the tears running down the big wolf's fur-covered cheeks. Caylen lay down on the blood soaked ground beside him, and cradling his faithful friend's big head in his hands, cried with him for the next two hours as he mourned the death of his loyal companion and his love.

***

It was nearly midnight as Caylen finally returned to the house. Walking slowly along beside him was a bedraggled, sad-looking Warrior.

"You can bury her in the morning, Shilah. I would like you to take Warrior with you when you do. He will be okay now." Caylen said to Shilah and Bill who sat waiting on the porch for his return.

"Now we need to plan what we are going to do next."Caylen said to Bill and Shilah.

"Before we do anything, we need to talk to Talisa as we discussed earlier. The more she can tell us the better chance we are going to have to get them back in one piece." Bill said.

"I shall speak to her first thing tomorrow." Shilah said. "She finally got to sleep."

"What do you think they want and how do you suppose they are going to get their demands to us?" Caylen asked. "I have to admit that I am getting more than just a little frightened. I know Hawk will hold his own but little Spirit is still just a baby and may not fare too well with strangers."

"Well, if they are like most kidnappers they will be asking for money. They have probably already left a demand letter somewhere or with someone who will have had instructions to deliver it to us." Bill replied. "That person is probably not involved in the crime itself but will have been paid to deliver the message to you. I also have to tell you Caylen, that in about fifty percent of these cases the perpetrators end up getting rid of their hostages."

"What do you mean by 'get rid' asked Caylen."Do you mean that they kill them?"

"That exactly what I mean." replied Bill.

"Well, I will only say that if any harm whatsoever comes to either of those two kids, those three men will suffer very slow painful deaths." Caylen said. "Now I think we should try to get some sleep. It will be a long day tomorrow."

***

The family was up before dawn. Sihu and Aponi prepared a large breakfast for everyone as it would probably be a long day. Thus far she had managed to maintain her composure in front of everyone but once alone with Caylen, she wept softly in his arms as he attempted to console her.

"We will have them both back in no time at all." he said."We will go up in Bill's plane tomorrow to see where their boat is and then we will take the speed boat out and run them down."

"But they might hurt Spirit and Hawk." Aponi said. "I don't think that I will be able to live with myself if they are harmed. I swear that I will never let them out of my sight again! "

***

Once breakfast was over, Bill and Caylen, along with Sihu and Shilah spent the next hour picking Talisa's brain for any details that she might remember about the kidnappers.

"I have an idea." Caylen said when the questioning revealed nothing new. "Sihu and Shilah, what would you say to my entering Talisa's thoughts?. By doing that I may be able to picture the men and get a better idea of their appearance as well as what their voices sounded like."

"You may try as long as it does not harm her." Shilah said. "But I thought you could not place your mind in another human's mind."

"Well you are correct. I cannot control another human but I can get into a child's immature mind and am then able to read his or her thoughts so if, once I am in her mind, I ask her to try and visualize their faces and to recall the sound of their voices, I may be able to identify them if I see or hear them in the future."

"Well, if you think it will help, give it a try. Should we tell her what you are going to do?" asked Sihu.

"That will not be necessary." Caylen replied."She will not even realize what is happening. All that will happen is that she may be a little confused for a moment or two but that will be over very quickly. Okay now, here goes."
Caylen then positioned himself so that he was looking directly at the still red-eyed Talisa. Projecting just a small bit of his powerful mind towards her, his thoughts easily entered her mind where he could quickly detect the sorrow, guilt and sadness that still filled her young mind.

"Talisa," Caylen said aloud but very softly. "I want you to now try to remember again in your mind everything that happened yesterday when those men came ashore. I want you to take all the time you need but I want you to try really hard to remember what they looked like and what their voices sounded like. You don't have to say anything aloud but I want you to try extra hard to remember all that happened even if it makes you sad. Could you do that for us, sweetheart?"

"Okay Uncle Caylen, I'll try."Talisa replied.

It took Caylen about forty five minutes to glean all the information he could from Talisa's young mind "That was kind of odd." he said to the others.

"What was odd?" asked Bill.

"Well it was the way the leader spoke, his voice sounded quite familiar. He sounded like someone I know or knew."

"Most of these kidnappings are perpetrated by persons known to their victims families." Bill said. "He was likely someone you met somewhere who knew how wealthy you are and figured to make an easy buck by grabbing your kids and making you pay for their return. Now, let's get that plane fueled up and in the air. This is going to be a big day. Shilah, what is that noise?"

"We have a boat coming into Tranquility Harbour." Shilah said. "I can only see one man on board."

"Well, let's go and see what he wants." Caylen said, as he grabbed his big hunting rifle.

The middle-aged man sat waiting for them as Caylen, Bill and Shilah walked out onto the dock.

"What's the rifle for? Are any of you guys Caylen Helms?" he asked.

"I'm Caylen Helms."Caylen said."What is it you want?"

"I have a letter for you. Last week this guy paid me fifty dollars to get it to you this morning."

"Give it to me."Bill said.

"No, I was told to only give it to a Caylen Helms." the man replied handing a sealed letter to Caylen. "Now, if you don't mind I'll be on my way."

"Unless you want to be shot you will stay right where you are until we tell you to go." Caylen said.

"Okay, okay." the man replied. "Do you mind if I get out and stretch my legs? It was a long boat ride from Atlin."

"Okay, but we don't want you leaving the dock until we tell you to go. We'll be back in a few minutes. Caylen replied.

The three men walked partway back to the house before Caylen finally stopped and tore open the tattered envelope and read aloud the handwritten notice:

"If you ever wants to see yer kids again you will take 500 pounds of gold to the western end of the river to Tagish Lake. You will see a big white cloth there tied to a birch tree on the north shore by a small crick. Put the gold in the clump of bushes behind the tree then takes the white cloth away and replaces it with a blue cloth. You has seven days to gits the gold there. Iffen you does this yer kids will be found four days later at the old log cabin on the little island at the West end of the river twixt Tagish and Atlin Lakes. We's will be watchin everyting you's does so's you's best do all this quick like and do's it by yerself. Onc't you; leaves the gold off you's aint to go nears that place fer four days. Iffen we's see anythin funny likes, yer kids will be fish foods and you's wont's be seein them agin. They's is both ok fer now so iffen you's wants to ever see' s them alive agin you's will do xactly as we says."

"I think we can tell that guy who delivered this letter to get out of here, Bill, but before you let him go you should probably see if he knows anything that might help. I will go up and tell Aponi what has happened and then I had best get the gold ready." Caylen said.

"Do we have that much gold here?" Bill asked.

"I'm not sure, I was going down to the mine for a load when all this happened. I will check our lock up and if I have to I will go and get some more from the mine. By the way, have you seen Warrior this morning, Shilah?"

"Yes, he was missing when I came out this morning. I figured that he was at Snow's grave so I checked and there he was, laying on top of her grave. I think he spent the night there and I could swear that I saw tears in his eyes again. He is the first dog that I ever saw cry. Oh, there he is now, back on the porch at his usual place." Shilah responded.

"Well, I don't think he is like any other dog or wolf that ever was with one exception, his father Abhaya. Warrior could be, if one did not know differently, a twin of his father. I think it will take some time before he gets over Snow's death."

"Well, I will go down and fuel up the plane. As soon as your ready, Caylen, we can get under way. I would guess that there is a good possibility that they took the kids through to Tagish Lake and are holed up over there somewhere not too far from where they want us to leave the gold. We will fly by and see if they have their white signal flag up yet. If they don't, we should hide nearby and watch for them. If we see them we can follow them to the kids or we could take them and make them talk." Bill said.

"I could make them talk real quick like." Shilah said. "Just get me one of them and he will very quickly tell you anything you want to hear."

"I hope it doesn't come to that." Caylen said."But I will do whatever needs to be done to protect those two kids."

***

Fifteen minutes later Bill and Caylen were headed West at about two thousand feet in altitude scanning every bay or inlet that looked big enough to contain a boat. As they soared above the river joining Tagish and Atlin lakes, Bill dropped down to nearly treetop level, flying close to the southerly shore so they could see the white flag tied to the tree if it had already been placed. As the seaplane roared past the river's inlet, they could easily see the big white sheet tied to the birch tree flapping wildly in the westerly winds.

"Do you want to land here now?"Bill yelled over the loud radial-engine noise."No, let's follow the north shore over to the lake and then come back along the south shore," Caylen said. "Our big advantage is that they don't know we have a plane so if they do see us they may not be overly suspicious. As we go along I will send out a mind-probe and see if I can pick up Hawk. I just don't know if he has developed any range though, so unless we are quite close he may not sense me."

***

After two hours of flying along the long coastline of the huge Tagish Lake, Bill turned the big single-engine seaplane around and headed back towards Tranquility Harbour and home.

"We have searched about one hundred miles north and another hundred south." he said."We haven't seen any sign of any boats or anything that even looks suspicious since we took off. I'm beginning to think we are not looking in the right direction."

"Well, I kept sending out mind probes but all is quiet. I know that Hawk can receive my thoughts up to a mile or so but I don't know if he can pick up my thoughts at any greater distances. We have six more days to get the gold there so that means that we have five days left to find them." Caylen said. "Let's get back home and get ready for another long day tomorrow."

***

Hawk and Spirit were tossed into the little cabin on the boat and the door slammed shut. They could hear and feel the boat surge forward as the leader fed fuel to the big engine. A small window at the front of the cabin afforded them a view directly to the front of the boat only. They could hear the men talking over the engine's roar but could not decipher exactly what was being said.

"I want my mommy!" wailed Spirit. "Did those bad men shoot all our dogs, Hawk? I hope White Fawn is okay."

Hawk did not immediately reply. He had clearly seen both Snow and the white daughter of Snow and Warrior fall dead before the onslaught of gunfire but he felt it best not to cause his little sister any more anguish than she had already suffered. Going to her, he placed an arm around her shoulder and said, "The dogs are going to be okay Spirit. Once we get back home we will bandage them all up and Aunt Sihu will give them some medicine that will make them all better. You will be playing with them as soon as Dad rescues us and kills these bad men."

Hawk kept looking out the bow window of the power boat as it roared ever westward. He had been over this route more than once with Caylen or Shilah on hunting, fishing and berry picking expeditions. They had even, on two separate occasions, travelled out of Graham Inlet and across the big Tagish Lake and up the fast-flowing river to Fantail Lake.

***

Caylen, accompanied by Aponi, Sihu and Shilah, Hawk and Spirit related to his companions how he and his mother had accompanied Fariss Lubak to the little wilderness cabin where he had spent three years of his young life before being forced to venture off on his own for his safety. On one of the trips they had even gone by canoe up the stream to the lake where to their utter amazement, they saw the little log and mud cabin for themselves.

"You actually lived here?" Aponi asked."I cannot believe how you and Lora managed to survive out here."

Hawk, when he now saw the speeding boat turn into the estuary of the vaguely familiar river leading to Fantail Lake, realized that they were a long way from Serenity Island and home. Looking at the now sleeping figure of his little sister, he felt the fear begin to grip and tighten his stomach and to make his entire body tremble. Crossing to where Spirit lay, he wrapped his arms about her and began to weep softly to himself so as not to awaken her.

"Oh, Dad, Mom, where are you? Please come and get us real soon." he murmured softly to himself as he finally allowed his tired little five-year-old body to ignore the roar of the boat's engines and succumb to much needed sleep.

***

Caylen and Bill, over the next three days, flew over the entire east and west coastlines of both Atlin and Tagish Lakes to no avail. They spotted numerous prospectors and fishing boats but none that looked like what they were searching for. Anything that looked even vaguely like the boat described by Talisa was enough to justify landing the plane and taxiing up to where they could question the boats occupants.

"We don't have much time left." Bill said on the fourth day. "I think we should get the gold in place pretty soon so we can position ourselves in a good spot to watch it. When they pick it up we will follow them to wherever they have the kids and then take them into custody."

"If either Hawk or Spirit have been harmed in any way, I am not too sure we will be taking them into custody." Caylen replied. "But I agree, let's get the gold in place and find ourselves a good hideout."

"One good thing about where they want the gold is that unless they are inland from it they will have to come by water to get it. We can see that spot from a long way off so there should be lots of good hiding spots for us. We should also bring the speedboat with us and hide it nearby. We will need it to chase them down once they get the gold." Bill said.

"I agree," Caylen replied. "We should be prepared for any eventuality. I wonder if we should bring Aponi and Shilah along?"

"I don't think that bringing Aponi along would be a good idea." Bill responded. "I know you don't want to even think about it but having her along if they have done something to the children would not be a good idea."

"Yeah, I guess you're right. I am not able to even think straight, Bill. This is the worst thing that has ever happened to me. I'm sure glad you're here to help me, 'cause I'm not sure I would be able to handle this by myself." Caylen said. "I don't know how I can ever thank you, Bill."

"We are family." Bill replied. "That's what families are for. Now let's go get that gold and plan our next move. We may be able to use Shilah but I don't want to leave the women alone. Maybe I will scoot on over to Atlin and bring back a couple of Mounties to watch over the place while we are away."

***

The following morning was the fifth day since the children had been taken. Warrior was still spending every night sleeping on Snow's grave so Sihu had taken a old wool blanket and spread it over the damp ground for him. She then constructed a little lean-to over the gravesite that would keep him dry should it rain.

Black Cloud's shoulder was healing nicely but he kept looking about for his brothers, sisters and his mother. He was limping about the yard but Sihu would not permit him to run free as she wanted to permit his damaged shoulder to heal properly. Warrior would, each morning when he returned from his vigil at Snow's gravesite, go to his son and to all who watched, he appeared to comfort him by licking his face clean.

Bill returned from Atlin with two Mounted Policemen. They had been fully briefed on the kidnapping and all subsequent events and informed Caylen that a third Constable was on his way over on a police launch to assist in the search and the manhunt. Caylen and Bill updated the pair on what was proposed and suggested that they accompany them to where the gold was to be left and that the third constable could remain at the house with the women and Shilah. The two constables would remain in hiding near the gold in the event the kidnappers approached from land. If that was the case they would be able to follow them as Bill and Caylen might not even be aware that they had taken the gold. They were to signal Bill and Caylen if that were to occur. Caylen and Bill then loaded the gold on board the speedboat along with sufficient food supplies for at least two weeks. They also quietly placed on board, medical supplies and warm clothing for the children in the event they were needed.

The following day dawned bright and clear. The four men were boarding the big speedboat even as the bright morning sun rose over the eastern mountains. Warming the boats big engines, Caylen sent a "Come, Warrior" mind=thought out to Warrior. Expecting him to appear within a few moments, he was still impatiently waiting ten minutes later.

"Shilah, would you please run over to Snow's grave and get Warrior, he doesn't seem to hear me."Caylen said.

Shilah returned a few minutes later to report that Warrior was nowhere to be found. Impatient to be off, Caylen, after deciding to leave the big animal at home, idled the big speedboat away from the dock and out into the big lake before opening the throttles and sending the boat up to planing speed.

***

Warrior, the night before, had gone at sunset, to Snow's grave. Settling himself down for the night, he had barely managed to close his eyes when he suddenly, with a start, jumped to his feet. Seemingly unable to resist the forces that now compelled his actions, he raced across the northern tip of Serenity Island and without a moment's hesitation, leaped into the cold waters of the narrow channel that separated Serenity Island from the mainland that lay just to the west. Approximately an hour later he was clambering up the rocky bank and into the thick mature spruce forests that seemed to go on forever in all directions. Shaking himself dry he turned to the southwest and raced off towards the south end of Tagish Lake.

***

Caylen, Bill and the two Constables arrived at the flagged tree two hours later. One hour after arriving, they had placed the gold in the thicket as directed and replaced the white cloth with a blue one. Looking about the site they discovered many animal trails leading out of the forest to the water. They could not, however. find any signs of human passage on any of these trails.

"No matter." Caylen said. "They may not have been down any of these trails yet but that does not mean that they won't approach from inland somewhere."

"I really don't think that's too likely." Bill said. "After all, five hundred pounds of gold is a lot of weight to carry. I'll wager that they come by boat."

"I think so, too." Caylen replied. "But I don't want to take any chances. My kids' lives may depend on us making the correct choices."

"We will get up on that little rise over there to the west," one of the Constables said. "From there we can see the flag and the gold. If they come by land or water we will see them. What do you want us to do when they do show up?"

"Well, that depends," said Caylen. "If they don't have the kids with them I don't want you to do anything. Just sit pat until they leave then get down on the beach and we will pick you up and then we will follow them. That applies if you don't see the kids, also. They may be locked out of sight in the boat's cabin. If you do see the kids, signal us with your signal mirror and we will be there in about three minutes. In the meantime do whatever you have to do to ensure their safety. Keep your weapons loaded and handy and please try not to make any noise."

"Well, we do have another day to wait." said one of the Constables.

"Not necessarily so." Bill said. "They might be watching us now and know exactly what we are doing. They may also cruise by this spot every day to see if the flag has been changed. We just can't take chances. You will just have to try and make yourself as comfortable as possible and remember, no fires!"

***

It took Caylen and Bill another hour, after dropping off the two men, to hide the speedboat and get themselves comfortably situated where they could see both east and west on the channel as well as the flag and the position of the two Constables.

"Now we just sit and wait." Bill said. "I cannot believe they will come after dark. I'm quite sure that they will show up about midday and just cruise past a few times to make sure the coast is clear before they land to get their gold."

"You know, I could probably take them out from here with my target rifle. It is only about four hundred yards. With this scope I could drop all three of them before they even realized what was happening." Caylen said.

"Unless we see the kids and they are in danger, I would not suggest that. If you were to miss even one of them or just wound them, they could harm the kids. We would be better off to wait until they think they are getting away with it before we make our move." Bill replied.

***

During the remainder of that day and all of the next they sat, hidden and waiting with the mosquito's and black flies swarming about them, gorging on their blood and nearly driving them mad. They did see a boat similar to the one described by Talisa pass by their hiding place four times on the second day. It approached from the west and cruised by quite slowly. Caylen, looking through his powerful binoculars could see only one man on board who appeared to be constantly scanning the shorelines on both sides of the narrow inlet. The boat went only about a mile to the East before it turned and cruised back to the West.

After the second passing Bill commented, "I'll wager anything that fellow out there is one of our kidnappers and that he is looking things over before he takes the gold tomorrow."

"I'm pretty sure he did not see us or the other two guys." Caylen said.

"If he did he sure was not letting on." said Bill. "I don't think he will be back today so we may as well get settled for the night."

***

"Hawk! Hawk! Wake up! Please, Hawk, wake up!" cried Spirit as the boat's bow crunched into the gravelly shore of the little lake.

"What?, What is it, Spirit?"Hawk asked as he came fully awake. He jumped off the small bunk where they had been sleeping and peered out the front window. "Where are we?"he asked. He could see nothing save the green of the thick spruce forests in front of the boat.

"I don't know where we are Hawk, I wants to go home!. I want my mommy " Spirit wailed.

"Be quiet, Spirit. These are bad men and they might hurt us if we make too much noise. We have to do what they say and not get them mad at us." Hawk said. "Dad will come soon to get us away from these bad guys and take us home."

"Are our puppies okay, Hawk?"Spirit asked. "I think these men hurt our puppies, Hawk. They are bad men."

"Dad will take care of them pretty soon, sis. He will be really angry when he catches them."

"He won't be mad at us, will he, Hawk?"Spirit asked.

"No, he won't be mad at us but I bet he'll be really mad at these men for taking us away."

***

"Okay you kids, c'mon out here, we have to walk up this trail a ways and then we'll be home." said one of the men as he opened the cabin door. "C'mon out here, you'll be okay. We'll gets you somethin to eats real soon."

The three men led the two children up the trail to a small clearing and a cabin which Hawk recognized as the home where his father and his Grandma Lora had once lived.

Entering the cabin, the bearded leader soon had a hot fire burning in the rusty old cookstove and a big pot of canned caribou stew simmering on its top. Filling two big bowls with the hot mush, he handed one to each of the children with a crust of bread.

"Now, you's two eats up and gets onto that there bunk soon's as you's is done." he said. "Now, alls we gots to do is waits a few days then i'sl go back and keeps an eye on that towel we tied to that tree. We's is goin to be real rich real soon."

"Is we goin to gives the kids back to that Helms guy Viktor, or is we goin to jest knock them on their heads and drops them in the lake?"

"Well, I figures iffen I gets the gold okay if's will come back here and then we's can figures out whats to do with them. Maybe we's will jest leaves them here fer the bears and wolves to git and maybe we won't. Maybe we's will takes them out to Carcross and maybe we's will slit their throats fer them. I jest don't know yet whats I's is goin to do."

***

Viktor waited four days before loading and fueling the fishing boat and heading back to cruise past the site they had marked for Caylen to leave the gold at. He went slowly past the site twice, scanning the shorelines for any sign of anything unusual. He could see that the white towel had been replaced with a blue cloth so he assumed that the gold was in place in the thicket as he had directed. After his second run past the site without seeing anything he cruised westward about one-half mile before dropping anchor. From this position he could still observe the drop site and see anyone who might attempt to approach it.

"Well, Fariss, big brother, we's is goin to gets even wit him now. Soon's I gits that gold, I's will go's back and burn that there cabin with the kids and my two "assistants "in it. Maybe I'll kills them first and maybe I wont's. Jest what's you think bout that, brother Fariss?. Will that be good nuff revenge or does you's wants more?. I could goes back and kills his purty little Hopi wife and her ma, too."

***

Viktor Lubak had arrived in Atlin shortly after his brother Faris had been killed by the evil Wendigo that resided in the forest to the west of Fantail Lake. While he did not know the real cause of his older brother's death, he knew from all the reports and rumors that Caylen Helms had been somehow responsible. The official police report gave little details other than to say that the fugitive Faris Lubak had fallen to his death while being pursued by Special Police Constable Caylen Helms and Police Sear gent Bill Tomkins.

It had taken Viktor nine years to formulate his plan on how to revenge his big brother's death. A small gold strike on upper Spruce creek finally provided him with sufficient monies to begin to implement his carefully thought-out plans. Killing Caylen was not enough. he wanted to do something that would cause him pain over a long period of time. He thought at first that he would capture Caylen and torture him but these plans changed when he found out that Caylen had two small children.

"He tooked my brother from me so I's will takes his kids from him and gits rich all at the same time." he explained to the two men that he had befriended and convinced to help him. The promise of one hundred pounds of gold for each of them was the only convincing necessary.

"At least you's thinks you's will be gettin it." he smirked to himself."But you's will be gettin somethin a lot lighter. In fact I thinks it only weighs bout two hundred fifty grains or so and it be solid lead!. And you's will gets it right betwixt yer dam eyes jest afore I's cuts them kids of Helms throats and feeds them to the fishes!"

***

Warrior finally stopped and drank deeply at a little ice cold stream that ran down out of the high mountains. He had been running steadily at a breakneck speed for over five hours. He had no concept of distance but if he did he would have realized that he had loped across and through nearly forty miles of spruce forest, swamp and glaciers. He had swam and waded across numerous streams, creeks, rivers and small lakes. He had startled moose, caribou, ptarmigan, snowshoe hares and on one occasion even a large grizzly bear foraging on the plentiful northern lowbush blueberries.

Warrior had no idea what was driving him. He had no idea where he was going or why he was going there. All he knew was that some force that was much stronger than he was impelling him ever onward to a unknown destination. After drinking his fill, he scouted around until he could detect the strong odor of hare. It took only a few moments for him to find and dispatch his meal of fresh rabbit meat before he flopped down and rested his big muscular frame. After about thirty minutes of deep slumber he rose, walked over to the stream and again drank his fill before whatever force that was controlling him caused him to head off, again at a dead run in a northwesterly direction.

Three hours later, tired and thirsty, he suddenly realized that he was in familiar territory. Even though he had been away from this area for over eight years, the big wolf dog could recall hunting and exploring this area with his master. He slowed his pace first to a walk and then to a stalking pace as he realized that he had reached his destination. Still unaware of what his mission was, he stalked quietly onward towards the old cabin that he once had called home. A moment later he stopped. A sudden waft of air brought to his sensitive nostrils familiar odors that he immediately recognized as emitting from his master's children.

Mingled in with those familiar smells were the terrible smells of the humans that he knew had been responsible for the traumatic deaths of his beloved Snow and their litter.

In less than a moment the big docile, playful wolf dog that a child could crawl over, maul and even ride on as though he were a pony turned into a cunning powerful, vicious killer, capable of taking down and killing a full grown caribou or a mature moose. Warrior had now reverted to a snarling, drooling, bloodthirsty northern timber wolf, hungry for the blood of those evil beings who had destroyed his family.

As he neared the cabin, the big carnivore crawled silently forward, growing ever closer to the sources of the terrible stench that the killers of his family were emitting from their body pores and their breath. Now, in totally familiar territory, the big animal eased his big head out from under the cedar tree that edged the little clearing. As he watched, one of the humans that had murdered his mate came out of the cabin and strode over to one side of the clearing. Before he knew what was happening, the big human was on the ground, straddled by a drooling two hundred and twenty pound Northern timber wolf with two-inch fangs at his throat. Less than a heartbeat later, this evil human was dead, his throat torn completely out and his life's blood soaking into the spongy peat moss of the northern forests. A moment later the big black wolf faded back into the dark forest to await the appearance of the other men.

***

The bright early morning sun peering over the eastern mountains confirmed to Caylen and Bill that the old fishing boat was still anchored just to the west of where the gold lay hidden. After a cold breakfast and their morning toiletries, they hunkered down to await further happenings. It was not until about ten a.m. that they observed the old boat begin to move. As per the previous day, the operator of the boat cruised slowly past the site where the gold was hidden twice before it finally stopped just offshore from where the gold lay. It sat motionless in that spot for about fifteen minutes before it moved slowly in to nudge its bow up on a sandy spot on the shore. A moment later, the boat's operator jumped ashore and was soon hurriedly loading the gold on board. Once the gold was safely aboard, the man reboarded his boat and took off at a high rate of speed to the west.

Once the boat was a reasonable distance down the lake, Caylen and Bill raced down to where their speedboat was hidden. Quickly removing the camouflage they started the big speedboat and ran it across to pick up the two constables who were now standing on the shore awaiting their arrival.

"He left you a letter, Mr. Helms." said one of the men, handing it to Caylen.

Caylen reversed the speed boat out into the channel and turned it to the west before opening the throttles to half speed, keeping the old fishing boat, now far ahead, just barely in sight. Only then did he open the sealed letter from the kidnappers. He quickly scanned the letter and, with tears forming in his eyes, handed it to Bill who proceeded to read it aloud, "If's you's has bin watchin me gits the gold and tries to follow me back, yer kids will be fish food afor you's kin gits to them. You's is to waits fer two days then foller these here insructions. Yer kids is still livin and will be okay as longs as you's does xactly as I says. You's should goes to that little island that is at the ends of Fantail Lake. Theys will be in that old cabin there. Theys will have foods and blankets and will be okay. Jest so's you's know's whose I is, I be Viktor Lubak and I be Faris Lubaks yonger brother. I done all this cause I know's that you's is the one that kilt Fariss."

"Well, according to this they are still alive."Bill said."But I don't think we had better let him get back to them before we stop him or they may not be. I would not trust him for a moment. He is after revenge and I believe he intends to kill them as soon as he gets back to them."

"I think your right Bill, but how will we find them if we take him now. He will never tell us where they are."

"You said that Hawk could send and receive mind-thoughts up to about a mile. Why don't you start sending them out now? Once you make contact we will catch up to and take Viktor into custody before he gets to them. Then we can go deal with the other two and bring the kids home."

"Sounds like a good idea." Caylen replied. "As long as Hawk is alive and is able to think properly, it should work. If I get through to him you will know because I will open these motors up. I will start sending as soon as we get a mile or so from that shoreline over there."

***

Warrior did not have long to wait. About five minutes after he had taken out the first kidnapper, the cabin door slammed open and the second man stood there.

"Rufus! Where in the hell did you gits to?. Gits yer sorry butt back in here. Yer suppers gittin cold! " Not receiving an answer or hearing any sound from his partner, the big man stepped out and walked around to the side of the cabin. The kidnapper was to never know what killed him. In an instant, Warrior's huge jaws closed over the back of the man's neck in a vice-like grip. The wolf's big fangs severed the spinal column at the same moment that Warrior shook his head, breaking the man's neck and killing him instantly. Releasing his grip as the man fell to the ground, the big wolf raised his head and gave out a long, eerie, mournful howl that was, a moment later answered by the wolf pack that currently occupied that part of the northern forests.

It was to take Warrior about five minutes to regain his senses and become once more the big oaf of a dog that could and would not harm a flea. He was never to understand what had possessed him and controlled his actions, guiding him across nearly one hundred miles of northern wilderness to the men that had slain his mate and their litter. Realizing that his jaws and mouth were covered with very unpleasant tasting human blood, Warrior ran over to the fast-running icy-cold stream that crossed the clearing and dipped his blood-covered jowls repeatedly into the cold water until they were completely free of blood. Looking about at the once familiar clearing with his senses now fully regained, he loped over to the open cabin door and entered.

***

"Warrior! Spirit, it's Warrior! Where did you come from, boy? Is Dad with you?" Hawk asked as Warrior ran over to the children with his big bushy tail waving back and forth and a big happy smile on his gray muzzle as he licked the two children's tear stained faces clean.

"We are safe, Spirit." Hawk said."Let's go outside and see if Dad is here. Maybe Warrior has scared those bad men away."

As Hawk exited the cabin he nearly tripped over the body of one of the kidnappers. Quickly turning, he shooed Spirit back into the cabin so she would not see the dead man. Leaving Warrior to keep her company he soon discovered the second body. Returning to the cabin he found two ragged blankets that he used to cover the dead men. Gathering a few heavy rocks he used them to pin the blankets to the ground so that the wind would not remove them. With the bodies now hidden from sight, he returned inside the cabin to get Spirit and Warrior.

The two children and warrior then proceeded down the trail to the little lake. The remnants of the still solid old dock jutted out into the lake about twenty feet just as it had been left. They walked out on it and sat with their

legs dangling over the edge and with Warrior lying between them.

"We will wait right here, Spirit. Dad will come soon
and take us home."

"I missed you, Warrior." said Spirit. "And I want to go
home, Hawk, I'm still scared and I want my mommy!"

***

The children sat on the old pier until the sun began
to set before returning to the cabin past the two dead
kidnappers. As they passed by the two bodies, Warrior
went to each of them in turn, sniffing at their stiffening
carcasses once before lifting his leg and urinating on each
of them.

***

Caylen kept the speedboat at half throttle as they
crossed the big lake. Viktor's old boat, although fitted
with a new engine, could only travel at about twenty
knots. Caylens powerful engines could easily propel his
big boat at about forty-five knots on a calm day.

"It looks like he is heading for the entrance to the
river that leads to Fantail Lake." Bill said. "Have you been
sending out any mind-thoughts?"

"Yes, ever since we sighted land." Caylen replied.
"Nothing yet."

***

Hawk didn't know what to do. He knew exactly
where they were but he also knew that Caylen would not
have any idea where to look for them. He also knew from
overheard conversations that the bearded leader of the
kidnappers would soon be returning to the cabin. From
the conversations he overheard, he understood that the
men had planned to leave them where they were and
somehow notify Caylen of their location. He now realized
that with the two men now dead that the leader, once he
returned, would not be too pleased with what he would

find. His young imagination was running wild as he imagined all kinds of scenarios occurring when he did finally appear. He thought that the man would be really angry and might kill his sister and himself. He then said to himself, *No, Warrior will protect us and kill him first.* Then he thought, *But what if he shoots Warrior?. Maybe we should hide in the bushes and maybe he will just go away. Dad, where are you?* he thought. Suddenly he remembered what Caylen once said to him when he was practicing his mind-games.

"If you are ever in trouble son, think really hard and send me your thoughts. I know you can't send them very far yet but as you get older and practice more you will be able to send your thoughts further and further. I am also quite sure that if you ever do get into serious trouble that your thoughts will travel a lot further than when you are just practicing."

Recalling his father's words, Hawk said to his little sister. "Spirit, I am going to say something to you and I want you to do exactly as I say. I want you to think really, really hard about Dad coming to get us. You have to really think hard. I want you to start now."

Hawk thought really hard and projected the thought, *"Dad!, we're here!. We are okay and Warrior is with us. Please come and get us. We are hungry and tired and that bad man will soon be coming back. We are at the cabin where you and Grandma Lora used to live. Please come and get us, Dad."*

***

"You know that once we get into the river that we will have to get really close to his boat or we may not see where he goes if he lands and goes ashore." Bill said.

"And if we get to close he will get spooked and do any number of things. He might start shooting or he might try to make a run for it. Either way we may never find the kids." Caylen replied. "I think we should just hold back and give him some time before we proceed. We'll just have to chance that he will go to where the kids are. There is no other way out of here other than this river unless he decides to go cross-country. With five hundred pounds of gold, I doubt that he'll take that route."

"Got it!" Caylen exclaimed. "I will take over that raven up there and keep an eye on him that way. Now what the ----."

"What's the matter?" Bill asked.

"Just a minute, Bill."Caylen replied. "I think I just got a message from Hawk! "

"Great! We must be getting close." Bill replied.

"Just what are you guys talking about?" asked one of the Constables. They were both unaware of Caylens abilities and had not heard the previous conversations about sending thoughts with his mind.

"I'll explain it to you later." Bill said. "What was the message, Caylen?"

"They are at our old house and Warrior is with them." Caylen said. "He must have come across country and found them. That nearly one hundred miles!. Oh, my God. Oh no."

"What is it?, What's wrong?" Bill asked.

"Hawk is telling me that Warrior has attacked and killed the two kidnappers who were guarding them. They are both laying dead out in the yard. Hawk has covered them so Spirit cannot see them. We need to get there fast before that character in the boat gets there."

"Well, if we know the kids are safe and okay, why don't we nail this guy now and be done with him before he gets any further." Bill said.

"I think that I would prefer to get to the kids and make sure they're safe before we do anything about him. That old fishing boat can't go anywhere but further to the west and then his only options will be to go cross-country or turn about and make a run for it back out to the big lake. He doesn't know his partners are dead so it will be interesting to see what he does when he finds out we are right behind him. He may think his partners will take care of us if we follow him to the cabin so I think that we will pretend to chase him past the river that goes to our lake. We know we can go twice as fast as he can but he doesn't know that. I will pretend that I can't quite catch up to him until he is just past our turn-off and then we will turn around, making him think we have given up. Then we can run up to the cabin, make sure the kids are okay, then come back and get him."

"That's a plan!" said Bill. "Let's do it; let's get close enough to him so I can put a bullet into his boat. That should give him a little more incentive to keep moving up the lake or maybe we'll get lucky and I can hit his engine and put it out of commission. That would leave him out here drifting around until we get back. We can even let him get a good look at these guys' police uniforms. That should help speed him along even more! "

As the speedboat exited the wide river and entered Fantail Lake, they could see the fishing boat plowing through the lake about two miles ahead. Caylen pushed the throttles ahead enough to make the big speedboat jump up into planing speed. Within a few minutes, they were slowing to a speed that matched the boat that was now only about two hundred yards ahead of them.

Bill took Caylen's thirty-ought-six target rifle and brought the crosshairs of the powerful rifle's telescope to bear on the stern of the old fishing boat. A second later the sharp crack of the rifle sounded and a large splinter was seen to break off the old boat's transom. Caylen, Bill and the constables then observed the boat's bearded operator turn with a start to look directly at the following speedboat. They could quite plainly see the shock on the kidnappers face as he realized that he was being followed by four men, two of whom were quite obviously North-west Mounted Policemen.

Viktor could not believe what he was seeing. Immediately behind him was a large, beautifully-crafted, polished-mahogany speedboat with two civilians and two mounted policemen aboard. Knowing that his only chance was to attempt to outrun them he slammed his throttle wide open. The old boat surged ahead, gaining about five or so knots per hour. A few minutes later he looked back to realize that he was in fact increasing the distance between himself and the following speedboat.

"Ha, "he exclaimed to himself."This old tub can outruns you. I'll just scoot on down this here lake until I gets rid of you's. Then I'll sit out heres till tomorrow afore is'l go back and take cares of things at the cabin. I don't knows if them cops knows what we's done but they's can't knows bout where we's got them Helms kids hid."

***

Caylen allowed the fishing boat to get about two miles ahead before swinging his big speedboat around and opening the throttles. Again up in a planing mode, they were soon zooming up the much smaller river that led to the lake where the old cabin and his two scared children waited.

Dad's nearly there, his thoughts went out to Hawk and Spirit. *I will see you at the dock in a few minutes. You two and Warrior get ready to come aboard.*

A few minutes later, Bill and the two constables were tying the speedboat to the old dock while Caylen was hugging and comforting his two children.

"Well, you two have had quite a time for yourselves." he said, wiping tears of happiness from his cheeks.

"Why are you crying, Daddy?" queried brave little Spirit. "We have had a real big adventure trip. We rode here on a smelly old boat that stank of dead fish. We had a good time though, didn't we, Hawk?, didn't we?"

"Warrior killed those bad men, Dad. Did you catch the other one yet?" Hawk asked.

"Not yet, but we will. Now I had best let your mom know that your okay. C'mon on board and we will get you some warm clothes, some hot food and then we will get you both into a cot so you can get some sleep while we go have a look at the mess at the cabin."

***

Early the following day Caylen and Bill left to find the last kidnapper. They had, after much discussion, decided to leave the children in the care of the two Constables while they pursued the last kidnapper. They instructed the two Constables to bury the two dead men and advised that they keep a watch in the event the kidnapper eluded them and attempted to return to the cabin where he had left his partners. Caylen also contacted Aponi and advised her as to what their plans were for that day. He told her that the children were fine and that he expected to be home late the following day and that if their plans were to change he would let her know.

In less than an hour, he and Bill were creating a huge wake on the big Fantail Lake as they powered West towards the lake's feeder stream.

"Do you recall the last time we were down this way?" Bill suddenly asked.

"How could I forget." Caylen responded. "I wonder if our friend is still living up in that case?. He still has about ninety years or so left before he has to feed again."

What Caylen and Bill were talking about was the evil forest spirit known to the native Indians as a Wendigo. The evil Wendigo could only live and survive in the wilds by consuming evil men who happened to trespass onto his domain. This evil being, in order to continue his survival, needed to consume at least one evil human every one hundred years or he would simply cease to exist on the earth.

The particular Wendigo that Caylen was speaking of lived in an area that encompassed the western end of Fantail Lake, the big tributary river that fed the lake from the western and southwestern mountains and the rocky crags that ran north and south about thirty miles from the west end of the lake. His exact northern boundary was unknown as no-one save Caylen, Bill and Fariss Lubak had ever dared venture into this evil being's kingdom in order to find out.

The end of Caylen and Bill's earlier pursuit of the murdering Fariss to this particular area had come quite quickly and early in their pursuit when the resident Wendigo had grabbed and eaten alive the fleeing Fariss. The being's territorial boundaries were quite easy to approximate as his entire territory was, for the most part, devoid of any of the birds and animals that normally abounded and resided in these northern woods.

***

As Caylen steered the big speedboat down the lake, Bill, using powerful binoculars, was scanning both shorelines for any sign of the fishing boat. As they entered the wide opening that indicated the tributary feeder river, Caylen slowed his boat down to about five knots and proceeded slowly up the narrowing river. Recalling that this river became unnavigable only a few miles upstream, he knew that if the kidnapper and his boat were here, they had to be close, he said to Bill, "We had best be prepared for anything now. If he is in here, we will be seeing his boat real soon. If he is nearby we may have to use extreme and deadly force to take him. If he has decided to try the cross-country route out carrying the gold, he will not be moving too fast."

"I am keeping our rifles handy." Bill replied.

A moment later, as Caylen was steering the speed-boat around a particularly sharp bend in the river he saw Bill suddenly stagger and fall to the boats deck as his chest turned bright red around the gaping wound caused as a heavy caliber bullet exited his chest.

Chapter 25

Miracles

Caylen, as Bill was still falling to the deck, spun the wheel of the speedboat and slammed the throttles fully open. The big engines roared with the sudden increased flow of fuel. The boat leapt into a planing mode in less than an instant. Racing around the bend and a few hundred yards downstream, Caylen barely felt the big bullet that grazed his left arm and ploughed through the boat's control console. As soon as he felt that he was out of sight and out of range of the shooter, he switched off both engines and knelt over Bill, who now lay unmoving on the deck with his eyes wide open on his paling face as his life's blood pooled around him.

"Bill! Bill!" Caylen said, tears beginning to well up in his eyes as he realized that his old friend and his mother's husband was now dying in front of him. "Bill, hang on. Bill. I'll get some bandages and stop this bleeding."

"Take it easy, son. There is nothing you can do for me that will stop what is about to occur. I'm a goner, son. Please tell Lora and Georgina for me that i died loving them. I want you to promise me that you will look after them for me, Caylen. I want you to also know, Caylen, that I have loved you as though you were my own son. Now, I think I have to go, I cannot see you anymore and I am really tired.

"Go with God, Dad, I love you and I will do all you have asked."Caylen sobbed, his tears dropping onto Bill's blood-soaked chest. "Goodbye, Dad; goodbye, Bill."

As Caylen watched and held Bill, he could feel the life force leave the dying man. He could also feel the terrible rage beginning to rise up within himself.

Picking Bill up, he carried him into the speedboat's small cabin. After gently placing him on the cot, he covered him with a wool blanket and went back up on deck. He picked up his heavy thirty-ought-six target rifle and fully loaded its five shot magazine with two hundred and twenty grain soft-point bullets. Caylen then went back to the controls and started the two powerful boat engines.

Turning the boat around with the engines idling, he looked about the sky and finally spotted a big eagle floating about on the drifting air currents. Projecting his mind up he was soon inside the eagles head controlling its actions and seeing through its binocular-like eyes. In full control, he soon had the eagle soaring along up and over the river until he spotted the old fishing boat tied to a tree along the north bank just below the steep rapids. With a part of his mind still controlling the eagle, he pushed the throttles forward until the big speedboat was planing upstream towards the fishing boat at full speed. With his eagle vision he could easily see the bearded man readying his boat for whatever he was planning. As Caylen watched through the eagle's eyes, he saw the man suddenly turn to look downstream towards where Caylen and his speedboat were rapidly approaching. It was clear that the man could hear the roaring of the high performance engines in Caylen's boat as he rapidly closed. An instant later, before the bearded kidnapper and murderer could react, Caylen rounded the corner in front of him. Caylen stopped his boat, permitting it to begin to drift slowly downstream as he picked up his big rifle. The fishing boat with the bearded man standing on deck was directly in front of him at about seven hundred yards distance. Bracing himself, Caylen sighted carefully and began

firing. He was not aiming at the man but at what he supposed was the boats engine compartment. At the fourth
shot he could see smoke coming from somewhere on the
old boat. Quickly reloading, he then riddled the boat at its
waterline with twelve more shots. Reloading again he
now directed his aim so that the heavy slugs would fly
past the man's head. At the third shot he saw the man's
arms raise above his head in surrender.

Still in control of the eagle, Caylen flew down to just
above the bearded man. Spotting the man's rifle leaning
against the boat's rail, he dove in and, as the man watched in amazement, the eagle grabbed the rifle in his talons
before rising up to drop it into the dark waters of the river.

Caylen then pushed the boat's throttles forward and
cruised up to where the kidnapper stood with hands still
raised. "Get on board, you scum "he said."Who are you?.

"I'm Viktor Lubak. I'm the younger brother of Fariss,
the guy you'se kilt a few years back. Be yer partner
dead?"

"Yes he's dead, just like your kidnapping friends are,
but my kids are safe and sound. And for your information,
and I really don't care if you believe me or not, but I did
not kill Fariss. Now, I'm going to stand here with this rifle
aimed at you while you transfer all that gold from your
boat onto mine. And be quick about it, cause if you have-
n't noticed, your boat is sinking."

It only took about five minutes for Viktor to transfer
the gold to Caylen's boat. Once it was loaded, Caylen took
a pair of handcuffs from the boat locker and secured Viktor to the boats railing.

"Whats you'se goin to do' wit me?"Viktor asked.

"I am going to take you to a place not far from here
where you will meet your brother Fariss." Caylen said. "I

think you and he will be quite happy to be together again."

"But I thot you's said he were dead." said Viktor.

"Your absolutely correct, he is dead, just like you're going to be. And if I am really, really lucky, you will die in the same horrible way that he did." Caylen answered.

"You's cant just kill me." Viktor said with fear mounting in his voice. "You is a police man and police men don't kills people fer no reason."

"No reason!" Caylen exclaimed. "You kidnapped my kids, you killed nearly all my dogs and you just killed my best friend and my father-in-law. No reason! You must be crazy!, How many more reasons would you suppose I would need to justify my killing you right here and now? At any rate, it will not be me that is going to kill you. It is, hopefully going to be the same thing that killed your murdering brother that is going to kill you."

Caylen then started his boat and began slowly to move upstream and across to the very spot where he and Bill had begun their foot chase of Fariss Lubak many years earlier. Tying the boat to a large tree, he loosened Viktor from the railing and recuffed him. Climbing ashore he assisted Viktor up the rocky bank and resecured him to a small birch tree.

"Have you noticed, Viktor, that there are no birds or any other wild things living around here?" he asked, relishing the fear in Victors eyes.

"Whats dat smell?" Viktor asked. "I's never smelt anyting dat bad in my lifes."

"That smell is the smell of the creature that is going to end your miserable life and send your damned soul to hell to be with your brother." Caylen said. "I can tell that he is nearby and will soon be here so I will just leave you here while I go and sit out in the centre of the river on my boat where I can watch you die. Goodbye, Viktor, and be sure to say hello to Fariss for me."

In the next instant, everything around him changed. Caylen's vision went totally dark for just a second. He could feel himself moving but had absolutely no control over the moving. A second later he found himself standing in a small, vaguely familiar, well-lit room that held only a large chair constructed of a white shiny material. The floor and ceiling seemed was of a greyish metal-like substance. All four walls were translucent like, but impossible to see through. They contained no visible doorways or visible light sources. Suddenly, with total recall, Caylen realized where he was. The aliens who called themselves the Travelers had again brought him aboard their ship that was obviously still within teleporting distance of the earth.

"Why have you brought me to your ship?" he asked. I was in the middle of doing something very important. You must return me at once."

"Must we again remind you that you need not make your speech with your mouth, Caylen Helms?. You need only to think what you wish us to hear and we shall know what you are thoughts are. We also would advise that you should not presume to command us to do anything."

But I have left another human fastened to a tree and my children await my return. Caylen said. *I beg of you, please return me so that I might complete what I have begun. I must get my friend's body back to his wife who is also my mother so that she might prepare his body for eternity. I must also get my children back to the arms of their mother.*

"We are very much aware of what has transpired in your life over the last few of your days. We are also very much aware of what has transpired in your life since last

we spoke with you when we aided your defeat of the Hellhound. We have watched as you have grown and used your gifts to better those of your kind. We have seen nothing but goodness in your spirit until now. We now see a blackness entering your body. We see hatred and rage in your spirit. This hatred and rage is attempting to take control of you and your actions. Do you not understand that if you permit the evil spirit that you call a Wendigo to consume the human that you now have control of, that you will then be as evil as he?. Do you not realize that if you allow the evil that resides in the forests to kill Viktor Lubak that you will be forever lost to the blackness that even now, tries to control your

"At this moment I care not that I might become evil. All I know is that my heart is full of sorrow, rage and pity. My sorrow is for my dear mother. She has had so much grief and sadness in her life and now the one who entered her life and gave her so much happiness is dead. Her heart will be sick with sadness once more as she lays to rest her lifemate. My rage is for what this evil man, Viktor Lubak has done by killing my mother's lifemate, my pets and for stealing away my innocent children. My pity is for my mother and my wolf dog pet and my wife for the suffering that they have been put through. I wish, at this moment only to end the miserable existence of that evil man that I have tied to that tree. Caylen thought.

"Is this the truth of your soul, Caylen Helms?. Is it pity for your birth mother and your lifemate that you feel in your heart? Is this the truth or is the real truth that you feel pity in your heart not only for those of whom you speak but for yourself over the loss of your pets and your friend?. Look deep inside yourself for this answer before you reply." the Travelers thought came. *"We also ask that you consider what you have said about not caring if you become evil. Do you wish to go*

through your life full of rage and hate like the human that you have tied to that tree?. We think not. We believe that you are a good man. We believe that you have much good to do before you join your father and your blood-brother. The great Sania, the Whakan Powwaw that befriended you and taught you how to use the gifts that Qaletaka bestowed upon you also watches over you as we do. His heart grieves for your losses even as he prepares a place for your friend Bill."

You have yet to tell me why you have brought me here to this place wherever it is. Caylen thought. *But you are right when you say that I am feeling sorry for myself. I do not like feeling as I do and I do not think that I can go through with what I had planned for Viktor Lubak even if he does deserve it.*

"We brought you here because we cannot permit you to be the one to allow that evil creature that lives in the forest to kill and consume that man. We recognize your pain at what has occurred and we wish to offer you a means to change that which causes you all this pain."

"What can you do that will stop my pain?. Can you make time go backwards? Can you make my pets alive?. Can you bring Bill back to life?. What will you do?" Caylen asked.

"No, we cannot make time go backwards and we cannot make your pets live again. Their souls have long since left your world for another. But, we can, if you so wish, return the life force and the soul of the man you call Bill to his physical body."

Well, do it. Please do it. Please give him back his life!. I will do anything you ask of me in return. Caylen pleaded.

"We shall do as you ask only if you agree to do something in return for us. What we will ask of you in return for this man's earthly existence will not be easy. It

will, however, bring great joy to you and your family."

"I'll do whatever you ask of me. Caylen vowed.

"Your friends spirit is now returning to his physical body. You must hasten to care for his body's injuries and take him where he may be cared for. The person you call Viktor Lubak has also been freed from his ties to that tree. He is now running through the forest of the Wendigo. This Wendigo shall, very soon, kill and consume Viktor Lubak just as he killed and consumed his brother Fariss Lubak. Your earthly justice in this matter has now been fulfilled. The death of Viktor is no longer yours to carry out. We are the beings who must now accept the responsibility for Victors death. Go now and care for your friend."

"But what is it I must do for you?"Caylen asked.

"We will return to you in twenty of your earth days to gather from you what you have promised in return for the life of your friend. Go now, he calls for you."

In the next instant Caylen found himself back on board his speedboat as it sat anchored in midstream of the river. As he stood regaining his bearings he could hear from the nearby forest, the agonized screams of Viktor as the savage Wendigo tore his body asunder. He could also hear, coming from the boat's cabin, the much more pleasing sound of Bills voice as he called out to him, "Caylen! Caylen! where the heck are you?. I think my wound has started to bleed again."

***

They all arrived back at Tranquility just as the sun was setting. Caylen, after rebandaging what was now a simple shoulder wound on Bill returned to the old cabin to pick up the children, the two constables and Warrior. The constables had taken care of the burial of the two dead kidnappers as they awaited the return of Caylen and Bill.

***

Aponi, Sihu and Shilah were overjoyed at the safe return of all and had prepared a huge feast in celebration of their homecoming. Warrior, upon their return had immediately gone to Snows gravesite and again, wept huge wolf tears over her for nearly an hour before returning to Tranquility just as the family was preparing for bed.

"I think that Warrior has completed his all night vigils at Snow's grave." Shilah commented as he watched Warrior settle down on his blanket beside his only surviving son Black Cloud for the night. "I do not believe that he will be going back to her grave quite as often now. I believe he is now back to being his normal old self."

"Well, I've still got a ways to go before I'm back to normal." Bill said a few days later. "By the way, Caylen, I am starting to remember what happened when I got shot. What I seem to recall is that I was hit pretty much dead center by that slug and that I was dying. The next thing I remember is waking up with one really sore and bloody shoulder. You also have not told me what happened to that last kidnapper. We are going to have to file a report with the boss in Whitehorse so maybe you had better tell me what happened after I got shot."

Caylen thought that now would be the time to tell all. He asked Bill, Lora, Aponi, Sihu and Shilah to settle themselves down. "Now make yourself comfortable cause what I am about to tell you will sound pretty farfetched. You were right Bill. You were shot dead center and you did die. That's when I got really mad and captured that last kidnapper that shot and killed you. I handcuffed him to a tree and told him that the same thing that had killed his brother would soon be there to kill him in the same manner. Yes, Mom, the kidnapper was the younger brother of Fariss trying to get revenge for Faris's death. He blamed me for Faris's death. Anyway, I had cuffed him to a tree and was waiting on the boat for the Wendigo to show up when the 'Travelers' took me back on board their ship. They said that they could not permit me to kill another human being and that they would take care of punishing Viktor. They also said that they would give Bill back his life if I promised to do something for them."

"Oh, my God!" Lora exclaimed. "You mean that Bill died and was brought back to life?"

"That's exactly what happened, Mom. Bill was absolutely and surely dead for about an hour before the 'Travelers' moved his wound from the center of his chest to his shoulder and revived him. After I gave my promise, they returned me to my boat. When I got back I could hear Bill yelling at me to come and rebandage his shoulder. They also had released Viktor from the tree. It didn't do him any good though because he just ran off into the forest. The last thing I heard from Viktor was his screams as the Wendigo ate him just like he ate Fariss. I suppose that there both together in hell by now."

"What did you promise the Travelers in return for my life?" Bill asked.

"Nothing as of yet," Caylen replied. "They said that they would return in twenty days to collect. I did not really promise them anything specific. I just said that I would do anything they asked of me."

"Well, let's just hope that they don't put too great a value on my life." said Bill with a smile.

"Oh, Bill! This is serious! "Lora exclaimed.

"Well, I believe that we must thank the Great Spirit as well as the Travelers for allowing us to have our children and Bill back." said Sihu.

"You are right, Sihu." Aponi said. "We must all remember to thank our God for keeping everyone safe and sound and returning them to us."

Chapter 26

A Promise to be Collected

The morning of the twentieth day dawned bright and clear. Caylen, as was usual, was up early as was Bill. Bill and Lora had decided to stay on with Georgina until Bill's wound healed. They were also curious and anxious to see if the Travelers would return to reveal to Caylen what they wished of him in return for saving Bill's life.

The family had barely completed their morning meal and were enjoying a second cup of Sihu's delicious brewed coffee when Caylen suddenly blacked out as he sat at the breakfast table. Caylen only became aware of what had occurred when he found himself in the now familiar room with the chair. Sitting himself in it, he sent out his thoughts to the Travelers.

Okay. You have me here again. I thank you for giving us back Bill. I suppose you're here to collect on my promise to you. Caylen said.

"You are correct in what you say. However, before we ask you to fulfill your promise we wish to inform you of many things that will soon occur on and to your world during your lifetime. These happenings and events may have a great influence on any decision you make regarding what we will ask of you."

Are you saying that you can see into the future and therefore can tell me what will happen in years to come?

"We say nothing but what we know. The future and the past are as pages in what you would call a book. The future has already been written just as the past has

been written. The difference is that the past is known and may be written with great accuracy. The future may also be written but it, if written, would have to be written in many different ways as there can be nothing at all certain or accurate about the future until it actually occurs."

Are you telling that you know what the future is even before it occurs? Caylen asked.

"We have told you nothing. What we will now tell you is that the future as it happens has yet to be recorded. What the future contains will depend on many things. These things that will govern the future could take many paths. A example of those things would be your friend Bill. Had we not brought him back from the dead, he would not be able to father and produce the many children that it will now be possible for him to father. Were he not to father those future children, the future would not be the same future as it would be had he remained dead. Who can say what Bill or his future children might do now that he is again alive. Who can foretell what difference his life and his future children's lives will make to your world or how those differences will affect the future of your world.

"Do you now comprehend how and why the future cannot be written or foretold with complete accuracy? There are many paths that could be taken as you and your people travel through life. Each of those paths taken will result in a totally different future than the paths not taken."

I believe that I now understand. Caylen said. Whichever path I chose to travel through my life will result in a future quite different from the future had I chosen a different path. Whatever I do in life will affect the future in some way but just how it will affect the future is impossible for anyone to forecast as who can know what things that I will do in the future.

"That is correct. We do however have knowledge of what is most probable for your world's future, given our knowledge of your people, your technical skills, your ambitions, your greed, your need for power and the callous attitude that many of your people have for the resources of your world and for others of your own kind. We will now reveal to you what we perceive in your world's future should your kind continue on their present course.

"A part of your world will soon have o powerful but evil leader. This man will strive to rid your world of a complete portion of its peoples. Many of this man's own kind will be led by him to believe in what he says. He will convince a great portion of his country's peoples to do his evil work and to slay many of your world's humans. Other evil leaders will also attempt to take advantage of your world's troubles and will also make war. These evil leaders will eventually be defeated by others of your species with a weapon of such power that it will be capable of destroying the entire world. Unfortunately, other evil men will then come forth who will use these weapons. Your world shall eventually, after the use of these weapons become a wasteland full of wandering humans who shall only survive by slaying others of your kind and robbing them of their belongings.

Your people are also destroying your world with your waste. Your seas and your very air will soon be contaminated by your wastes to where these environments will have difficulty supporting life of any kind. Many of the forms of life that exist or once existed on your world have already become extinct or will soon become extinct due to your overuse, your wastage or your pollution of your world. Chaos, starvation, disease and death shall be as common in these soon-to-be-days as your very breath is today."

Is there nothing that can be done to save our world?. What you have forecast for us is that the end of our world is coming and there is not much we can do to stop it. Caylen thought.

"There is much that could be done to change what we have seen in your world's future. What we have seen and related is what your world will become should it continue on its present course. Many things could occur that will alter your world's future. We have only said what is likely to occur if your peoples continue as they have. The future of your world and the future of your peoples will depend on their actions now and in the future."

Will you now tell me what it is you wish of me? Caylen asked. Your future predictions for my world have not been pleasing.

"We wish, first of all, to tell you that for the previous millenniums, we have been developing a planet that is very similar to your own earth. This world is three hundred twenty light years distance from your earth. It is nearly the same size as your earth but is slightly smaller. Its day is only twenty one of your hours long and its year is only three hundred and forty of your days in length. This world also has two satellite moons that are similar in size to your own. At the present time there is no intelligent humanoid life on this world. We have given this world many kinds of plants including edible fruits and vegetables. We have also filled the lakes, rivers and seas with many edible fishes, crustaceans and other kinds of edible life and plants. The lands also teem with numerous edible animals and birds. What we have not done is to place any creatures, large or small, on this world that would be dangerous to those of your kind.

We have placed creatures such as your wolves there that will control to some extent the spread of the edible species. We have also given this world insects that will assist in the propagation of the plants and fruits that will feed this world's creatures."

Why do you tell me these things? Caylen thought. *Surely, you do not need me to assist you with your development of this world.*

"But you are wrong in your assumptions. What this new world still lacks is an intelligent species that will utilize that world's many resources. What this world lacks is a peace loving species that will multiply to become masters of the universe and who will eventually evolve as we have. We would hope that the species we choose to populate this world will, at some point in time, assume the roles and responsibilities of ourselves. Our time of existence in this universe is now limited and we wish to pass on our responsibilities to others who will, as we have, watch over and care for this universe and its many civilizations."

All that may be true. Caylen thought. *But you still have not said how it is that you wish me to repay my promise to you.*

"What we wish of you is - - You, yourself, Caylen Helms! We wish for you to be among the few humans that we choose to populate this new world. We wish for you to be the leader of the group of humans that we have selected to populate this new world!"

"You must be joking! "Caylen exclaimed aloud. "Are you telling me that you wish for me to go with you to this new world that is hundreds of millions of miles from our earth and populate this new land? Why would you want me? Why would you think that I would leave everything I have here? What of my family? Who else would be going? There are so many questions that you would need to answer before I could even consider such a thing!"

"We understand your concerns and we shall answer all of your questions. First, we want you to go and we want you as the leader of this group because we know of all your powers and how you have so wisely used them. Your powers exceed those of any other human on this planet. You are also the most intelligent of all the humans possessing powers similar to yours. Only those with such powers shall be given this opportunity to populate our new world. There shall be one exception to this prerequisite. You, and you alone, shall be permitted, as the leader of this group to take with you, your mate, your children, your mother, her husband, their child and up to ten others of your own choosing. You shall also be permitted to take your wolf dog and his son. You may also take plants and seeds from your world as well as clothes, tools and other items that you might deem necessary for this great adventure. You may not however, take any of the weapons of your world other than what you call knives, spears, bows and arrows and fishing equipment. You shall also not take any equipment powered by fossil fuels or electricity. You would be well advised, however, to take with you, fire starting materials, clothing, bedding, sewing equipment, axes, saws and other such items that would be required to survive were you to be left on a remote land with naught but your wits with you. What you take with you shall be all you will have until you and your people develop and construct your own required items on this new world. There will be no source of any of these or any other of your needed items other than what you are able to manufacture or have brought with you. We shall also grant all who make this journey a life span that shall be the equivalent of one thousand of your earth years. You

shall, during that time, be immune from any disease or illness that might befall you. We cannot stop you or your people from injuring yourselves but we will provide you, Caylen Helms, with the power to heal any human or creature of any injuries that might befall them during this time period. During this extended life span, each of you shall be expected to reproduce yourselves and produce your own required foods and supplies. You will also be expected to populate all areas of this new world as your numbers increase. We, the Travelers will be a resource that only you, Caylen Helms, as this group's leader, may call upon, during that thousand years, at any time for our advice and assistance should it be required. We go now, Caylen Helms. You shall now be returned to your world to ponder our thoughts. We shall return in twenty of your days to hear your thoughts and to listen to your further questions on this matter. Go now, Caylen Helms, go back to your world and speak of what we have imparted to you to your family and to your friends."

"Caylen! Caylen!" Aponi was exclaiming. "Bill has asked you twice now if you wanted another cup of coffee. Your mind must be off somewhere else."

Caylen realized instantly that his experience with the Travelers had occurred in an instant of time to everyone else at the breakfast table and that only his spirit had been transported to their ship. Unable to speak for a few moments, he merely nodded to Bill, who filled his cup with his third cup of hot coffee. A few minutes passed before he spoke.

"You guys are not going to believe what just happened to me." he said.

"Whatever do you mean?" asked Aponi. "Nothing just happened to you that we could see. All we know is that you seemed to have your mind on something and that you were not paying attention when Bill asked if you wanted another cup of coffee."

"Well, you had all better grab yourselves another cup and sit down. I'm about to tell you something that will, if you're not sitting down, make you fall down!" Caylen said. "Now I want you all to just listen to what I have to say until I am finished talking. Then I want you to ask away everything you can about what I will have said. You may not believe what I am about to say but I swear that everything I will say is exactly what I have been told."

"Whatever are you talking about?" asked Lora.

"Do you recall me saying that the 'Travelers' exacted a promise from me in return for Bill' life?" Caylen asked.

"Yes, but they have yet to tell you what they want. Lora said. "I'm sure that we can easily afford to give them whatever it is they want!"

"Well," said Caylen. "Before you say that you had best hear just what it is that they want. You're going to have a hard time believing this but here goes."

***

Caylen spoke steadily over the next four hours. The family sat in stunned silence and amazement as they listened to him relating the thoughts of the 'Travelers' and their request to him regarding their relocation to some far away world. Finally, after completing the unbelievable story of his latest visit to the 'Travelers' ship to his family and his friends, Caylen sat back in his chair, saying. "Okay, folks, that's about all they want in return for saving Bill's life. In short, they have chosen myself and a few others from our planet that have powers similar to mine. They have taken over and nourished a brand new world that is presently uninhabited save for plants, insects, fish, birds and other edible creatures. They now wish to populate this new world with humans that have extraordinary powers in the hope that these chosen people will eventually develop themselves to become as they, the 'Travelers' are and not destroy this new world as the peoples of this planet are now doing. Now, what do you all think of that? Any questions?"

Chapter 27

A Clear and Starry Night

The weather was clear and the summer night quite warm four weeks later on Serenity Island. The old leader of the Matah Kagmi sat quietly on the big log that lay just below the wide entrance to his and his family's cave. The night sky over the island sparkled with the millions of specks of light that seemed to the Matah Kagmi to mysteriously appear each and every night when the dark rain clouds were not present. The old leader's thoughts were clearly and easily understood by his young grandson who sat with him enjoying the spectacle of the flashing colorful Northern Lights as they raced to and fro across the dark night sky.

"Do you, my favourite son of my son, see those many colours that the Gods have painted our skies with?"

"Yes, Grandfather, I see all those wonderful paintings that cover our skies. Oh, Grandfather!, do you see that bright light?. It seems to come from the wood and stone cave of the humans who live below us on the shore of the big water."

"Yes, my young friend. I see that light. That light is the means by which our human friends that once lived below us have begun their travels to a new home and a new beginning. We shall no longer be visited or be able to visit those beings. They have gone with the Travelers and all their friends to make their home on one of those specks of light that you see in the sky."

Chapter 28

A New World

Caylen woke quite suddenly. His eyes ached from the sudden brightness that struck them and roused him from his deep sleep. As his senses slowly came back to him he sat suddenly upright on the edge of his sleeping platform and looked about the large, brightly-lit room he was in. He could see thirty-two other containers very similar to his own that contained Warrior, Black Cloud and the thirty still sleeping others that had agreed to accompany himself to the new world promised them by the Travelers.

"Are you awake, Caylen Helms?. Are you once more in control of your senses?"

"Yes, I am awake and in control. My muscles feel just a bit weak but I should be able to function okay." Caylen replied.

The trip through space from Earth had taken twelve earth years. The passengers selected had all been placed in deep sleep immersed in a thick viscous liquid that supplied all their bodily needs. They remained in a coma-like state for the duration of the long journey. The warm liquid, flowing constantly through the containers, was then thoroughly filtered and cleaned of all the bodily wastes produced by the containers' occupants during the journey.

"We are now in orbit above your new world. If you wish, you may observe this world through the viewing port that is just to your front."

Caylen rose on unsteady feet and walked over to the large viewing window. Steadying his still shaky body with his hands he gazed out at the beautiful world that lay beneath him. What he saw made him gasp in amazement and awe. Far below lay a land so spectacular it was beyond description. Oceans and lakes glittered in the bright sun. Huge forested areas blanketed the rolling stream and river-filled continents. The forests were interspersed with green grass covered rolling plains. Mountains and mountain chains were clearly visible to Caylen on all the land masses that were visible to him. The poles were quite similar to Earth's own North and South Poles in that they were blanketed in white that Caylen assumed was snow and ice.

"If you would see your new world in a closer and clearer way, Caylen Helms, turn the dial on your left. This will enlarge your view to show you as much detail as you wish. You may also direct the view to show you any part of the world that you wish to see."

Caylen directed the view to show the middle of a large plain close to a lake on the largest of the continents. He then turned the dial on the left as he had been instructed. To his astonishment, the scene enlarged to encompass an area of about two square miles. In that two square miles he estimated there to be approximately one hundred deer-like animals. Moving his view to the lake itself he could see uncountable numbers of geese-like waterfowl. As he swung his view even further past the lake, he could see buffalo-like animals, what appeared to be elk and then huge flocks of turkeys and what looked like large sage grouse feeding on the rich grasses.

"That place looks so serene, it reminds me of my island home back on earth. I believe that I would like to call this planet Serenity." said Caylen to no one in particular.

"And that Serenity shall be forever your home. Caylen Helms. Now you must go to your people and awaken them so that we may transport you all to your Serenity."

Caylen went first to Aponi's container. All that was required of him to awaken each container's occupant was for him to flip a switch that was located on the very top of each container. As soon as the switch was turned to the off position the fluid inside the container was drained quickly away to be replaced by a rich mixture of oxygen and another reviving gas that worked almost immediately to revive the cylinder's sleeping occupant. A few seconds later the container's cover swung open, releasing its now awakened occupant. Within a very few minutes the large room was full of stiff, stretching and groaning settlers ready for transporting to the planet's surface.

***

"Welcome to our new home." Caylen said. "In case you are wondering, I have taken the liberty to call this new world Serenity. You may each have a good look at Serenity from this window before we select where we wish to be placed. I would suggest that we choose the area where I have pointed the viewer at as it seems to contain everything we will need to get ourselves settled. I could see streams and lakes, wooded areas as well as clearings for cultivation and numerous varieties of edible animals and birds nearby. I have also seen what appears to be caves in that rocky area near that series of lakes and rivers. I have been assured by the 'Travelers' that the waters teem with fishes and the lands contain many edible plants, fruits, berries and nuts. As we know, the only carnivores on Serenity are wolves that were left to provide some control on the herbivores. I have been told that there are no other animals, insects, mammals, fishes, birds, snakes or any other creature on Serenity that could cause harm to our kind. Now, will each of you please give me your thoughts about where we should settle on this beautiful new world called Serenity."

***

Following an hour or so of excited discussions, it was agreed that the entire party of settlers would land on the shores of one of the bigger lakes near where a small river emptied into it. This river ran down from a whole chain of other lakes that began about two miles upstream. Just off about one-half mile to the east of the river were the cliffs that were peppered with numerous deep caves that from space had looked quite appropriate as temporary or even permanent homes for the settlers.

***

'Travelers', we have made our choice as to where we would like to be placed on this new world. Caylen thought.

"We have heard your thoughts in that regard, Caylen Helms. Your supplies have already been placed high on the shore of your chosen lake awaiting your arrival. We shall transport you and your people next. We, the Travelers shall then depart for other worlds and other experiences. We wish you well, Caylen Helms. Do not forget that we will respond to your requests should you require our aid at any time. Go now, Caylen Helms. Go to your New World with your people. Go and populate this beautiful world that we have created for you. Go to your world and remember to treat your Serenity as a place of Serenity for all time."

***

A moment later, Caylen found himself standing on a warm, sandy lakeshore of Serenity surrounded by his family, his mother, Bill and Georgina, Shilah, Sihu Talisa

Warrior, Black Cloud and twenty other settlers from the far away planet they once knew as Earth.

"The End "

or possibly

"Just the Beginning "